Wine of Violence

Wine of Violence

Priscilla J. Royal

Poisoned Pen Press

Poisoned
Pen
Press

Copyright © 2003 by Priscilla J. Royal

First Edition 2003

10 9 8 7 6 5 4 3 2 1

Library of Congress Catalog Card Number: 200311196

ISBN: 1-59058-088-5

Poisoned Pen Press
6962 E. First Ave., Ste. 103
Scottsdale, AZ 85251
www.poisonedpenpress.com
info@poisonedpenpress.com

Printed in the United States of America

Hear, O my son, and receive my sayings;
and the years of thy life shall be many.
Enter not into the path of the wicked,
and go not in the way of evil men.
For they eat the bread of wickedness,
and drink the wine of violence.

Proverbs 4:10, 14, 17 (King James Version)

To my mother,
Betty J. Hallenbeck Royal (1905-1998),
who taught me the joy of reading
and the love of a good story.

Acknowledgements

To the Every Other Thursday Night Writers' Group (Kris Brandenberger, Bonnie DeClark, Liz Hartka, Anne Maczulak, Sheldon Siegel, Meg Stiefvater, and Janet Wallace). Your encouragement and insights have been invaluable.

To Katherine V. Forrest and Michael Nava, my first mentors. Had it not been for you, I never would have achieved this.

To Peter Goodhugh for being so generous with his time to an unpublished writer and sending wonderful photographs, pamphlets and books as well as answering all my questions.

To Judy Greber (Gillian Roberts), a fine writer and teacher, who got me started in the right direction with this book.

To Sara Hartley, M.D., another fine teacher, for patience, wisdom and good humor.

To Henie Lentz for, among many things, finding all those wonderful medieval histories.

To Katherine Neville and Sarah Smith for invaluable guidance in the joys of historical research and warm encouragement to budding authors in all fields.

To Joanne Pence for encouragement as well as telling me about Book Passage and the California Writers Club.

To Barbara Peters, Robert Rosenwald and Monty Montee at Poisoned Pen Press for making my 50-year-old dream come true.

To Elaine and Bill Petrocelli and the staff at Book Passage in Corte Madera, CA, with gratitude for providing classes—and mystery conferences—to die for.

To Barbara Truax and the Marin Branch of the California Writers Club for providing speakers and a supportive environment for writers of all genres.

Foreword

Although Tyndal Priory and its inhabitants never existed, the Order of Fontevraud most certainly did. It was a very powerful religious institution from its founding at the turn of the twelfth century by Robert d'Arbrissel until shortly after the French Revolution. Like the Order of the Paraclete (once headed by Heloise, whose correspondence with her husband, Peter Abelard, is one of the treasures of medieval literature), Fontevraud was one of the rare Orders of double houses where a woman was in charge of both male and female monastics.

A "double house" is a religious living arrangement where nuns and monks work and live in the same enclosed setting. Before celibacy became the rule in the western Church, the term meant a monastery where married monks and nuns, as well as single ones, could live together and raise their children. After celibacy became the required norm, a few double houses continued to exist, although the men and women were very carefully segregated for most of their daily activities and the head of such an establishment was almost always a man.

Fontevraud was an exception. Founded in France, the mother house was in Anjou and was headed by an abbess. Parts of that abbey remain. Although the Order was a favorite amongst aristocratic women, it also accepted nuns from other social classes as well as women who had been prostitutes, a unique practice in any religious community at the time.

There were four daughter houses of Fontevraud in England, all under the control and direction of the abbess in France. Technically, they were each headed by prioresses, although the leader of Amesbury was often called an abbess, in part because the community had once been a Benedictine abbey and in part out of courtesy for its prominence. Amesbury was certainly the most important of the four and the most famous. Two queens, Eleanor of Aquitaine (Henry II) and Eleanor of Provence (Henry III), retired there in their last years. Eleanor of Provence was buried at Amesbury; Eleanor of Aquitaine was buried at the mother house in France. Today, all that is left of Amesbury Priory is part of the parish church. As mentioned in this story, Grovebury was a small administrative center. Nothing remains of it now. Of the other two houses, the site at Nuneaton is being excavated, but Westwood lies buried under a parking lot.

Unfortunately, I have been unable (so far) to locate a complete architectural plan for any Fontevraud house. The Cistercians in the thirteenth century also had double houses, and reasonably complete designs for some of their priories are extant; however, they so disliked the idea of having women in their Order at all in the medieval period that their nuns were virtually walled up and allowed almost no freedom of movement. Just how segregated men and women could be in a Fontevraud house, which was run by a woman, is an interesting question. The architecture of the place must have allowed for much more interchange and freedom of movement between the two—at least by the prioress and prior. Without an adequate outline of a Fontevraud house, I have used my imagination to come up with a generic Tyndal, although I have tried to temper fantasy with what did exist. Since I made Tyndal a Benedictine house originally, and almost all single-sex monasteries of the period had relatively similar plans, I have used those generic designs for fictional Tyndal from sources, some of which are listed at the end of this book.

The accuracy of historical details is one problem, but how to portray people, their thoughts and feelings, from an era so distant from our own is another. The fiction author inevitably walks a very narrow line between making the characters sound too modern to be of the period or making them so different that the modern reader feels little in common with them. Yet histories, literature and other written work from any era suggest that people have changed little in unspoken thoughts and feelings, although different language is used to express them and symbols may have different meanings.

We often judge people in earlier times to be more ignorant and less socially progressive than we; yet no insight bursts upon the world fully formed like Athena from the forehead of Zeus. As the writer of Ecclesiastes pointed out, there is no new thing under the sun. It is certainly true that a particular concept may be given wider or fuller expression in one period as opposed to another (democratic government is one example), but it is unlikely that the concept was absent in the minds of thoughtful people in other times.

Nor should we be smug about whatever progress our generation might make. Not only is history full of dark ages following enlightened ones, but each era has its share of savagery. In the West, we may no longer literally burn people at the stake for heresy, but weren't the blacklists of McCarthy a form of punishment for a "heresy" of the era? And how many examples can any of us come up with these days where religion raises some to greater compassion and wisdom while lowering others into ignorance, anger, bigotry and even murder, just as it did in the medieval period.

The medieval society is seen as a violent, harsh and cruel one. It could be and often was. Wars were frequent. Life expectancy was short. The slightest illness or wound was cause for serious concern, although medical knowledge in the Arab world was quite sophisticated and vastly superior to that in the West. Sanitation and literacy were minimal but certainly not as nonexistent as many suggest. Torture to obtain a confession was not uncommon, yet the fictional Ralf's dislike and distrust for the practice were shared by many historical figures. Traitors were executed by publicly hanging, drawing and quartering them. Religious as well as sexual heretics were burned at the stake, although some executioners tied bags of gunpowder around those to be burned so their suffering might end quickly or garroted them prior to the burning. Indeed, each generation may have its unique brutality, but it holds its special mercy as well.

Thus period language, symbolism and dated references aside, it does seem reasonable to conclude that some people from 1270 might well feel and react much as some do today. They might even have come to a few of the same conclusions that a few of us have. Some controversial examples in this book of such a conclusion, however, bear some additional discussion.

Many of us in our middle years equate the life of nuns with Audrey Hepburn in *The Nun's Story*. However, most religious women in the medieval period not only were free to move about but were expected to do so if secular matters (especially family ones) demanded. One prioress of Amesbury from the early 1300s, Isabel of Lancaster, spent much of her time not only outside the priory in family visits but also at court and with friends. No one at the time thought this strange or condemned her for it.

Nor were all nuns unworldly, and ignorance of secular life was not even considered a particular virtue. In fact, the founder of the Order of Fontevraud specifically suggested that a widow (albeit an upper-class one) should become the Abbess of Fontevraud because she would know how to run a household and how to deal with both men and women more effectively. Heloise of the Order of the Paraclete, who was an abbess by her early twenties in the 1120s, wrote quite openly about her sexual feelings for Abelard even after they both took vows of celibacy. She was considered an exemplary religious. Hildegard von Bingen (1089-1179), given to an anchoress at the age of eight to be completely closed away from the world, became famous for her practical advice and common sense. Not only was her counsel widely sought by men within the higher ranks of the Church and secular life, but her medical works are interesting for their graphic descriptions of sexual acts and sensations.

Chapter One

During the dark morning hours of a winter day in the year 1270, an aged prioress realized she was dying.

To her surprise the dying was much easier than she had ever imagined. The crushing pain in her chest was gone and she felt herself drifting upward with an extraordinary lightness. She was floating above the rush-covered floor, over which a dusting of sweet-scented petals had been scattered, and away from that narrow convent cot where her earthly remains lay so still. Indeed, she wasn't frightened. She was very much at peace.

Below her, a semi-circle of nuns continued to chant with haunting harmony, their warm breath circling around her in the bitterly cold air. Many had tears in their eyes at her death, she noted, especially Sister Christina, whose grief meant the most to the old prioress. She could not have loved the nun more if she had been a child of her own body, but Christina had become the child of her soul instead, and, knowing the young woman would remain in the world, the old prioress could leave it with an easier spirit. She smiled.

Still sitting by the convent bed was Sister Anne. The sub-infirmarian to the priory was pale with fatigue and her shoulders hunched as she bent over the hollow body that the prioress had just quitted. The old prioress shook her head. No, good sister, she thought, now is the time for prayer, not your concoctions.

How often had she told the nun that when God wanted a soul, all those earthly herbs and potions would be useless? Yet the kind sister had been able to ease the mortal pain of her passing. For that I am grateful, the old prioress thought, and as she watched the nun lean over, testing for breath from the quiet body, she hoped Sister Anne would, as she should, find a comfort in having given that relief.

Against the wall stood Brother Rupert, in front of her favorite tapestry of St. Mary Magdalene sitting at the feet of Our Lord. The good brother's eyes were red from weeping, his head bowed in grief. How she wished to comfort him! He looked so frail to her now, his monk's habit far too big for his diminished frame. Maybe he would join her soon?

She mustn't hope. Earthly associations should have no place in Heaven, but she was insufficiently distanced from the world not to believe Heaven would be a happier place with Brother Rupert by her side, as he had been for more years than either could truly remember.

Heaven? Was she really going to Heaven, she wondered. A cold gust of doubt cut through the warm breath of the nuns and chilled her. Was that invisible hand lifting her young soul from her age-ravaged body really the hand of an angel of God?

She shivered. She had always tried to be worthy of God's grace, serving Him to the best of her ability. She had tried to be humble, dutiful, and she thought she had confessed all her sins to Brother Rupert just before falling into the strange sleep that had preceded this freeing of her soul.

An icy uncertainty nipped at her. Had she remembered all her sins? Might the Prince of Darkness have blinded her, making her forget some critical imperfection? Some sin of omission perhaps? Was her soul truly cleansed or was there some small rotting spot that would fling her into a purgatorial pit where pain was as sharp as the agonies of hell?

An unformed impression, a memory, something nagged at her.

It wasn't too late, she thought. Brother Rupert was standing near. Surely she could still reach him if she could just think of…

Then it came to her. Oh, but the mercy of God was indeed great! He had granted her the understanding to see the tragic error both she and Brother Rupert had made. Now she must get the message to the good priest. She must!

She struggled to reach her confessor, willing her soul toward the weeping man.

"Brother! Brother!" she cried. "I must tell you one thing more!"

She stretched out her hand, struggling to grasp him, reaching for the crude wooden cross he wore on a thin leather strap around his neck.

But something seemed to hold her back; some black force scrabbled to keep her soul from deliverance.

The priest had not heard her cry. He did not see her fighting to reach him.

She must tell him. She must! After all her years devoted to God, Satan should not win her soul over such a misunderstanding, a judgement she'd made with imperfect knowledge and mortal blindness. An innocent person would be hurt, even die, if she did not. She could not have that fouling her conscience.

She fought harder to reach her confessor, twisting, crying, moaning for help.

Suddenly a hand materialized from the tapestry. It grasped the old prioress firmly and pulled her back to the ground. It was a woman's hand, and the touch was warm.

The old prioress looked up and saw St. Mary Magdalene smiling.

"Tell me, my child," the saintly voice said. "I will tell Our Lord." She gestured to the glowing man at whose feet she sat. "And He will forgive all as He always has."

The old prioress wanted to weep for joy.

"Please tell him that I accused wrongly. It was not the one we feared, but rather the other!" she gasped.

And with that, the world turned black.

II

His heart pounded. His lungs hurt as he gulped cold ocean air through his open and toothless mouth. Stinging sweat trickled down his reddened, unevenly shaven face, and Brother Rupert rubbed the sleeve of his rough robe across his age-dulled eyes.

Once he could have walked the familiar path between town and priory with ease. Now his legs ached with the effort of climbing and he had to will himself to the top of the sandy, scrub-grass covered hill.

"I'm getting old. I am getting old," he muttered, as the moist wind stabbed each one of his joints.

At the hilltop, he stopped to rest and looked back into the distance. The morning sun of early spring had burned off the thickest fog, but the walls of Tyndal Priory, a double house of priests and nuns in the French Order of Fontevraud, were mere shadows in the drifting haze.

It didn't matter. He could have shut his eyes and seen each stone of every building clearly. Since the winter of 1236, when Eleanor of Provence had come to England as the now aging King Henry's wife, Brother Rupert had been chaplain, scribe, and administrating secretary to the recently deceased Felicia, Prioress of Tyndal. He had lived at the priory long before that, however, indeed from a day in his thirteenth summer when his rich merchant father proudly dedicated him to this woman-ruled Order so favored by kings, queens, and other elite of the realm. His father might have given him to the religious life as an oblate, but the boy came as a willing and eager offering. The monastic walls provided a secure refuge from a world he found frightening, a world filled with violence and lust.

Suddenly his eyes overflowed with tears, and he wiped his gnarled fingers across them hurriedly. "Ah, but I loved you, I did, and I miss you," he said, watching as a swirling gust of mist seemed to lift his words into the sky and scatter them. "And for the sake of all our souls I will put the matter right, my lady. I promise you that."

His words were fervent with an almost prayerful intensity.

Then he sighed, stretched the stiffness from his legs and started down the hill, tentatively at first, unsure in his footing. Once protected from the sea breeze, he could feel the warmth of the sun, and his steps quickened.

His mood improved and he smiled. Indeed, in the warmth he now felt he could almost sense that the eyes of God were upon him.

They were not. They were human.

Chapter Two

"Sister Christina will be here in due course, my lady." A scowling nun, of middle years and pockmarked face, bowed with perfunctory courtesy in Eleanor's direction. Despite the warmth in the crowded chapter house, Sister Ruth's words fell with a chill on the prioress's ear.

Eleanor of Wynethorpe, recently named the new head of Tyndal Priory, sat with stiff spine in her high-backed chair, looked down at the forty-odd wimple-encircled faces in front of her, and knew she was not welcome.

Nor could she blame them. Her appointment to the position of prioress had nothing to do with competence. It had all to do with her father's unwavering loyalty to King Henry III during Simon de Montfort's recent rebellion, her oldest brother's close friendship with Prince Edward, and her mother's devoted support of the queen during a crucial time in the royal marriage. As each one of the nuns sitting in front of her well knew, none of these things meant Eleanor was personally qualified for the high office she now held, only that her family was in favor at court.

After the recent peace settlements, King Henry had had little spare land and even less free coin, thanks to Prince Edward's recent departure on a crusade. Thus the genuinely pious, increasingly ill king had decided that the prayers of many nuns at Eleanor's behest would be of greater benefit to her father than worldly wealth, a conclusion with which the good Baron Adam might have disagreed but which he accepted with appropriate gratitude on his daughter's behalf. In short, her appointment had been convenient and the wishes of the priory itself were set aside.

Although it was not uncommon for kings to honor priories by placing their own choices in superior positions, the royal selections usually carried some important benefit besides the king's fickle favor to sweeten the decision. Sweetening was certainly needed here. Each house in the powerful Order of Fontevraud had always had the absolute right to name its own head. Tyndal had been uniquely thwarted.

"Is Sister Christina habitually late to chapter or is there a special reason she is not here?" Eleanor asked the nun at her side. Perhaps by deferring to this older woman's experience and seeking her advice she might begin to dispel her obvious bitterness.

"She is our infirmarian," the elder nun replied after a silence so cold it felt like ice pressed against Eleanor's heart.

Eleanor swallowed a sharp retort. Last night, at her first private dinner in her new chambers, Brother Rupert had told her that Sister Ruth had been elected to succeed Prioress Felicia, albeit not by an overwhelming vote. This sour-faced nun had been in charge of Tyndal from the death of the former prioress until the announcement of Eleanor's appointment early in the summer. Of course, the woman's disappointment at being so unexpectedly supplanted had been profound, and the elderly monk had also suggested, with the understandable hesitation of one religious telling tales on a fellow, that Sister Ruth's current thoughts about Eleanor might be less than charitable.

"I am aware of Sister Christina's responsibility to the sick," Eleanor replied. "However, she must often absent herself from them for good and proper reasons. Surely she has some reliable lay sister or brother she can leave in charge when her other duties require her attendance?" Eleanor hoped she had succeeded in keeping her voice devoid of the anger she felt at Sister Ruth's insolent manner.

"She is never late for prayer, my lady."

Eleanor bit the inside of her cheek, regretting that there had been nothing, or at least nothing obvious, offered to sweeten her arrival at Tyndal. Indeed, she could list two more good reasons for her charges not to accept her. Having been raised at Amesbury Priory since the age of six, she lacked the secular world experience required of most Fontevraud prioresses; moreover, she was only twenty, very young compared to most of the other nuns here. Each shortcoming, indeed all three, might mean little to a king giving gifts to a loyal lord, but to the women who were quietly studying her, none were trivial. With sharp pain, she felt each one of her deficiencies. Compared to the woman who might have sat in this prioress' seat, but for the grace of kings, Eleanor knew she fell far short in the eyes of those sitting before her.

"I see," Eleanor, said, though in truth she did not. Nor would she. Although tempted, she would not explain to Sister Ruth the need to balance God's work with prayers to God, nor would she chastise her in public for rude and arrogant behavior to a religious superior. It was Christina who needed counseling on maintaining balance and Ruth who required delicate diplomacy if Eleanor was ever going to win her allegiance. Embarrassing this woman in front of the other nuns, as appealing as that course was now, would not accomplish that.

Eleanor glanced up at the rough beam rafters above her. I may not be your elected choice, she thought as she looked back at the nuns sitting on the stone seats surrounding the chapter house wall, but chosen I was and there is naught any of us can do about that. Let us only pray that God will grant me sufficient wit to guide you well despite all the misgivings we share.

"We shall delay the start of Chapter for a few minutes more." Eleanor nodded at her charges, then took a deep breath.

There were over forty women to whom she must attach names and a few salient facts about familial background as well as position within the priory. While they waited for the absent sister, she could use the time to put faces to names. That would keep her temper cool. To call a sister by her name without hesitation and ask after her kin helped create an aura of authority she desperately needed. Brother Rupert had given her a succinct summary and description of most of the nuns last night. She had quickly memorized it, but if she did not apply that information to the actual person, she would soon forget the details. She looked to the woman on her far right and began a mental recitation.

The nun on the last seat was easy to remember. She was the tallest in the convent. Sister Anne had come to Tyndal in her late twenties after several years of marriage, Eleanor recited in her head. She and her husband had left their apothecary shop and the world together, he to the Fontevraud brothers at Tyndal and she to the sisters here.

Now which brother was he? She hesitated. No, Brother Rupert hadn't mentioned his name, but then he hadn't had time to tell her about all her charges at the priory. She made a mental note to ask him later.

Eleanor glanced up at the nun, then quickly lowered her eyes to avoid the discourtesy of staring. According to Brother Rupert, Sister Anne seemed content enough in her vocation and served competently as assistant to the infirmarian. There was, however, a sadness about the woman, evident in her bent shoulders and in the manner she held her bowed head. The observation was, she felt, worth further thought.

The seat next to Sister Anne was empty. That would belong to Sister Christina, the infirmarian, a plump and youthful nun who spent much of her time in chapel praying while Anne actually ran the hospital. Eleanor was beginning to suspect that habitual tardiness to everything except prayer, and perhaps meals, was another salient fact about this young woman.

Eleanor heard a muffled cough and looked at the door, hoping to see the tardy nun arrive. She hadn't. Eleanor closed her eyes and offered a quick prayer for patience in dealing with Sister Christina, but in truth, she had never felt charitable toward the unreliable.

With a suppressed groan, she opened her eyes. The nuns were sitting with great patience, hands tucked into their sleeves and eyes demurely lowered as if continuing their prayers from chapel. Indeed some were thinking godly thoughts. And some were not. Two of the latter were on the left of Christina's seat.

Sister Edith and Sister Matilda were actually blood sisters, children of a minor lord, who had come to the convent together because they apparently could not bear to live apart. Yet the two bickered constantly. Even now the thinner sister jostled the stouter one for space while muttering what Eleanor suspected were less than Christian sentiments.

Sister Edith, lean, pale and restless, was in charge of the kitchen, a position for which she had neither interest nor talent if last night's anonymous food was any indication. Sister Matilda, on the other hand, was red-faced, rotund and in charge of the kitchen garden. From the drooping state of its few pallid vegetables, little had survived her less than tender care over the summer growing months.

Eleanor looked up as she heard scuffling outside the chapter house from the direction of the cloister walk. The sound made her think of a large mouse running in soft leather shoes. Sister Christina rushed through the door and almost tripped over raised spots in the worn, uneven stone floor. All eyes, lowered though they were, watched with great interest the round nun's graceless progress to her assigned seat and their new prioress's reaction.

"I am late!" The nun panted the obvious.

Sister Anne gently smiled and moved to one side to make room for her.

Eleanor lifted one eyebrow and waited in silence for the nun to offer some explanation.

"I was lost in prayer to Our Lady." Christina's face was rose-red. She twisted her hands, round and around, as if she didn't know why she had such strange things attached to her arms and was trying to discover a use for them.

The prioress did not smile.

"It will not happen again!"

Out of the corner of her eye, Eleanor saw Sister Ruth nodding to the young woman with an almost benevolent smile twitching at her thin lips. The habit of authority is rarely surrendered with ease, Eleanor thought, as she ignored Sister Ruth's act and gestured in silence for the young nun to sit.

The flustered Christina wiggled herself into the space allotted to her.

Sister Ruth's careless attitude about the young nun's absence suggested that it was both habitual and accepted. Why had the former prioress permitted this breach of discipline, Eleanor wondered. Again, Brother Rupert would know the reason. She had so much she needed to ask him.

She looked around again. Although the elder monk's attendance was not obligatory, it would have added some weight of legitimacy to her own presence at Tyndal had he come to her first chapter. He understood that she needed all the support she could get from those respected inside the priory and had pledged his loyalty last night. That the old priest had not shown up was therefore inexplicable. Although aged, he had seemed vigorous enough at table. The meal may have been one of the worst Eleanor had ever eaten, but surely it had not made the good monk ill. Perhaps an emergency had delayed him.

Eleanor looked over at Sister Christina. "Did you see or hear Brother Rupert on your way from the church, sister?"

The nun opened her eyes and blinked as if she had just awakened from a deep sleep. "No, my lady."

"Then we shall start without him," Eleanor said, with what she hoped was a significant look at Christina. "Punctuality is a virtue without which we fail in our obligations to God as well as to man." Her voice sounded sufficiently stern to her own ears, and she prayed it also sounded more mature and forceful than she felt.

With that, Eleanor, duly appointed head of Tyndal Priory, clutched her staff of office with a firm hand, looked with steady eye across the granite slabs marking the graves of her noble predecessors, and began her first official act as prioress.

Chapter Three

From a small clearing at the edge of the forest, an auburn-haired young man mentally measured the distance over the diminishing hills as they rolled and slipped into the misty horizon to where he knew the North Sea lay. The late summer sun had warmed the trees, and he delighted in the tangy scent, but the sharp breeze from the ocean chilled his freshly tonsured head.

He raised his hand to cover the round bald spot, then dropped it. He would have to get used to this strange lack of hair. With any luck the scalp was now properly weathered after the long journey from London to this forsaken part of the East Anglian coast. Certainly he did not want any questions from his soon-to-be Fontevraud brothers about his recent commitment to the cloistered life.

He put his hand back on his horse's neck, stroking the sticky, stiff brown hair gently, and looked to his left. Tyndal Priory sat in a small valley between two low hills. He could see the stone walls of the outer court, some outbuildings on the rise of the hill, and the dark, rectangular bell tower. To the right of the priory, a large stream curved lazily as if it was in no hurry to meet with the sea, and he could see where it disappeared into the same valley. A grove of trees hid where it passed into the priory grounds. A stream might mean Tyndal had a mill and fishponds, but those were hidden from view.

The village was further to the left and beyond the priory. A fishing village, he assumed, and grimaced at the thought of how it must reek. London might not smell sweet to a countryman's nose, but he was a city man and preferred the familiar stench of civilization to that of dead fish wafting in from the garden, sheep dung next to the porridge pot, and decaying seaweed everywhere else.

His horse snorted, shook its head, and shifted with a definite but gentle show of equine impatience. He patted its neck and sighed.

A man coughed behind him. "My lord, perhaps we should…?" Although the phrasing was polite, the tone was not.

"Your 'my lord' was mocking, Giles. Please let us be done with that."

"Perhaps 'your holiness' then?"

"May you roast in Hell for that sacrilegious remark."

Giles' laugh was scornful.

Indeed, the young man thought, it was he who should be roasting, if not in Hell today, then surely at the stake. He squeezed his eyes shut until they hurt and shook his head 'til the bones in his neck cracked in protest. He still feared he'd wake from this dream to the smell of his own crackling flesh and guts. He took a deep breath to keep from crying out.

"Very well then," he said in a choked voice. "Let us get on with it."

His companion grunted and shifted in his saddle. "You'll find chastity does have merit, Thomas."

Surprised, Thomas turned. The man's tone held a hint of compassion, perhaps even some leftover affection, and, for the first time since they had left London, his companion's expression was not totally contemptuous.

"Aye, I'll not miss the pox," Thomas replied with a hollow laugh. "I am pleased to leave you with the whores' smiles."

"I'd rather the smiles on the whores' faces at my coming than their tears at my failure to properly attend them," the man said with a return of his sneering tone.

"You're rude, knave."

"Neither, I think. A knave is a dishonest man. And of the two of us, I do not qualify as the dishonest man. And if I be not dishonest, then it must be equally true that I am not rude to speak the facts."

Thomas laughed in spite of himself. "I will miss your wit, Giles, and I grieve for what has come between us."

"And I grieve for the man I once believed you to be. What you are, I hate with all the passion of a true Christian." He spat on the ground between them.

"Then there is no more to be said. It is time."

With that, the two men turned their horses away from the small clearing and guided them with care back over the soft, thick ground covering of rotted wood, vines and woodland flowers, to the path leading from the forest. In silence they rode single file, a finely dressed courtier on an even finer horse, followed by a simple monk on his very plain mount.

Chapter Four

Eleanor burst through the chapter house door and into the open, covered walk that surrounded the tranquil and fragrant gardens of the cloister square garth. Her step was brisk but light, and her soft shoes made almost no sound on the smooth stones. The nuns had left to start their tasks. She had survived her first chapter. Now she needed to be alone, think in peace, plan her day, to walk, walk, and walk until the tension built up from pretending to feel little when she had in fact felt so much had dissipated.

She entered a dark, narrow passage, cool even after a long summer's warmth, which ran between the chapter house and the warming room, unlocked the thick wooden door that protected her encloistered sisters from the world, and stepped into the outer court of the priory.

Beyond the carefully locked quarters where the monks and nuns lived, but still on monastic grounds, the charitable and practical businesses of Tyndal were conducted. The outer court was a largely public area. As Eleanor emerged, she looked to her left where the monks' quarters, brewery, mill, fishponds, stables, barns and livestock lay. The warm and dusty smells of well-tended animals mixed with the sharp odor of fermenting ale were sweet scents to her. They reminded her of her younger years at Wynethorpe Castle before her mother's death, when she and her two older brothers fought and played together with that fresh innocence of childhood. The memory brought both pain and joy to her heart.

She stood for a moment. Although the details of these particular priory grounds were still unfamiliar to her, the general design of Tyndal was very much the same as that of any other monastic house. In the middle of everything, and separating the monks' from the nuns' quarters, was the parish church, a dark and dominating structure of wind-battered stone. To her right would be the nuns' cemetery, then the gardens and orchards that provided food for the priory.

She shut her eyes to picture what stood beyond her vision. Lying in front of the priory grounds would be the main gate, near which lay the primary charitable business of Tyndal, a hospital. Just outside that main gate was the almonry where alms and food were given to the poor. Immediately inside the gate was the porter's cottage. The monks' cemetery lay near the stables and just beyond the hospital. It was a respectable distance from that of the nuns and sited against the wall of the outer court.

Eleanor turned right toward the gardens, and, after a short walk along the windowless wall of the nuns' dormitory, she rounded the corner at the stone-enclosed garderobe and stopped to look at the orchard across one of the streams that passed through the priory grounds. The trees were well established and properly pruned, she noted, and a gentle breeze carried the sweet scent of sun-warmed, ripening fruit. *Even if the vegetables don't survive the less than gentle touch of Sister Matilda, we should at least have dried fruit over the winter season,* she thought wryly.

Immediately in front of her and near the kitchen were the vegetable gardens. Just beyond them grew beds of both culinary and medicinal herbs, and further on was planted a garden growing flowers to adorn the altar. In a short while, lay brothers and sisters under the supervision of Sister Matilda would arrive to weed and harvest the raised beds. Sister Anne and a few of the nuns might also come to gather and tend the herbs, but for the moment all was quiet. Eleanor needed only a short time to concentrate her thoughts, relax her taut muscles.

As she walked along the edge of the beds toward the flower gardens that lay just beyond the hut where the medicines for the hospital were made, she slowed her pace and took in a measured, deep breath. The morning air was still moist and chill from sea fog, but the sun was warm and soothing where it peeked through the light mist drifting above her. She closed her eyes and listened to the birdsong, the distant whoosh of ocean waves, and smelled the slightly tart scent of seaweed carried on the light breeze. She smiled. It was lovely here, she thought, but she was still homesick for Amesbury.

After the death of Eleanor's mother in childbirth, Sister Beatrice, her father's elder sister and head of novices at Amesbury Priory, had taken the frightened six-year-old girl back with her to the convent. There Sister Beatrice had raised the child with warmth and kindness, and, having recognized the eager, intellectually curious Eleanor as a small version of herself, had wisely fed her niece's mind with all her own learning as a complement to feeding the child's soul.

Sister Beatrice's grandmother had come from Aquitaine as a lady in waiting to the equally famous and infamous Eleanor, wife of Henry II, and was known to suffer neither the ignorant nor fools gladly. As strong-willed and independent as her queen, she had no tolerance for intelligent women who pretended to be stupid and had taught her equally strong-minded daughters to use and be proud of their good wits. Thus, unlike most women of their class, they were taught to read and write not only in French and English but in Latin and Greek as well.

And little Beatrice had learned the same from her mother, who also ensured that her daughter was comfortable with arithmetic. These skills served Beatrice well during her marriage. While her husband was away at war, she ran the estate with competence and kept good accounts. Thus she was able to turn profitable lands over to her eldest son after her husband was killed, and happily take the veil at Amesbury, dedicating the rest of her life to the training of young girls.

It was true that Beatrice secretly hoped her niece would one day become Abbess of the entire Order of Fontevraud, a position that would assure great honor to the Wynethorpe family and secure places in Heaven for its more profane members. Such a worldly ambition she kept hidden in the deepest recess of her heart, and any such hope took second place to her love for her niece and concern for her happiness. Had marriage and children meant contentment for Eleanor, Sister Beatrice would have sent her back to the world, albeit shedding tears later in the privacy of her chamber. Meanwhile, before the child had to make her choice between the cloister and the hearth, Beatrice made sure little Eleanor learned and practiced the skills necessary to lead others and to manage priory assets in a profitable way. In a world of mortal men, wealth would always be the key to power, no matter whether the community be secular or religious.

Beatrice need not have worried about losing her niece to the world. For Eleanor, happiness was the cloister, and when Baron Adam wanted to take his child back to Wynethorpe Castle and a good dynastic marriage, Beatrice had stood up on her behalf like a mother lion protecting her cub. After long arguments, Beatrice and Adam did come to a reasonable compromise: the girl would be sent back to the world for one year to test her vocation. After that year, Eleanor chose to return to her aunt's welcoming arms at Amesbury and take her final vows. What Sister Beatrice understood and her brother did not was that the world and Wynethorpe Castle to Eleanor meant the sound of her mother's screaming and the memory of her death from childbirth. The convent, on the other hand, was a home filled only with love and peace.

Although she had rejected a marriage that would have gained her father both allies and land, Eleanor was not insensitive to the concept of familial duty. Indeed, she had wept bitterly in her aunt's arms at the thought of leaving Amesbury when she was told of her appointment to head Tyndal Priory, then quickly washed the evidence of grief from her face, stood with dignity before the king's messenger, and accepted the position with proper expressions of gratitude and modest joy. She knew full well the honor it had brought to her family, and she was determined to be adequate to the task.

⟡

Eleanor stopped by a bed of Madonna lilies commingled with Apothecary's roses, both grown in honor of the Virgin Mary, and happily breathed in their heady fragrance. This part of the priory gardens bordered on the plot containing plants used by the hospital for potions and other remedies.

A small woman, Eleanor had to stand on her toes and stretch to look over the lilies at the raised beds of healthy medicinal herbs, some still glistening with drops of morning dew. Sister Anne's ability to coax plants from the dank earth was impressive. As opposed, Eleanor thought with bitter amusement, to Sister Matilda's abuse of innocent vegetables.

She reached out, gently touched a silky white petal of the Madonna lily where it was lightly marked with gold from the stamens, and pulled her thoughts away from Amesbury and back to her problems at Tyndal.

She knew the priory was having financial difficulties. Prioress Joan of Amesbury had told her so before Eleanor left for her new home. Until she could study the problem in adequate depth and make more far-reaching plans to regain solvency, one of her first undertakings had to be a review of the assignments of tasks within the priory to make sure that Tyndal at least was run as efficiently as possible. So far, Eleanor had been amazed at Prioress Felicia's reasoning behind matching nun to occupation. The former prioress's decisions appeared arbitrary and without merit, at least on the surface. Talent for the task did not seem to have weighed with the old prioress, Eleanor thought, as she reviewed the responsibilities assigned to the Sisters Christina, Edith and Matilda, in particular.

She had to be careful not to change things quickly, and not to change anything without understanding why the previous decision had been made. Prioress Felicia had been revered. Eleanor was not. However efficient changes might be, she knew they had to be done slowly and with diplomatic skill. Any changes made without full agreement of the community would be undermined out of sheer resentment, and Eleanor was painfully aware of both her inexperience and youth compared to her predecessor. She would and must show due respect to the former prioress.

It was regrettable that she could not turn to Prior Theobald for advice and insights. He had been in charge of the monks and lay brothers at Tyndal for many years and would have been a logical mentor for her. However, after Sister Beatrice had consulted with one of her vast number of knowledgeable contacts, she had warned Eleanor against him. The prior, it seemed, was a man uncomfortable with detail, one who avoided the effort of well-considered decisions and left the day-to-day work to others. Thus he rarely knew what was happening amongst those he supposedly oversaw. Instead, her aunt had advised her to seek out Brother Rupert, a man known to be quiet but competent and who had worked closely with the former prioress.

At their initial meeting, Eleanor had gained some valuable insights into the priory overall, but she needed to question Brother Rupert in detail about much. The good brother had still not appeared, a perplexing failure that filled her with a growing concern. She closed her eyes against the tender beauty of the gardens and turned back to her quarters. She must find him without further delay.

As Eleanor walked back along the pathway between stream and gardens to the narrow passageway leading into the vine-covered trellised arches and flower-lined paths of the cloister garth, she tucked her hands into her sleeves for warmth against the sea breeze and bowed her head. Mentally, she started a list of the most pressing questions she had for the monk.

As she emerged from the walkway, however, something caught her eye. Eleanor stopped in shock. Near the fountain, a very tall nun knelt in the grass. Half-lying on the ground in front of her was a man in monk's garb. With one arm she embraced his shoulders, holding him close to her body. Her chin rested on the top of his head and she caressed his neck with great tenderness. Eleanor could not see the man's face.

"Sister!"

Sister Anne gently lowered the man to the ground and rose. As the woman turned to face her, Eleanor noted the dark streaks on the arms of her habit, the stains of grass and damp earth about her knees, and the tears streaming down the cheeks of the habitually sad nun.

"My lady," Sister Anne said, her voice shaking, "Brother Rupert is dead."

Chapter Five

Giles rode away. Thomas stood in the dark shadow of the priory walls; his hand raised to ring the gate bell; his back turned from the road. He knew there would be no backward glance from the rider, only a swirl of dust kicked up by the horses' hooves.

Brother Thomas, as he now must call himself, pressed a hand against his chest. Pains of longing and grief stabbed equally and unmercifully at him. Both the lack and the loss of loved ones were all too familiar to him, yet he had never been able to inure himself to either.

Thomas was a by-blow. His servant mother had died of some fever soon after his birth. His father, an earl, had taken him up, tossed him into the arms of a wet nurse, fed and clothed him with some decency, and then mostly forgot about the boy as he habitually dismissed all his offspring, whatever their legitimacy. In both war and bed, the earl was a man of passionate action. Consequences merited a more limited interest.

The earl's presence in Thomas' life was just frequent enough, however, that the boy could neither forget nor ignore him, and he longed for his father's rare attention and even more infrequent praise. Thus the lad searched out the men most favored in the earl's circle and began to study how they spoke, stood, and gestured, so that he too might catch his father's eye and approval. This may have started as a boy's desperate attempt at attention, but Thomas soon developed a talent for shadowing older men, eavesdropping on their bragging tales, and watching them do the things men do when they do not know they are being watched. And with the precocious intelligence of a parentless child, he quickly figured out the significance of what he overheard when secrets were whispered.

One day, the boy begged an audience with his father and imparted something of such import into his ear that the earl developed a true, albeit belated fondness for him. As a reward for warning him of the malicious plot being brewed, the earl gave Thomas a thump of genuine affection and sent him off to cathedral school.

Thomas might have preferred more direct forms of affection and, from the beginning, made it clear he had little taste for the Church. At his father's insistence, however, he did take minor orders. The earl told him with well-intentioned candor that Thomas' birth precluded inheriting either title or lands and that taking such orders would give the boy a fine future with men in high places who would value his talents. Indeed, as he began his sometimes less than strictly clerical duties for some of the more ambitious men of the Church, Thomas learned to enjoy assisting in the earthly power games played by his priestly masters.

Sharing this love of intrigue had been his boyhood friend, Giles, who was also sent to cathedral school as the proper place for a younger, and in this case legitimate, son of one of the earl's barons. Giles was more than just a childhood friend. They had been brothers in toddler mischief, adolescent buffoonery, and finally the more serious sports of wining and wenching.

Then one bright spring morning, after a night of sharing the lush favors of a serving maid from a pilgrims' inn near Saint Edward the Confessor's shrine at Westminster, Thomas was awakened from a sweet but unremembered dream by church bells ringing out with their particular joy. He looked at Giles' naked body next to him and had begun to caress him with an inexplicably tender longing. Indeed, never before had Thomas felt so unreservedly happy nor had he ever been able to show love so freely.

Giles later claimed he knew nothing of what had happened before the maid began to scream and a horrified pilgrim ran to fetch the archdeacon's chief clerk, but Thomas knew better. He remembered how ardently Giles had returned his kisses and fondling, how Giles had begged his friend to thrust his sex into him. And as he began to do so, Thomas felt an almost holy joy.

Yet the man who dragged him from Giles had screamed "Sodomite!" and the dungeon where Thomas had soon found himself was a cold, foul, and brutal hell.

One of his jailers raped him, all had taunted him, but two took especial joy in loudly recounting tales of how Giles had spent his days since, tearing at his garments and howling like a wolf. He had been locked away in his father's castle tower until he begged his father to take him to the chapel. Arriving at the door, Giles had ripped away his remaining rags and plunged naked into a bed of stinging nettles. The priest had exorcised Satan from the young man's writhing body, after which Giles had fallen into a deep sleep and, when he awoke, claimed ignorance of all that had transpired in bed with Thomas.

Now cleansed of evil, Giles had walked barefooted to a nearby shrine in penance and in gratitude. Shortly thereafter, he was married to an old and wealthy widow of his father's choosing. Thomas' jailers recounted this last news in especially ribald detail just outside his prison door. The onetime rape he might have endured, swearing to castrate the man in good time. The tauntings were only words even his dulled wits could match, but these jailers could not have chosen a better torture than this tale to bring him to his knees, whimpering like a beaten dog, in grief for his friend.

Why Thomas hadn't been burned at the stake was still a mystery to him. Perhaps it was his father's doing. Perhaps it was some bishop who had benefited from his murmured advice. Whatever, he had wanted to die by the time he was finally wrenched from his prison bed of rotten straw, rat feces, and his own filth. The brightness of forgotten sunlight had seared his eyes, and the encrusted chains had rubbed his bloody ankles to a point beyond

pain. He would have begged for death, had he not lost his voice
in a world where darkness made a mockery of human speech.

Although the tonsure would suggest the man was from the
Church, Thomas had no idea of the somber one's identity as he
sat in the warden's room and silently examined the disgusting
wretch Thomas had become. Whoever the man was, he had
quickly ordered a stool brought for Thomas to sit on and some
watered wine for his rusted throat.

"I have a proposition for you," the black-robed man had said,
his voice undistinguished by any particular tone.

Thomas had stared at him.

"A slow death at the stake and your soul condemned to
Hell…"

Thomas blinked.

"…or your sins forgiven in return for becoming a priest
with unquestioning obedience to a master whom you will
never meet."

Thomas said nothing.

"Do you hear me?"

Thomas dipped his head.

"Do you understand the choice?"

Thomas nodded.

"And?"

"The Church," Thomas whispered. "I know Hell and wish
no more of it."

And so they had cut the chains from his flesh, bathed his
filth-dyed and rat-bitten body, put poultices on the worst of
his festering wounds and shaved a monk's tonsure on his head.
When he was strong enough, they trained him further in priestly
rites and draped chastity, poverty, and obedience over his head
with a monk's rough habit.

But Thomas didn't mind what he had been forced to
swear.

He only minded forswearing Giles.

And who, with such sadistic humor, had chosen the penitential Giles to lead the ravaged Thomas to Tyndal Priory and

leave him like an abandoned child to be encloistered with monks under the rule of women?

Thomas hoped he never found out.

⌘

Thomas rang the bell, then turned and looked down the road. There was nothing to see, not even settling dust, but Thomas continued to stare into the distance as tears slipped down his cheeks. Shamed at his weakness, he wiped them away but bowed his head as the ache of grief burst into his hollowed-out heart. The pain would linger for a long, long time.

The sound of the heavy wooden door opening on its metal hinges caused him to turn around. In front of him was a small monk of indeterminate age with deep blue eyes and a head so bald a tonsure was unneeded.

"Thanks be to God! And welcome to Tyndal Priory, brother," the man said with ritual greeting and a deep bow. "I am Brother Andrew."

Chapter Six

"We will, of course, handle the problem of our poor brother's body, my child… ah, my lady. Please don't worry yourself about it. A great shock it must have been for you to find him lying dead in your cloister. And a great tragedy for you to lose his counsel, to be sure." Prior Theobald of Tyndal shifted in his ornately carved wooden chair, a slightly musty odor emanating from his dark robes with the movement. As he resettled, he grimaced, and in so doing brought his bushy gray eyebrows into brief collision.

He was a dour man of advanced years with an unusually large abdomen despite an otherwise skeletal frame. Resting on his stomach was a heavy gold cross, attached to a soft rope that looped around his birdlike neck. His long, bony fingers first clutched, then stroked the crucifix with a broken and irritating rhythm.

Eleanor lowered her eyes, not out of modesty but to prevent him from seeing her fury. The prior's tone had been dismissive from the moment she arrived at his quarters, and he had just interrupted her in the middle of a sentence. Again. At this rate, it might be the midnight hour before she was able to tell him the exact and very serious nature of Brother Rupert's death. Did he think she had nothing else of importance to do with her day as a result of it? She took a deep breath to calm herself.

She knew she had only herself to blame for his disrespectful behavior. Her aunt had given her good warning about what to expect at Tyndal. Although the clerical world, and indeed the secular one as well, found the idea of Eve leading Adam uncomfortable, the founder of Fontevraud had specifically declared that female leadership would be the rule in his Order of nuns and monks. The old prioress had not always been diligent in exerting her rightful authority over both men and women as the supreme head of a Fontevraud double house. Sister Beatrice had told Eleanor that she would have an upward battle to reestablish the rule.

"I am sure your assistance will be greatly appreciated, Prior," she replied, unclenching her teeth.

Some would have argued that Eleanor's first concern should have been to reestablish her authority immediately, despite the alarming circumstances and implications of the old monk's death. She knew that. Of course she should have summoned Prior Theobald to her chambers where she could look down from her raised chair and enforce obedience from that symbol of her superior status. Instead she had chosen to go to his chambers, in the monks' quarters to the south of the parish church, out of consideration for his advanced age and the effect she assumed the news would surely have on him. In going to him as if she were the inferior, she had committed a tactical error and further diminished her authority in the eyes of those who venerate form over substance.

Eleanor glanced up at the smug expression on the face of Brother Simeon. The receiver and sub-prior, who stood next to Theobald and idly stroked the grooves in the top of his prior's chair, was one who appreciated the power of symbols. Perhaps even better than his master, she thought. Ideally, such worldly games should have no place in a house dedicated to God, but Eleanor was not so naïve as to think a religious vocation stripped men and women of ambition. She would have to learn to play the game of symbols far better if she were going to succeed here, or anywhere else.

She glanced over at Sister Ruth to see her reaction to the confrontation. The nun sat with hands folded in her lap and eyes staring in rapt concentration at the prior and Brother Simeon. Eleanor had no allies in this room, if, indeed, she had allies anywhere in Tyndal. Eleanor closed her eyes for just a moment. They burned.

"We will need a priest immediately to hear confessions, attend the dying at the hospital, and perform Mass. The crowner has been summoned," she continued, concentrating on the rushes under her feet so as not to betray her feelings.

The prior blinked fretfully. "With all due respect, my lady, this is not a matter for the crowner. We need no such officer of a secular court to investigate and hold an inquest for our brother's death. I will send one of the monks to examine the body, if that would allay your fears that the death might be questionable, but there is no doubt that Brother Rupert died a natural death. He was an aged man. Surely, God must have called him..."

"I did the preliminary examination with the aid of Sister Anne."

"What!" The prior rose halfway out of his chair, his face as pale as his wispy hair. "This was not proper for..."

"Prior Theobald, as you well know, I am in charge of this priory and such actions are within my responsibility. A dead man's body is hardly a shock or a temptation to sin." She raised her hand as the old man opened his mouth. "Nor am I ignorant of the differences between bull and cow. Indeed, Brother Rupert did not die of age, he..."

The prior flapped his hand in the air as he eased himself back into his chair. "Disease of the lungs. Of course. Not uncommon here, but I was unaware he was so afflicted. Although I may have heard him coughing..." He glanced tentatively at the towering and well-fleshed monk standing beside him. Brother Simeon smiled down at Theobald with obsequious agreement.

Frustrated with the prior's inability to listen long enough to hear her out, Eleanor dropped all attempts to soften the news. "His lungs were not at issue. He was stabbed and castrated." She sat back in her chair, raised her eyes, and waited for the expected reaction, but the taste in her mouth was bitter.

"Castr...castrated?" Prior Theobald's voice shifted up an octave in shock. He pulled his cross over his heart. "Brother Simeon! Why was I not told that Brother Rupert was troubled with such lust? Why was he not brought to me for prayer and counseling?" His voice cracked.

Eleanor blinked at this unexpected interpretation and looked over at Sister Ruth with hope that she might have some understanding to give to her. The nun looked away but not before Eleanor saw that her face was bright red.

Simeon smiled without humor and showed a few gaps in his yellowed front teeth.

"Surely, my lord, you remember when I mentioned my concern over his, shall we say, unusual attachment to..." he nodded in Eleanor's direction and lowered his voice "...our revered Prioress Felicia? However, since her death, I assumed, in your wisdom, you had..."

Eleanor muttered a short prayer under her breath for the renewal of a patience she was quickly losing, then snapped. "Prior, he did not castrate himself. It was done to him. After death. A knife in the chest killed him, Sister Anne believes, but the blade was broken off..."

His face scarlet, Theobald leaned toward her. "How could you..."

Eleanor was about to tell him exactly how and why she could when a gentle rapping at the chamber door stopped her.

Theobald jerked upright in his chair. "Yes?" He squealed as his elbow hit the edge of his chair.

When Brother Andrew emerged from the doorway, he looked at the expressions of those in the chamber, then backed up and ever so slowly reached behind him to feel for the door. He gently pushed it shut before continuing. "My lord, the priest we have been expecting has arrived," he said. "He is a young man as you hoped. What shall I do with him?"

Brother Simeon's face softened as he bent to Theobald's ear and put his hand reassuringly on the prior's shoulders. "I suggest you bring him in to us here first, my lord. As a young man, surely he would have the energy to take over all a priest's responsibilities with the hospital and nuns. And, perhaps, he might help our prioress settle this matter of our poor brother's death in an expeditious fashion."

Theobald exhaled as if he had been holding his breath and relaxed in his chair. "My thoughts exactly," he said. "Bring him in, Brother Andrew."

Eleanor raised her hand. "Just a moment, brother."

The monk stopped in mid-step, but instead of looking to either Theobald or Simeon for direction, he turned to her. Perhaps, she thought with mild relief, she would not have to reeducate the entire priory.

"I have some questions before you bring him in. I was unaware we were receiving another priest; therefore, I must know something of his background and why he was sent here before I agree to his assignment as the spiritual advisor to my nuns and the afflicted. It would be discourteous to discuss this in front of him. We shall do so now."

Sister Ruth's eyes widened.

Simeon coughed and looked quickly in the direction of Theobald.

The prior nodded.

The interchange was not lost on Eleanor.

"In brief then, my lady," Simeon said, "Brother Thomas has been sent by our English administrative community at Grovebury. Beyond that, we know little more except that his appointment to Tyndal has the approval of our Abbess at Fontevraud." He smiled. "As yours has as well."

Eleanor did not take the bait and said nothing. The silence grew long and tense as she waited for the receiver to give her the *little more* information she should have as head of the priory.

Simeon looked at Theobald, his forehead furrowed with irritation. Perhaps the receiver did not want to lose this battle of wills to a woman, but Eleanor noted that the prior gave him no support. Instead, Theobald looked away, leaving Simeon to flounder on his own.

Simeon cleared his throat and continued with some degree of dignity. "We had requested an additional chaplain, a young man we hoped. Many of our priests, poor Brother Rupert among them, are aging and no longer able to perform all their duties. Our few novices are too young."

Grovebury, a tiny Fontevraud priory to the east of Amesbury, often provided monks for administrative help to the English houses of the Order. That connection alone would be sufficient recommendation to accept the new priest. The specific approval of the Abbess should suggest even higher merit, Eleanor thought, but as you well noted with such sarcastic tone, good brother, I received the same approval. How competent has that made me in the eyes of those here? The young priest's credentials were indeed all too sketchy.

The problem of qualifications aside, what troubled her even more was the lack of sense in what Simeon had just said to her. Although Brother Rupert had that frail look not unusual amongst those who fasted often, she had not noted any remarkable physical weakness in him. That was the first inconsistency. Moreover, even if one were to assume he was far weaker than he had appeared and so advanced in age that he no longer had the energy to perform Mass or even hear confessions, how could anyone conclude that he burned with such uncontrollable lust that he would castrate himself? The whole thing was just ridiculous. It gave her no great peace of mind to know she had monks in charge of accounts and the estates who could reason no better than that.

She ground her teeth in frustration. The inability of either the prior or his receiver to think logically should be the least of her worries. She would, after all, be taking over the management of the priory herself. Of greater concern was the fact that she was not just starting her tenure with potentially incompetent monks, an inexperienced priest, and no support from her priory, she had a murdered priest in her cloister garth. A murderer had been able to enter both the outer court and the locked nuns' quarters without being seen. The latter fact was especially disturbing.

She prayed the crowner would prove more competent than at least two of the people in the room with her and that he would capture the perpetrator quickly. She already had more to deal with than the average new prioress without having to worry about a murderer on the loose.

"Very well, then," she said, looking at each man until he shifted uncomfortably. "Let us see this young priest who will serve my sisters and succor the dying at our hospital."

Chapter Seven

Simeon thumped Thomas' shoulder with such enthusiasm that the young man staggered. The older monk's face might have beamed with jovial greeting, but his dark eyes studied the younger with grim intensity. "You have just arrived from Grovebury then, brother?"

"Yes, my lord." Thomas wanted to rub his aching shoulder, but he had been through such silent examinations before and knew when he was being appraised. This might be a world dedicated to God, but the unspoken rules were no different from the secular one. Acceptance at Tyndal was crucial to his success with this first assignment given by his grim new master, and he knew better than to show weakness of any kind. The ache in his shoulder receded.

A flicker of approval passed over Simeon's face, and then he nodded to the porter. "Brother Andrew, bring some wine to wash the dust from our new brother's throat."

"I would be most grateful for it, my lord," Thomas replied with calculated courtesy. As he smiled in thanks, he would have sworn the short, bald monk winked at him before dropping his eyes modestly and limping dutifully toward the wine pitcher. Brother Andrew slopped some deep red liquid from the ewer into a gold goblet and handed it to Thomas.

He gazed down at the object in his hand. It was an unusually opulent thing to find in such a remote house, Thomas thought.

The priory's uncharacteristic financial downturn had tweaked the interest of some high churchman, at least enough to use it to test Thomas' investigative skills, yet clearly its members had not felt sufficient distress to sell any of its valuable plate. Despite its plain design, the goblet was still gold and well-crafted. Then he glanced at the table and noted four similar goblets. Odd too that such rich possessions would be brought out for daily use, and by the prior, who was not even responsible for the entertainment of important guests under normal circumstances. He wondered what quality of plate the prioress had in her lodgings.

Thomas sipped the smooth and mellow wine. It was of superior quality as well. If Tyndal had a generous patron who guaranteed a good supply of fine wine to make diminished wealth more palatable, Thomas' human raven had failed to mention it. Or perhaps he didn't know about such a benefactor. Or perhaps he was misinformed about the entire situation. Ignorance of what really happened in places or amid people deemed to be of minor or no importance was not unusual amongst those at the pinnacles of power. Thomas remembered some of his former masters with mild derision and enjoyed another sip of the wine.

"You elevated me beyond my station, however." Simeon's words were humble, but as Thomas looked up at the tall monk's expression, he knew he had quite pleased the man.

"I am Brother Simeon, receiver and sub-prior of Tyndal."

Thomas bowed graciously.

Simeon gestured to the man at the head of the table. "Prior Theobald leads us."

"My lord." As Thomas humbled himself once again, he noted the prior's blinking eyes and aimlessly fumbling hands. A pathetic and ineffectual old man, he decided, and hardly the real center of power here. That, he concluded, was Brother Simeon, whose formidable size and vitality overwhelmed the room.

With a sharp stab of pain, Thomas once again missed Giles. In the old days, they would have made Theobald into prime fodder for parody. Now there was no one with whom he could later mock such a feeble, aged master in the time-honored tradi-

tion of young clerks. Then with some surprise Thomas realized
he felt sorry for the old prior. Maybe the days were past when
he could find joy in mocking men whose manhood existed only
in memory. He snorted quietly. Was he much different himself
from this impotent prior? Thomas lowered his head to keep his
moist eyes from public gaze.

"Excuse me, brother, but I did not hear your name?"

Thomas started. The voice was distinctly feminine and quite
melodic.

Simeon stepped aside.

Sitting at the table behind the receiver were two nuns. One
was a woman of middle years, stout about the hips and waist.
The other was youthful and quite diminutive. The first must
be the prioress, Thomas thought. She looked sour enough, her
forehead deeply ridged in what must be a perpetual frown, and,
although her eyes were lowered, he could sense their look of
constant disapproval. The young one, however, looked directly
at him, her gray eyes alert with curiosity and her complexion
flushed a healthy pink. Too tiny all over for my taste, Thomas
thought with irreverent amusement.

Simeon cleared his throat. "Forgive me," he said, rudely pointing his finger at the young nun. "Prioress Eleanor of Wynethorpe
has just arrived from Amesbury but a day or so ago." With far
greater courtesy and warmth, he gestured toward the elder. "This
is Sister Ruth, our esteemed porteress for the nuns."

Thomas blinked in surprise. He watched as Prioress Eleanor's
eyes briefly narrowed in what he suspected was carefully con-
trolled anger, then quickly cleared and began to appraise him.
Perhaps, he thought, it might not be wise to dismiss this young
woman, as Simeon appeared to be doing. Had the person in
front of him been a man who could control his emotions with
such iron will, he would have accorded him more respect.

Thomas bowed. "My lady, I am Brother Thomas. Here to
serve your will."

"And what skills do you bring me, brother?"

"Humble ones. I have come lately to the priesthood."

"Indeed, but previously a clerk, I see. What brought you to choose a cloistered vocation over the earthly rewards at a king's court?"

Thomas paled. Surely this prioress could not know his real background. His black-clad liberator had promised him anonymity in exchange for his oath of fealty.

"Do not be so surprised, brother. With such soft hands, you are surely no man of arms, although I wonder why not with your height and that breadth of shoulders." She smiled warmly, then laughed with a straightforward heartiness.

Sister Ruth pressed her lips together into a rigid white line.

Thomas smiled in return with more warmth than he felt. *You, my lady prioress, are more observant that I would expect from a woman of your youth and vocation*, he thought, *and more than makes me comfortable.*

"Indeed," he said aloud, "I was a clerk, thus I have some knowledge of Latin and law. As for my choice of the cloister, my shoulders may be broad but my soul cried out to serve God in a more contemplative setting, not on the field of battle or in the courts of kings."

"Well said, brother. I think our sisters will be lucky to have such a priest as their spiritual guide."

Her phrasing was smooth as river rock. As he bowed his head in humble thanks at her courtesy, Thomas knew by her amused smile that she was not deceived in the slightest by his fine and empty words.

⁂

When Eleanor first looked at Brother Thomas, as he walked into the prior's chambers, and saw blue eyes the color of the summer sea and hair the shade of burnished copper, she felt heat, then shuddered as if chilled. He had all the legendary beauty of Satan's own angels.

The suddenness, no, the strength of her attraction to the young monk startled her. This was not just a playful, almost innocent tickling of pleasure to be enjoyed for a moment, confessed, then forgotten. She felt as if a bonfire had been set alight in her entrails. This was no easily ignored and set aside desire. This was lust. And why had God chosen now of all times to give her the added burden of conquering such a passion? Didn't she have problems enough?

Yet God had not completely abandoned her. Even as she felt her face flush, she had struggled, then regained control of her reason and calmly questioned the man. He had seemed oddly taken aback at her observation that he must have been a clerk. Perhaps he had been insulted, assumed she thought he was of a rank too low to be trained in the knightly arts of war, or had not thought him man enough. Nevertheless, he had quickly recovered and shown the smooth tongue of one at ease with courtly manners. A younger son of someone of rank sent to make his way in the Church with or without any calling to it, she thought. Or else a by-blow. If the latter, she might be better off. Her aunt had said that those born to the mighty without the benefit of legitimacy often understood the ephemeral nature of worldly rank and comforts better than a younger son who had grown up in the ease of it.

Whatever his lineage, he was a priest with some training in law. She could see no reasonable grounds to refuse him as the offered replacement for Brother Rupert. Without a priest to perform sacraments for her nuns and the hospitalized dying, the priory could not function properly. She herself must have an educated man to assist her in the administrative work. For the moment, she would have to put her own feelings aside and accept him, but deep inside she trembled for her own emotional security. How she wished Sister Beatrice was waiting for her in her chambers with comfort and advice.

"I am grateful to you for your offer of Brother Thomas to fill the position we so desperately need." Eleanor turned to face Theobald and Simeon, hoping that they could not see her slight trembling.

"I believe it to be best…" Prior Theobald began.

"And I accept your recommendation. At least for the time being. Our immediate concern, of course, must be Brother

Rupert's murder. The effect on our priory and indeed the implications for our very safety within the walls are paramount. Once the crowner has examined his body and decided what must be done to apprehend the killer, we can discuss further and in greater detail how the monks and lay brothers should be used to run our hospital and priory as well as serve the parish efficiently. At that time I will decide whether Brother Thomas can fulfill all his duties to my sisters without assistance. In the meantime…"

Thomas coughed. "Forgive me, my lady, but did you say *murder?*"

"Yes, brother. We have suffered a monstrous slaying in our midst. Brother Rupert, an elderly priest of our house, was found this morning in the nuns' cloister garth, stabbed and castrated."

Eleanor studied the young monk's face. He had paled a bit at the news but otherwise showed little emotion. "In your studies of law," she continued, "did you ever have occasion to investigate questionable deaths?"

⌘

The news that someone had been murdered and the prioress' query about questionable deaths took Thomas' mind back to the nights when he was a young lad and had heard muffled cries and scufflings in the dark passages of his father's castle just outside the room in which he slept. He was never sure if the sounds were those of ghosts and demons or were of human origin, but he remembered how rigid he had lain in his tiny bed, his eyes focused in terror on the wavering shadows and pale shifting lights that danced tauntingly on the walls of his room. As soon as the gray morning light illuminated the familiar forms of straw and wood, he would slip outside his door, where he'd sometimes find brown stains on the stones, then he would tremble with fear at what might have happened all too close to him in the hours of darkness.

Even later on in his adult years, there was the morning he had entered the chamber of a well-hated deacon to find the man's frozen and twisted body on the bed. Oh, he was told by a grinning servant, the master must have died from eating a dinner of bad eels. Did anyone die of food poisoning with such an expression of agonized horror on his face? Thomas suspected not but knew better than to voice his doubts.

So had he ever had occasion to investigate questionable deaths? No, he said to himself, he'd had more sense. Aloud, Thomas replied, "My education was academic, but both the study and practice of law require the exercise of reason and observation."

"Indeed. I hope you have a strong stomach as well. Brother Rupert is not a pretty sight."

Thomas lowered his eyes to hide his surprise at the bluntness of his new prioress. This woman did not behave like any of the other young women he had known. The sight of a tiny, live mouse was enough to cause them to scream and throw themselves into the arms of the nearest man, but this one was quite calm in her discussion of a man's mutilated corpse. He might have expected an older, married woman to be this composed. After all, he'd heard tales of how some wives successfully defended castles while their lords were elsewhere, but a woman of the prioress's youth? Never. Perhaps whatever changed some aging women into more manlike creatures happened to women of any age who devoted themselves to God? Thomas could think of no other explanation.

"My stomach will be strong enough, my lady," he replied at last.

"Good," the prioress said. "You must examine Brother Rupert's body now, if you will. Perhaps you will see something both Sister Anne and I missed. After that you will arrange to take his body to a more fitting place to lie. I have forbidden the nuns access to the garden until the crowner has done whatever examination he deems fit, but Brother Rupert should rest in peace in a chapel tonight. It is unseemly that the poor man remain exposed in the cloister garth until the morrow."

Thomas glanced over at both Prior Theobald and Brother Simeon for guidance. The good prior was stroking his cross, his eyes vague and his expression confused. The receiver stood with chin in hand, gazing at the prioress with a slight frown, then he turned and gave Thomas a quick nod.

"Of course, my lady," Thomas said. "As you wish."

Chapter Eight

Eleanor pressed her hand to her heart, then bit her lip. She was not surprised at the brief exchange between Thomas and Simeon. She should have expected that the young priest would seek approval from the two older men before obeying her. Still the gesture had stung her with a disproportionate pain. Thomas must be new to the Order, she told herself. Like both Simeon and Theobald he would soon learn that it was she who was in charge at Tyndal. Once he did, he would look to her for direction, not them.

Then she winced. Oh, don't be such a fool, Eleanor, she said to herself, shaking her head in disgust. It's not your position as head of the priory that you want him to recognize. You want him to see you as a woman. A worldly creature you still are, whatever your vows. Your muscles were like water walking so near him down the stone stairs from the prior's chambers, and you tremble with the sickness of lust. If God meant to purge your soul of any pride in becoming prioress to the religious at Tyndal, He has succeeded well.

She had always thought obedience would be the vow with which she'd struggle most. She was quite amply endowed with a high spirit. For cert, the vow of poverty had never been a problem for her. She had grown up in comfortable simplicity at Amesbury and such was her definition of poverty. Being used to that life, she even preferred it.

But lust? Virgin she might be, but innocent she was not. Not after living with two older brothers and a castle full of young men in the year she'd spent with her father before she had taken her final vows. She had played at courtly love and quite enjoyed the feints and parries of it all, but it was only a game to her and she had never lost sight of or the desire for her vocation. This was surely the first test of her vows. And, she thought with grim determination, I shall win the contest.

As they stepped into the dappled light of the monks' cloister walk, Eleanor glanced at Sister Ruth walking next to her in silence. The nun's eyes were downcast, and her mouth was pursed as if she had just tasted something bitter. Had the older woman recognized what her young prioress was feeling? Perhaps God was kind and she had noticed nothing. Certainly Eleanor did not need any further marks against her in her new community. Or perhaps the porteress had never experienced lust and would not recognize the symptoms.

For just an instant, Eleanor felt a tinge of envy.

The trio passed in silence through the covered cloister walk, keeping a modest distance from the few monks strolling there, and on toward the passage leading into the outer court.

She heard a muffled laugh and glanced quickly over her shoulder. The young monk was smiling in some private amusement. Seeing her turn to him, he looked down quickly. Had he noted the effect he had on her? Was that the source of his mirth? She scowled, hoping he noted her severity just as well. Then her own eyes turned traitor and quickly feasted on all of him from head to foot before she was able to drag her gaze back to a more seemly concentration on the stone walk at her feet.

He did look more suited to charger and armor than cowl and tonsure. Still, tonsured and cowled he was, whatever the true reason for his recent calling. She certainly did not believe the glib tale he had told her. He had shown a courtly manner and physical comfort with his body rarely found in younger monks. Although he towered over both Sister Ruth and Eleanor, he seemed in control of his size and strength and kept an easy, slow pace behind her as they walked into the dark, narrow passage under the monks' dormitory and up to the heavy wooden door.

"This is the path you will take when you come to serve us. And you will use it to return when you are done." Eleanor inserted a large key, unlocked the door, then turned and handed the key to Thomas. "This is now yours as priest to my nuns and the sick. Besides you, Prior Theobald has such a key and Brother Andrew also because he is porter. Of the nuns, only Sister Ruth as porteress, Sister Christina and Sister Anne, who are both in charge of the hospital, and I may have such keys. Please keep it safe and lend it to no one. These locked doors keep us protected from the world." Eleanor heard a sharp intake of breath from the nun beside her and winced. At least the doors had done so until the death of Brother Rupert, she thought.

"I will take you to the hospital before the crowner comes and introduce you to Sister Christina, the infirmarian. Sister Anne, her assistant, you will meet shortly. Until I can review the assignments of all the brothers at Tyndal, your duties will include service to the sick as well as priest for the nuns."

As they walked through the gate and approached the church, Eleanor pointed out the sacristy door that led to the priests' changing room and the altar. When they approached the entrance to the nuns' cloister, Brother Thomas bowed to Sister Ruth, who stepped back so he could take her place by the prioress' side.

"Since you have already examined the body, my lady, what specifically do you wish me to look for?"

Eleanor turned so quickly he almost trod on her.

"I did not mean…"

Eleanor was pleased that he looked abashed as he stumbled backward. At least there was little aggression to fear in the man. One prone to violence would have looked angry to be placed so suddenly at disadvantage.

She smiled with pleasure at her impromptu trick and at his flustered reaction, then nodded acceptance of the apology.

The boyish grin he gave in return was not only ingenuous but also calculated, Eleanor decided. The look did not extend to his expressionless eyes. Nonetheless, unwanted warmth rushed once again to her face. She quickly turned away from him and walked in determined silence to the nuns' gate, unlocked it with her own key, and led the two others into the cloister garth. As they reached the fountain where Sister Anne guarded the body, Eleanor finally stopped and turned to Thomas.

"Your opinion and observations, brother, would be both welcome and useful. Indeed Sister Anne and I did examine the body quite thoroughly. However, if the crowner is like most, he would more likely listen to the details and take them more seriously from you than from us. The world outside our small Order is unaccustomed to open female command and for me to assert this unusual authority as head of Tyndal might so unsettle him that he could be distracted from a timely pursuit of justice. I understand he has never had occasion to visit here before. I trust we will never have to invite him to our priory again. Therefore, in the interest of a clear-eyed, efficient hunt for the person who did this horrible thing to our brother, I think the issue of who runs Tyndal may remain a moot one."

"If I may be so blunt, my lady, you show rare judgement for…"

"A woman?"

"For any child born of sin."

Clever man with words you are, Eleanor thought and could not help smiling at him. She might fear Thomas and the unwelcome feelings and confusion he caused her, but she did like his quick wit.

Chapter Nine

Thomas retched. The sight of Brother Rupert's mutilated corpse had turned his stomach despite his brave words to the contrary. If he'd been alone in the garth, he probably would have instantly vomited the good wine he had just enjoyed, but he would never show such weakness before women. Now that he was by himself, he could throw up in peace. Bracing against the stone wall, he retched again into the tall grass.

Still sweating, he shook his head. How two women could have examined that body with apparent composure and thoroughness was beyond his understanding. He at least had seen death in some of its uglier forms; neither stabbings nor poisonings were pretty, but to castrate a man like that?

"What horrible thing could an old priest have done to warrant such treatment? And who could have defiled him so?" He spat. Such desecration of manhood was usually reserved for the most hated of men. Traitors to a king came first to mind, although there was Abelard who'd been gelded as well as that unfortunate lover of a nun at Watton Priory.

After some dry heaving, nothing was left in his stomach. Thomas kicked up some dirt and tore some of the dry grass to cover his leavings, then locked the door to the nuns' quarters and headed down the gravel path to the monks' lodgings. At the nave of the church, he stopped and looked up at the granite and slate building. Moss streaked the shadowed stone and blackened what might once have been colored light gray. The windows over the high altar were narrow and dingy, and something brown was growing from the corners and joinings which must further inhibit light from illuminating the inside of the church.

"What cold and soggy land have I been sent to?" he asked himself. A sudden chill shook Thomas in the afternoon sun. Damp and mold permeated all. Everything reeked of gradual but inevitable decay. A black mood descended on him, and the manner of Brother Rupert's death seemed in keeping with the ambiance of the place.

Just as his thoughts grew grim, he looked around, then smiled in spite of his sad temper at the incongruity he had just observed. Women might run Fontevraud houses but they still lived to the north of the church, the side that symbolized benightedness, while the very monks they ruled lived on the south, the side of enlightenment. What did his new prioress think of that? Had she even noticed it? He shook his head. A more apt question would be whether there was much of anything she hadn't observed.

A single cloud scudded across the sun, briefly darkening the day with its shadow. Thomas watched as more clouds followed the first, dark bottomed and close to the earth. Rain was coming, he decided, as he felt the air turn slightly damp against his skin. He turned away from the nave and walked on.

"Surely the prioress has recognized what a strong adversary she has in Brother Simeon," Thomas muttered. "Now there is a man who shows very traditional views on whether it is Adam or Eve who should rule. He would have no doubts that men were the more capable sex and that women should be guided by them."

How did such a man ever become a member of this religious order, founded in seeming defiance of established wisdom? Thomas shook his head. Perhaps he had arrived as a child and been more willing in his youth to obey a woman's command. If so, he had clearly changed in the passing years. Thomas had seen how little the now forceful monk cared for the equally forceful new prioress. "Without question, there will be a struggle for supremacy between the two. Perhaps I should not wager on which will win," he said into the dank wind.

And what were his own feelings about Prioress Eleanor and her authority over him? Thomas wasn't sure. In his father's court, women had seemed peripheral to the lives of the men he had watched, but he had never thought they were either unneeded or unappreciated.

When he was a little boy, women had looked after him, although he had little memory of his wet nurse. A flash of warmth, a bit of color, perhaps. Thomas did not remember if she had died or been sent away, but he did remember his father's cook who had taken him on afterward, a soft-fleshed, jolly woman who smelled of good things to eat which she freely gave him along with just the right number of hugs.

After her death when he was thirteen, he no longer attached himself to any woman and kept them all in the background of his life, like the men he sought to imitate. As a boy, he had always given due courtesy to each of his father's wives and had grieved deeply, albeit privately, at the death of the one who had been especially kind. Various maidservants and ladies had ruffled his soft hair, planted kisses on his downy cheeks, then stepped back to look at him differently when his voice dropped and his shoulders broadened.

In truth, he had given little thought to women for most of his life. He had shared the favors of many with Giles, enjoying the joint couplings more than those he'd had alone. The lusty joustings had been pleasant for the most part, rather akin to scratching a slightly unreachable itch.

Thomas chuckled. "For cert, this prioress will not stand in any man's background, at least not for long." Nor, he suspected, would she dutifully scratch any man's itch. She might be young and small of stature, but when she stood over him, watching as he examined the body of the old priest, he knew he had rarely met men tested in battle who exuded such iron control.

Despite the mettle he saw behind a soft woman's form, her smile was warm and her deep laugh suggested more earthiness than he would have expected in a virgin with a religious vocation. Of course he had heard stories of nuns who had lost the fight to remain chaste, not that he had known many nuns, virtuous or otherwise. Neither he nor Giles had had any interest in bedding a nun, no matter how willing she might be, when there were women enough outside the Church to satisfy them. The daughters of Eve who dedicated themselves to God might be holier than monks, according to the Church, because of their greater battle with unquenched lust, but neither he nor Giles had wanted to risk the future comfort of their souls by testing any nun's vows.

Thomas kicked at the stones in the path. Whether Prioress Eleanor of Wynethorpe was a struggling or willing virgin was really of no interest to him. There was nothing about her that had stirred his manhood. Had Giles been here, perhaps he would have indulged in and enjoyed some speculation, but without him…

Thomas stopped. In the quickly growing shadows of the late summer's afternoon, something caught his eye near the sacristy door. He quickly knelt and reached into the high yellow grass and leathery weeds. Lost in the tangle was a small, roughly hewn wooden crucifix attached to a thin leather strap. He pulled the object toward him and into the light. The strap was broken, and it felt stiff when he grasped it. Both the wood and strap were darkly stained.

As he quickly parted the grass around where he had found the cross, he thought the ground looked darker in spots. Could the marks on the ground and the stains be dried blood, he wondered? He quickly slipped the crucifix and strap into his sleeve. Something to look at later or give to…

"Brother?"

The voice startled Thomas. He stumbled as he rose, spun around, and then stared into the green eyes of a tall, wiry, but well-muscled monk standing behind him.

"Did you drop something, brother?" The voice was deep. The tone was not warm.

"A pebble in my shoe, is all."

"Soft feet to go with a clerk's soft hands then?"

"My history follows me, it seems."

The man did not laugh. "Brother Simeon wants to see you in the prior's chambers." With a look as thorough as that of a butcher appraising a cow bought for slaughter, the monk turned and left Thomas alone in the path.

⁊⊶

"Sit, Brother Thomas, and have some wine."

Brother Simeon poured a berry-scented wine into a goblet set in front of Thomas. There was no sign of the prior, but the receiver seemed quite at ease alone in his superior's chambers. And in using the gold cups.

Thomas watched the monk as he settled himself on the bench just opposite him. Of middle years, the man was large in every sense of the word and seemed more paternal than forbidding, or at least that was Thomas' impression. And, he noted with gentle amusement, Simeon was vain. The receiver had let his light brown hair grow longer at one side so he could pull it over the top of his head and in front of his tonsure, which he wore further back from his forehead than most monks.

"So what did you see in the garden? What happened to our poor Brother Rupert? Did he die with a smile on his face after a frolic with a wayward nun?" Simeon winked, his laugh deep and hearty, his smile good-humored.

This man may be more aware of human frailty than the usual androgynous monk, Thomas thought, but I find no humor in what happened to the old man. Why does he take it so lightly? "There was little enough to see. The poor man was stabbed in the chest. Sister Anne felt something odd when she checked him for signs of life. Then she and the prioress looked further and they found the remnants of a knife buried deep in his heart. The hilt had been broken off and lost. Only the shaft was left in the poor man's body."

Simeon's countenance darkened. "This all you have observed yourself? You are not just taking the word of the nuns?"

"Such was my observation after examining the corpse, my lord."

Simeon sat back, smiling slightly, and studied Thomas for a long moment. "Perchance the knife was from the nuns' kitchen and we still have some errant nun to bring before the Church courts?"

"The shaft was the breadth of a dagger and well made. I'd say a man's weapon."

"Breaking such a good knife would take more strength than a weak woman would possess. I'll grant that."

Having seen Sister Anne lift and move a man's dead weight with ease, Thomas was not quite so sure that there weren't women strong enough to have broken a good blade. In most cases, however, women did not possess such strength. He nodded.

"And the cutting?"

Thomas coughed and turned red. Simeon reached over and punched him sympathetically in the chest with a softly closed fist. "Of course, lad. Take your time."

"He held his…. Well, in his hand, they were. We found no other knife."

"Then he gelded himself. We had noticed that he was spending an unusual amount of time with Prioress Felicia before she died. Not that we thought either had actually broken their vows… I pity the poor man. The guilt over his lust for her must have been great. Perhaps he was in such pain that he fell on that knife and it broke. Like a Roman falling on his sword. There is no other knife, brother. He killed himself with the same. The hilt will come to light, no doubt. Probably trampled into the flowerbeds by those light-footed women. Prior Theobald is right, of course. This is not something for which we should have involved the crowner…"

"Beg pardon, Brother Receiver, but when I lifted his habit, I found there was blood around the wound in his chest but little where his privates…were. Sister Anne says that it is usual to have little bleeding when there is injury *after* death. She believes he was stabbed first and then castrated…."

Simeon waved his hand in a dismissive gesture reminiscent of the prior. "Ah, our worldly sister! She's a very *physical* woman." He wiggled his fingers in disgust. "I almost suspected she was his slayer until we realized he must have killed himself. Sister Anne's a trial to us, I'm afraid. What did you think of her?"

Thomas hesitated. "Indeed, I have not had your long experience with her, but she did seem very…perhaps *direct* is the word?"

"*Immodest* or *ill-advised* are better ones. Has an unwomanly arrogance about her, which you will learn from your work at the hospital. Her judgement is unsound and she will not listen to those wiser than she. A word of advice to you, brother. The infirmarian, Sister Christina, is a woman whose understanding of the spiritual roots of physical ill far surpasses that of Sister Anne." Simeon snorted. "And I have good reason to know that, in certain respects, Sister Anne has never left the world."

Thomas nodded. "She was appointed sub-infirmarian, I understand."

"One of those mistakes made by our late prioress and condoned by Brother Rupert, blinded as we now know by lust. I would have set Sister Anne to cleaning pots in the kitchen to teach her humility. When I heard that she was the one to find our poor brother, I knew that any conclusions she came to would be questionable. That is why I took them so lightly, but now that you have examined the corpse, I feel more confidence, brother." Simeon sighed and gave another dismissive wave. "But please amuse me. What outlandish explanation did our obstinate sister have, if he did not castrate himself?"

"Murder. She also noted that his robes had been changed after he died."

Thomas expected Simeon to whoop with laughter. Instead he paled. "What?" the monk asked, his voice hoarse.

"You see, there was no tear in his cloak where the knife went into his chest, and little staining on the garment."

"Surely she just didn't see the tear or the blood. Sister Anne thinks she knows everything, but women haven't a man's ability to reason and observe. Perhaps I had better look myself…"

"I did, my lord, and with great care." Thomas hesitated. "There was no tear. There was not the expected amount of blood on his robe."

For a long time, Simeon looked at Thomas without speaking, his expression inscrutable. Then the receiver reached for his goblet and took a long, pensive sip of wine. "In truth, brother, then I believe we do have a murderer to find," he said.

Chapter Ten

"Woman, get out of my light and get thyself away from my ears if you must moan so balefully! No man can think with such flapping around him." Crowner Ralf swatted in the general direction of Sister Christina as if she were an annoying insect, then turned his broad back to her.

It was the day after the sad discovery of Brother Rupert's mutilated corpse, and Christina had been interrupted by the arrival of the crowner while she was kneeling in the Chapel of Saint Mary Magdalene that lay on the cloister side of the nuns' choir. Except for Brother Rupert's body, she, a servant of the spiritual King, was completely alone with this loud and abrupt retainer of the secular monarch. Her quiet prayers interrupted, she wrung her hands and continued to make piteous cries of uncertainty. She was not only alone in the chapel with this worldly man, she was quite sure such unchaperoned contact was forbidden. She was absolutely terrified by him.

Ignoring her distress, the local representative of King Henry's justice bent over the body of the late Brother Rupert and resumed his careful examination while continuing to wave one hand absent-mindedly at the nun as if she were a pesky fly to keep at bay.

⁐

Eleanor stepped into the chapel, took one look at the young nun rocking from side to side in near hysteria, and called out: "You may go, sister. We will deal with the crowner." Then she turned to Sister Ruth and asked in a low voice, "Was Sister Christina here when you let the crowner in?"

Ruth looked genuinely distressed. "Forgive me, my lady! In my rush to announce him and bring both Sister Anne and Brother Thomas to accompany you, I did not notice if anyone was here. If I may, I will escort her away."

"Do. Please. She looks quite pale. Perhaps a sip of medicinal wine would be in order in view of her distress."

"Immediately, my lady." The elder nun stepped forward, took the arm of the trembling younger one and led her with speed and surprising gentleness toward the cloister walk. Whatever Eleanor may have thought of Sister Christina, this was one time she felt sorry for her. However severe Sister Ruth might be with Eleanor, the porteress was showing kindness to the terrified girl. That was worth remembering.

"I am Prioress Eleanor of Tyndal," she announced to the man, who had not even turned to acknowledge her presence. An unkempt and careless man, she thought, as she glanced at the clothing he wore. It was in need of mending, and where mended it was badly done. His back was stained from sweat and other liquids of less well-defined origins. Here was a man with little time for fashion and even less for the good opinion of others, Eleanor decided with grim humor. Was he even sober?

"A fine thing to find in your garden, my lady," the crowner said, continuing to bend over the monk's body.

His voice was steady, his words unslurred. At least he wasn't drunk, Eleanor concluded with some relief.

"Not a proper sight for virgins." He grunted as he turned the corpse over on one side and yanked up the corpse's robe to expose the mutilation. "Seeing this mess would be good for a few Hail Marys to ease the shock, I'd think."

Brother Thomas coughed, then gagged at the sight of the putrefying mutilation.

"Oh, and a man of God too. Well, this is the most blood you'll ever see, brother. Thank the good Lord for that, unless you're a fighting bishop that is." Ralf was the only one to laugh at his joke, but he seemed neither to notice nor to mind. The crowner continued his examination.

"You'll not find much blood to mark his lost manhood, Crowner." Eleanor's voice was stern. No one in her family had ever spoken favorably of the lower ranks assigned to administer the king's justice. Indeed, she had always assumed such men were mostly dishonest, or lazy and incompetent at best. She'd rather hoped this one would be different. At least his study of the dead priest was unhurried and seemed careful. Perhaps the crowner had merit, despite his clothes and rather earthy smell.

"And how would you know that, my lady?" The man sighed with barely concealed annoyance at the continued interruptions.

"We looked."

Crowner Ralf straightened up slowly, put one hand on his hip, turned and glowered equally at Eleanor and Thomas.

"Indeed. And what are your conclusions then, good people? Did God strike him down in your priory for his sins? Or was it for your sins? Do you think I'll close my eyes to all human intervention just because the corpse's a monk and you're a bunch of…?"

"Shush, Ralf! You are being impious. Be silent, and let us tell you what we did find." Sister Anne stepped out of the shadow behind Thomas, shook her finger at the crowner, and glared with a ferocity equal to his own.

Eleanor and Thomas both turned to look at her in shock.

"Well, Annie," the crowner said, his face relaxing into a surprised but delighted smile. "I'd hoped you hadn't lost all your sense when you left the apothecary shop for the convent."

Sister Anne turned to Eleanor. "Forgive me for speaking without permission, my lady. We knew Ralf, my husband and I, when we were in the world."

Ralf nodded. "Aye, and leaving it was the world's loss. You saved my lazy brother's life with that green and foul smelling poultice when the boar gored his leg, you know." He looked over at Eleanor. "He that is sheriff and too busy with the affairs of the high and mighty to attend to such matters as this." He gestured at the corpse.

"It was my husband who…"

The crowner's face reddened. "S'Blood, woman! 'Twas you, not that sexless, bloodless thing you called husband."

"Ralf! You forget yourself and where you are."

The man turned and bowed to Eleanor. "Perhaps. Forgive me, my lady. Sister Anne has reminded me that I have strayed from my task. You had observations you wished to share?"

Eleanor smiled in spite of herself. However crude the crowner might seem, his blunt speech and ill manners seemed based more in choice than nature. Indeed, she could understand impatience with hollow gestures when something important had to be done. She struggled herself with them at times, she realized, remembering her recent encounter with Prior Theobald. Then she noticed that the crowner was looking at her with some intensity as he scowled. He isn't just staring, Eleanor thought with surprise; he's studying me.

"Sister Anne discovered him," she said quickly and nodded in the nun's direction. "She should tell you what she noted. Brother Thomas and I came to the site later. If need be, we will confirm or add to whatever she says."

As Ralf looked at the tall woman beside her, Eleanor caught a fleeting look of sadness in his face. Something must have happened between them before Sister Anne left the world, she thought. Indeed, the entire interchange between crowner and nun had intrigued her.

"He's been moved since his death, Ralf. That coloring on the body you can see for yourself, but his clothing has also been changed. There was no tear from the entry of the knife into his garment, nor was there blood on the ground where we found him. And little staining on the inside of the robe near the chest wound. None near his genitals. In fact, as you see, there is but little blood around the mutilation itself."

The crowner had been listening intently. Suddenly, he laughed. "So you did not clean up the corpse. I wondered when I found it so neatly placed here in the chapel with little evidence of bleeding where I most expected it and a fresh robe."

"Our prioress forbade the washing until you had been here to examine the body."

Ralf acknowledged Eleanor with a slight smile. "And did you all examine the earth around as well?" he asked.

The three nodded.

"And did none of you find blood?"

The three shook their heads.

"Nor any dagger hilt?" He touched the spot where the knife had entered.

"None," the trio said, almost in unison.

"Well, now, what have you left to tell me?"

"One thing," Thomas said, pulling the crucifix from his sleeve and handing it to the crowner. "I found this near the sacristy door on the path to the monks' quarters yesterday afternoon after I left the garden. The ground may have been stained with blood. I couldn't quite tell and was interrupted before I could confirm my suspicions."

Ralf turned it around in his hand and held it up to the light. "Blood stains on the cross itself, and I'd say the cord was soaked with it. You were wise to pick it up, brother. Given last night's summer downpour, any trace of blood in the earth will be washed away, and the rain might have cleansed this as well if you hadn't taken it." He looked around. "Can any of you confirm if it belonged to him?" He waved at the corpse.

"Look at it, please, sister. You would know best," Eleanor said.

Anne reached out, and the crowner dropped the thing lightly into her hand, carefully not touching her. She looked at it for a moment, her eyes closing as she briefly shut her hand over the cross.

"It was his, my lady. He carved it himself. 'A simple cross for a simpler man,' he said to me once." Then the tears began to trickle down her cheeks. "He was a good man, my lady. A very good man."

Thomas and Ralf looked down at the floor.

Eleanor reached out for the nun's hand and squeezed it. "Who did not deserve what was done to him," she whispered.

Anne wiped the moisture from her face. "We must find who did it..."

"I will that, Annie. I promise you."

"Then hear this as well, Ralf. I believe the person who killed him was left-handed and either did not think about what he was doing or was in a hurry."

The crowner raised one eyebrow.

"If you were gelding a man, you would hold the genitals in your left hand as you cut with your right." Sister Anne held up her left fist as if she had just done it.

Ralf swallowed and nodded.

"And then you would take your victim's left hand thus and place them in his grasp so it would appear he had done it himself." She demonstrated, using Eleanor's hands as an example.

Ralf blinked. "Aye?"

"But Brother Rupert held his severed organs in his right hand."

"He did indeed."

"Brother Rupert was right-handed. If the murderer wanted us to believe our priest had done this act himself, he would have put his genitals in his left hand, a natural enough thing to do if the murderer is also right-handed, but not if he is left-handed. Come now, Ralf! Don't look at me with such doubt. If you were going to geld yourself, wouldn't you hold your balls in your weaker hand and cut with your stronger one?"

"That I would!" he said.

"Well, our murderer forgot."

Chapter Eleven

"Please join me in some refreshment before you go back to the hospital, sister."

Eleanor put her hand on Anne's arm. The unusual animation she had seen in the tall nun's face during the exchange with the crowner had faded back into her habitual look of sorrow.

Anne glanced down at the ground. "My lady, I overstepped my bounds today and I beg forgiveness." Her voice was soft.

"Come." Eleanor gently squeezed her arm. "Explain what you mean. After that, I have some questions for you."

"You are too kind, my lady."

Eleanor looked over at Thomas. "Brother, please take the crowner to the cloister to examine the spot where Sister Anne found the body and answer any questions he may have. Should either of you need me," she nodded to the men, "I will be in my chambers." Then the prioress gestured to Anne to accompany her down the nuns' choir to the private steps leading to her rooms.

"Do you mean I am too kind when I offer wine after your trying encounter with our gentle crowner?"

Anne gave her a faint smile. "It was not trying. I have known Ralf since childhood and understand the good heart under the dark looks and singular manner. No, I meant that you were kind to tolerate my outspokenness in front of you and Brother Thomas."

"I asked you to speak your mind."

"You asked me to tell what I saw, not what I had concluded."

Eleanor frowned. "I do not understand. Your observations and conclusions were astute. None of us noticed the details as you had, or put together the facts as well as you did. I must believe you made the crowner's task easier."

Sister Anne looked away. "I must tell you that our late prioress found my ways arrogant and chastised me often for lack of humility."

Eleanor stopped and in silence looked up at the ceiling of the long choir. The simple triangular design of dark wooden braces and supports, repeated along the length of the pitched roof, was soothing in its geometrical certainty. If the minds of mortal men were so formed, as many believe they should be, we'd have no cause for dispute, she thought, then prayed briefly for greater wisdom than she possessed.

"It is true that although we are made in the image of God, we must never forget we are flawed. In that, Prioress Felicia was right," she said, "but to ignore inspired insight is also a sin. I saw no sin in your words. I saw unusual perception, a gift from God surely. Would my predecessor not have agreed?"

"As you say, my lady."

Eleanor caught a fleeting smile of amusement on her companion's face. Perhaps the older prioress had not appreciated the questioning intelligence and independent mind of the sub-infirmarian. These were not qualities that fit easily and amiably into a standard conventual life, but Eleanor had not grown up with meek and spiritless nuns at Amesbury. Sister Beatrice was not the only religious who believed mindless humility often suffered from its own form of sinful pride.

As they continued their walk, Eleanor reached over and touched Anne's sleeve. "Tell me why Sister Christina was put in charge of the hospital and you were made sub-infirmarian." She asked the question not just for the information but to see how it was answered.

"Sister Christina is ardent in her prayers for the sinful souls of the sick. Prioress Felicia said that it is sin that brings sickness to a person, and thus prayer for them is the most effective treatment for their disease. My herbs and potions treat only symptoms, not the cause. Indeed she felt I should pray more and spend less time with my secular treatments."

"And what did you think?"

"Surely you do not expect me to contradict my superior!"

"By your heated response, I must assume you did contradict her, in thought, if not in words." Eleanor looked up at Anne. The woman's eyes were as unblinking as those of a child awaiting chastisement for some misstep. Did she think Eleanor was trying to trap her into saying something for which she would be punished? Eleanor shook her head in answer if that was indeed the unspoken fear. "When I ask for honesty, I do not punish it even if I disagree with what I hear. Tell me, sister, what you really thought of her conclusion."

Sister Anne stood silently, her face averted. Then she turned and looked straight down into Eleanor's eyes. "My lady, I have no desire to offend with my frankness and limited understanding. If I do so, I beg your pardon. To answer your question, I did not resent or disagree with Prioress Felicia's decision. Sister Christina gives much comfort to the ailing with her prayers. The sick who come to us are frightened. They not only fear their own physical pain and the effect of their deaths on their families but they are also terrified about the fate of their souls. In comforting their souls, Sister Christina has often cured their bodies. This I have seen."

Eleanor nodded. "And?"

"I have also seen the good effects of the remedies I was taught by my father. He was a physician and studied manuscripts brought back by those who had been to the Holy Land. Before his death, he was famous for his treatments."

"And he taught you, his daughter?"

"Aye, my lady, he did." Sister Anne smiled. "I loved to follow him and help whenever he would let me." She measured a short distance from the floor with her hand. "When I was this tall, he let me grind herbs and make simple potions. He spoiled me, I fear."

Eleanor looked at the height of the nun's hand, then glanced up at the top of her head. "You were young indeed to begin such learning!"

For the first time, the laughter between the two women was comfortable.

"I did interrupt you, sister."

"My lady, I work best with the physical body, but Sister Christina labors more effectively with man's immortal soul. Since she is better at curing the sinful, it was wise of Prioress Felicia to choose her to head the hospital instead of me. I was, and I am, content."

"Then I shall make no changes, sister, at least for the time being. Someday you must tell me more about your father, however, and what he learned from the Holy Land."

The two had almost reached the top of the stone steps when the wooden door to the prioress's chambers flew open, booming loudly as it crashed against the wall. A bright orange streak with a large, dark object gripped firmly in its mouth flashed by, just ahead of a swinging broom.

"Shoo! Out! Begone!"

The female voice behind the broom had a quite un-Norman, very local cadence to it.

Eleanor put her hand on Sister Anne's arm, cautioning her to stay where she was, then climbed the few remaining steps and stuck her head around the door.

A short but sturdy-looking girl, of just marriageable age, with heavy blond hair twisted into two long braids, stood staring at her. She held a broom raised to strike in her hands.

"You meant me, perchance?" Eleanor smiled.

"I did not see you, my lady. Forgive me!" Flushed with apprehension and embarrassment, the young girl dropped the broom, lowered her eyes, and curtsied.

"Fear not. I do not bite."

Eleanor stepped into the room and gestured to Sister Anne to follow.

"What just passed us on the steps?" the prioress asked, glancing back down the dark passageway.

"That wretched cat! Prioress Felicia hated him. Dirty, sneaky thing, she called him. He'd slip in when the door was open, then hide and drop mice at her bedside. She ordered me to drown him, but I could never catch..." The young woman blushed again and turned her head away, unable to finish an obvious lie.

"Dead ones, I hope?"

"My lady?"

"He left only dead mice at her bedside?"

"Aye. He's a good hunter, he is."

"And your name, child?"

"Gytha, from the village. I served Prioress Felicia."

"And well?"

The girl straightened herself to full height and looked at Eleanor with pride. "I am honest, my lady. Neat and efficient."

"And you would serve me as well?"

"If you'll have me." The girl then dropped her head and stared at the rush-covered floor.

And if I won't, your family will suffer, Eleanor thought. Even more than two hundred years after William the Great's conquest of England, life for someone not of Norman descent was beset with trials, regardless of education or former status.

"What complaints did Prioress Felicia have of you, Gytha?"

"I sometimes forgot my place and spoke out of turn."

"And?"

"She caught me feeding my dinner scraps to the cat."

Eleanor tried not to smile. "Do you not take direction well?"

The girl hesitated. Her face was square, body lithe but strong, and her gaze was guileless. "In all but the matter of the cat."

"Then I must assume you had words together over the cat?"

The girl's blue eyes flashed with indignation. "A house of God is no place for killing, is what I said! She told me killing *that filthy thing* was against no law. But I couldn't do it. I pretended I couldn't catch him." The look of outrage faded quickly and Gytha lowered her voice. "It really was hard to catch him, my lady. As you saw, he is very quick."

Eleanor sighed. "I think you would be a trial to one's patience, child."

Gytha looked as if she were about to cry.

"Which is why you should stay and serve me. I fear I need the ordeal for the good of my soul."

"Bless you, my lady!"

Gytha fell to her knees, reached out and kissed Eleanor's hem. Then the girl began to weep.

"Child, never do that again! I am not Our Lady and am certainly no saint." Eleanor lifted her up and hugged her.

"Nonetheless, you are kind." Gytha smiled and rubbed her hand across her eyes.

"Perhaps, but let us be clear on a few things."

The girl nodded eagerly.

"The cat? Oh, be at ease, child! He stays. Indeed, a house dedicated to God is no place for killing a harmless creature. If he is such a fine hunter, the kitchen will find good use for him. We have few enough things from our garden as it is without the mice taking a share. I will introduce him to Sister Edith. Should you see him in here, however, let him be."

"Of course, my lady, and willingly!" Gytha grinned.

"But keep your own dinner scraps for better use. I will make sure the kitchen trades him meals for mice. After all, we do pay for good service. And lest you fear he will lose in this bargain, I will have his food sent here where you may feed him yourself."

The girl grinned wider. "Agreed!"

"And one last thing, Gytha."

"Yes, my lady?"

"I will expect you to always speak your mind to me." Eleanor hesitated. "Although it might be best if you did so only when we were alone together."

Gytha giggled.

"And I must trust you always to tell me the truth. Is that agreed?"

"Always, my lady!"

As the girl went to bring wine for the two nuns, Eleanor turned to look up at Sister Anne. The expression of absolute delight and understanding she saw in the older woman's face brought her a warmth and comfort she had not felt since she had left Amesbury. Perhaps she had gained one ally amongst her nuns.

Chapter Twelve

A morning mist with the softness of tears caressed the faces of those who stood, heads bowed, on the day Brother Rupert was buried. As befitted a cleric vowed to chastity, only the monks clustered around the simple grave of their brother. Prioress Eleanor and the nuns of Tyndal honored him by standing at a distance sufficient to show respect for his vows even after death. Prior Theobald, supported by Brother Andrew and Brother Simeon, quietly spoke the last words that ever would be said over the priest's now discarded, silent, and rotting body.

For those whose first thought was for Brother Rupert's soul, it was a time of joy. For those who had loved the kindness of the mortal man, it was a time of very human grief as well as horror at the manner of his leaving them. When Eleanor looked around her, she saw more tears slipping down the cheeks of her charges, many of whom lowered their heads to hide them. Only the wide blue eyes of Sister Christina were free of tears and raised to heaven. Only on her smooth face was there a smile of happiness.

The service ended. Eleanor turned and gestured to the nuns, allowing them to return to the cloister, but Sister Ruth remained, lost in thought, her eyes moist as she gazed down her long, narrow nose at the damp grass around her feet.

Eleanor reached over and put her hand on the nun's shoulder. "Walk back with me, sister."

Ruth nodded. Her eyes, raised to meet Eleanor's ever so briefly, were black with sadness. For once the familiar look of bitterness was absent from them.

"He was a good man, Brother Rupert," Eleanor said.

The nun hesitated. "For a mortal one, yes." Her voice was harsh from soundless weeping.

"And one who did not merit such a death."

The two women walked together in silence. Their breathing and the gravel grinding under their feet with a harsh scraping noise were the only sounds in that rain-laden air.

"I wonder that no one saw anything strange that day," Eleanor asked at last.

"I saw nothing, my lady," Ruth replied, pursing her lips in what was becoming a very familiar expression. Eleanor wondered if the look was indicative of anger or just plain stubbornness.

"I am sure you did not or you would have reported it to me," Eleanor said, rather doubting that the porteress would have done any such thing. "Brother Rupert's corpse did not find its way into the cloister garth by itself, however. Haven't you heard anything from anyone who might have seen something out of the way?"

"This horrid act might not be the work of a mortal man. Satan is capable of wondrous things."

"The Evil One rarely expends such energy unless his purpose in astounding us is clear and will bear good fruit, however. The point of leaving our poor priest's mutilated body near the fountain remains a mystery. Thus I doubt bearing it there was the direct action of Satan, wondrous though he may often be."

Ruth sniffed audibly and raised her head. "Brother Simeon believes it is a warning against lust. He noted that Brother Rupert was far too fond of Prioress Felicia and was spending more time with her than was seemly near the end of her life. I, too, noted that with some dismay."

"If his mutilation was a warning against lust," Eleanor said, feeling somewhat uncomfortable on that subject in view of her own weakness for the auburn-haired Brother Thomas, "it was no work of Satan. The Prince of Darkness would surely choose to paint a more appealing picture of its consequences." She took a deep breath. "Tell me, was my honored predecessor ill long?"

Ruth blinked at the sudden shift in subject. "Not long at all. She felt pain in her chest and collapsed at Compline. By Matins her soul had left us."

Then most likely her death was a natural one, Eleanor thought. "And her age? I was never told."

"We understood she had entered her seventh decade." Sister Ruth's expression had changed to one of puzzlement.

Eleanor shook her head. Brother Rupert had been of much the same age, perhaps a few years younger. She discounted uncontrollable lust between priest and prioress or even in the heart of the priest alone as the cause of his death. As the all too palpable dream of Tyndal's young new priest that had visited her last night had taught her, the pain of passion burned with unbearable sharpness in youth. It was as consolation that her aunt had told her that the sting grew more blunted in well-advanced years, although it was never entirely banished. How she wished she had reached that stage of life!

"Did you have further need of me, my lady?"

Eleanor blinked. She had been woolgathering over her dream of last night and hadn't realized that she and Sister Ruth were now standing in the passage leading to the nuns' quarters.

"One moment more, sister. On the first day of my tenure here, Prior Theobald honored me by leading us all in prayer. I understand Brother Rupert usually did so when Prioress Felicia was still alive and would then attend her chapters."

Sister Ruth nodded.

"Did you expect Brother Rupert to come to my first chapter?"

"Prior Theobald had sent me a message through Brother Simeon that he might not. His absence from nuns' chapter was infrequent but not, certainly, uncommon."

Sent a message to Sister Ruth, Eleanor noted with irritation, but not to her as prioress. "Did he give a reason for the absence?" she asked, her voice calm.

"It was not my place to ask."

"Yet you said nothing when I asked Sister Christina if she had seen him. You knew I was expecting him."

"You did not ask me, my lady, and I would never presume to know what is in the mind of my superior."

Despite the sharp retort, Eleanor noted with interest that the nun had paled slightly. Indeed, she suspected that Sister Ruth either knew more about all this than she was telling or that she simply would not give even an inch of cooperation to the woman who had displaced her. The moment of human weakness Ruth had shown at the burial had passed, and the nun's expression hardened into a mask. Eleanor knew she would get nothing more from her.

"Very well, sister. I will not keep you longer."

As the prioress watched Ruth walk hurriedly through the cloister toward the Chapel of St. Mary Magdalene, she could not help wondering if her haste was due to something other than an urgent need to pray.

Chapter Thirteen

Thomas' eyes stung with hot tears as he sat by the bedside. The body lying there had been a boy of no more than six years. Now he was a corpse without age, slack-jawed and staring atop a reeking puddle of black flux. *This fate will befall us all,* he thought with bitterness. *Brother Rupert lies a week in the ground, melting into worm food. This child dies. Death cares naught for goodness, beauty, innocence nor wit. In the end, we shall all stink just the same.*

"Grieve not, brother. You gave him comfort, which is more than many of us are able to do for those facing death."

Thomas started. The hand on his shoulder was not that of Sister Anne.

Brother Andrew smiled, a look that held no humor but some gentleness. "I have seen you sitting with the dying, and I over-heard you tell this child that Our Lord would have a puppy for him to play with in Heaven," he said, gesturing tenderly at the soft corpse. "Your words made him smile. That was kindness, brother. You made it easier for him to endure his pain. I think you have a talent for comfort, a talent I've not often seen, let alone in someone of your priestly inexperience."

"You are kind, brother." Thomas stood and looked down at the small monk. "But you look as if you are in pain. Are you ill?"

Andrew snorted. "My leg. It distresses me when the air turns chill or damp. I am used to it, although I still have little patience despite much prayer. Sister Anne has remedies which ease the aches."

"Surely you are too young for an old man's pains," Thomas said, grinning.

"They are from an old wound, brother, gotten in a battle for a cause which died with its leader but not, perhaps, in the spirits of men."

"You have returned from the Holy Land then?"

"Nay. I was with Simon de Montfort and should have died on the field from my wounds. Or else been hanged, drawn, and quartered as a traitor to King Henry."

"My apologies, brother. I should not have pried."

Andrew looked up at Thomas and laughed, eyes sparkling with good humor. "Nor would I have told you except you remind me much of the man who gave me this bad leg and then saved me from a traitor's death by granting my wish to retire from the world. He was an earl who fought on King Henry's side, but he showed a knight's compassion toward this humble man whom he deemed a worthy opponent in face to face combat. Oh, but he was a fine fighter!" The monk smiled at the memory. "Indeed, you have his voice, his look and his breadth, although not his coloring. Strange, that."

Thomas felt his face turn cold, then blazing hot.

"Methinks I, too, have pricked an old wound? But fear not, brother. You may keep your secrets. It is part of the human condition to have something buried deep in the heart, and we monks of Tyndal are no different from any other mortal man in that."

"Even Prior Theobald?" Thomas asked, his laugh harsh with fear at the monk's quick perceptions. It would be wise, he decided, to maneuver the conversation into safer and more profitable areas. Indeed, that earl might well have been Thomas' own father.

"Even he, although his more spirited sins must now be as shriveled as ancient husks. We are used to his failings, yet respect his office and, out of kindness, pretend that all orders are his rather than issuing from others with his voice. I am not alone in feeling only pity for him."

"*Others* being Brother Simeon?"

"A man of great competence and perhaps even greater ambition, but the latter serves both the priory and God well. We may lose him one day to Amesbury. If God is kind, he may stay with us and become prior here when Prior Theobald is called to Heaven."

"Then surely Brother Receiver has no dark secrets."

Andrew folded his arms and lowered his head. "His ambition for advancement within the Church is no secret, but he exercises a shrewd humility. Although Brother Simeon has long ruled us here at Tyndal, he gives credit for everything he does to our prior. Such humility will serve him well with others of higher rank who would profit from competence in underlings but wish the glory to fall on themselves. No, if our receiver has a secret, it may be his grief. He once said that he admired his father above all other men, but less than two years ago, his father died. Brother Simeon was inconsolable for many months. We feared he would lose either his reason or his faith. Once in chapel I overheard him praying that the cup be taken from him. Apparently, God was gracious. The good brother has since regained his spirit and strength."

"He does not seem happy with our new prioress."

"Prioress Felicia was not a forceful leader. She was happiest working with the nuns or the hospital and let Brother Simeon run the estates as well as rule the monks and lay brothers on Prior Theobald's behalf. Prioress Eleanor seems more in the tradition of Fontevraud women. He will find the change difficult."

"And what think you of being ruled by a woman?"

Andrew chuckled. "Our new prioress, despite her youth, reminds me much of my own mother. Now there was a woman who knew how to order about the sons of Adam! And we all loved her, we did, including my father. This will be no change for me, brother. It is like going home."

Thomas knelt in solitude on the rough stones of the darkening Jesus Chapel, the monks' private place of prayer on the left of the church nave. The boy's death earlier that day had dug into his soul like a dark-hued worm, and he needed a comfort no mortal could give.

But he could not pray; his thoughts hugged the earth with a fierce tenacity. In truth, he had been unable to pray since the day he was thrown face down on the slimy straw of that rotting dungeon floor. After his release and transfer to Grovebury, a downy-cheeked priest had told him that failure at prayer proved Satan's hand clutched his soul. He advised Thomas to battle against such possession with the whip, the hair shirt and rejection of all earthly desires. Although he had smiled with some acidity at the young priest's naïveté, he did feel as if some malign force was crushing all spark of light from his spirit. And so he did try them, the whip and hair shirt, but they had accomplished nothing.

If Satan was offering bribes for his soul, he was doing it in a very unorthodox manner. Thomas no longer suffered from fleshly passions. He did not lust after women, either when he was awake or during the vulnerability of sleep. He ate because food was placed before him but did so with neither hunger nor eagerness, and he drank only to keep his throat from drying to dust.

And as if some part of him was truly eager for it, he needed no awakening for prayer. Indeed he was grateful when they all shuffled down to the chapel for Matins. It was torture, lying motionless in his bed with neither thought nor action to pass the interminable black minutes before sunrise. Although his eyes burned and his body ached from lack of rest, it was during Matins when he felt nearest to prayer, surrounded by the warmth and breath of his brother monks.

Now he was alone. His prayers swirled briefly in the air like lightly disturbed dust before drifting to the floor as soon as he had said them. He dropped his hands, leaned back on his heels, and turned his thoughts to more worldly things.

Although he had been sent to Tyndal to test his investigative prowess in what would probably be a minor and temporary matter of priory insolvency, he found himself settling into the place as if it were a new home. Despite the desolate location, the inhabitants were much like the men he was used to, although some of those *men* now inhabited the bodies of women, he thought with a smile. An interesting twist on traditional views, for cert.

However, if he wished Tyndal to be the place where he could lift his spirits and refresh his soul, God had played an ugly joke on him. Instead of granting Thomas peace and distance from his tortured memories, God had greeted him with the sight of Brother Rupert's horribly mutilated dead body before he had even spent a night within the priory walls. No matter that the murderer would be found eventually, Thomas would keep the image of Brother Rupert's obscenely mangled corpse forever in his collection of night terrors, which visited him on those rare occasions when he actually slept.

Would that the murderer be quickly found! The idea that he might strike again in such a blasphemous way was a thought too macabre to live with. Despite the astute observations of Sister Anne and Thomas' own discovery of the dead monk's crucifix outside the sacristy, however, Crowner Ralf had yet to find more evidence and apprehend the culprit, secular or religious.

If only Thomas knew why the monk had been so treated, perhaps he could await the murderer's capture with less terror, knowing how to protect himself from a similar fate. But he did not, and his imagination, colored with abnormal fatigue, sometimes let loose images of such ghoulish morbidity that he started at strange, demonic shapes he thought materialized in the shadows of his restless nights.

Thomas heard himself mewl like a babe in fear and he ground his hands into his eyes, forcing himself to turn his thoughts to the mundane task he had been sent to investigate. He took in a deep breath and just as slowly exhaled. With an exasperating sluggishness, calm returned to his overburdened soul.

Brother Simeon. He was, without doubt, a vain man, even pompous, but he was also competent. That reputation was known at Grovebury, and Brother Andrew had confirmed the general opinion. Thomas had also found the receiver vigorous and jovial, the kind of man who drew boys, just on the brink of manhood, to him. A man who'd stand, legs splayed, with a waster in hand, one of those blunt wooden practice swords, and invite the lads to fight with him. Afterward he'd cuff them like a great bear; show them skills to save their lives, which he'd call little tricks; praise them for their recklessness, which he'd call courage; and then slip them treats like the children they still were. Thomas had known a man like that when he was a boy and the memory warmed him briefly. Of course a man like Simeon would emerge a leader in this world of sometimes childlike monks.

That aside, someone had obviously thought there was a problem with Simeon or Thomas would not be here. An anonymous message with vague suggestions of even vaguer improprieties had been sent to the Abbess at the mother house in France. Thomas suspected some monk at Tyndal had become jealous of Simeon's growing reputation, but so far he had neither heard nor seen anything suggestive. Perhaps someone was just trying to blacken Simeon's name, or at least tarnish it a bit, so his promotion to prior at either Amesbury or Tyndal might not be considered such a foregone conclusion.

Thomas shrugged. He had yet to persuade Simeon to show him the account rolls. In fact, despite the receiver's frequent invitations to join him in a cup of good Gascon wine and talk about the new priest's day with the nuns and at the hospital, Simeon seemed disinclined to take Thomas on as his apprentice as Thomas had hoped. It would have made the task of investigating the lost income so much simpler. Now Thomas would have to wait until the prioress ordered the receiver to bring his accounts to her and trust she would invite Thomas to the meeting as a man familiar with law and with contracts and grants.

So far, she had not done so. The discovery of the mutilated corpse well within the sanctity of the priory gardens had profoundly terrified all at Tyndal. Not only did the prioress have to calm them, she had to question each, on the crowner's behalf, to discover anything that may have been seen on the day Brother Rupert's body was found. All this had delayed any review of revenues.

Perhaps the postponement was just as well, for Simeon had shown no dread of presenting his accounts. This suggested that the whole problem rested, not with the receiver's incompetence or even malfeasance, but rather with a resentful troublemaker who only wished to throw a little sand in Simeon's face.

Who might that be? In Thomas' opinion, the use of anonymous and vague accusations was a weak man's weapon. Could Theobald have finally rebelled against the man who had dominated him for so long? It would not surprise him. He had met a few others like Theobald in the higher orders. For the most part, they were harmless and vacant men, although often personable, who had been raised to positions that bewildered them. Indeed their advancements so far exceeded their abilities that even those more experienced in Church politics were often mystified by their elevation. The reason for their prominence usually involved the accident of high birth in combination with the ambition of men of lesser rank who used them as a shield to push themselves forward into positions of influence they could never otherwise reach. Such men then taught the Theobalds to say the words they themselves had no authority to speak, and if the ambitious men were competent and wise, well then, there was no harm and perhaps even some good done in the name of those who held the title. If they were not wise or were tainted with malevolence, however...

Was Simeon a wise man as well as a skilled administrator? Thomas did not doubt the monk's intelligence, but Simeon seemed uneasy with the new prioress and had treated her in a disrespectful manner at their first meeting. That was a surprising mistake for such a worldly and ambitious man. Perhaps it was a mere stumble. After all, the prioress had just arrived and he had had no chance to learn how to deal with a woman of will, something the Prioress Felicia had not apparently been.

Willful women! He smiled. In truth, Thomas had met more such in the house of God than he had ever encountered in the world of men, but he rather liked at least two of them. Even the crowner, a blunt, rough man and no courtier in his dealings with either monks or women, had shown respect for Sister Anne's logic.

And Thomas himself liked the evident but understated intelligence of the youthful prioress. She listened to others, a tactic the wise man learned quickly if he wished to survive into old age. Those high in the Church who had successfully kept their positions over decades of endless, sometimes daily, contradictory political storms would probably agree. That she had already learned it made him feel more confident about her strength and permanence as a leader. Perhaps that was why he chose to tell the prioress about finding the wooden cross and not Brother Simeon, about whose skills Thomas was still unsure. Choosing to show her the crucifix he had found was his way of aligning himself with the prioress and whatever faction of power she represented outside Tyndal. An unorthodox choice to be sure. Had he made a mistake? Thomas had honed his instincts on who was best to follow since he was a child. He had to trust himself.

A door creaked loudly as it opened.

Thomas froze. He heard the sound of steps and whispers. From the tone of their voices he knew the men who had just entered both wanted and expected to be alone. Thomas slipped to the ground and crawled quickly out of the dimly lighted chapel to a pillar in the dark nave closest by him. He had learned long ago that it was prudent and useful not to be seen by those who whispered together in darkness.

Thomas waited until the voices came no nearer, then carefully looked out from the shadows. At some distance away, he could see two men kneeling and facing each other. Neither was identifiable in the gloom of the monk's choir. Their words were muffled. Then one began to sob, neither child nor quite a man by his voice. Thomas watched as the other man reached out and drew him into an embrace.

Then the youth pushed the man away, leapt up, and, covering his face with his hands, ran through the nave to the sacristy.

With a hoarse cry, the man jumped up and raced after him. As the monk passed through a pale stream of moonlight from the window over the high altar, Thomas saw his face. It was the grim and green-eyed monk who had summoned him to Brother Simeon.

Thomas got to his feet and followed.

Chapter Fourteen

Eleanor finished her prayers. She opened her eyes and looked toward the high window over her small altar. The early morning sunlight shone down with a damp but welcome warmth, and, as she rose from her prie-dieu, she could hear the sounds of the awakening, hungry livestock from the stables and pens across the southern branch of the priory creek. The light rain had finally stopped and sunshine, weak as it was, lifted her spirit.

Today she had vowed to fast and drink only watered wine. Perhaps that would help quell the unwelcome and distracting emotions the new priest had inspired. Thomas was indeed a handsome man, but she had met his like in earlier days without feeling more than a fleeting interest. And those days had been before she became a bride of Christ. If those longings had been but negligible aches of transient lust, now they surely qualified as the more serious sin of infidelity, in thought at the very least. She had prayed the feelings would pass just as quickly as they had before.

They had not. Like an incubus, his image came to her at night, promising earthly pleasures to match those of Heaven, and when she fled from his illusory caresses into the safety of wakefulness, she found her body wet with the very worldly sweat of passion. Her raw fatigue was hindering her ability to concentrate on the needs of Tyndal, and she had been remiss in dealing with problems that demanded immediate attention, like the accounts. She knew she had to put all this behind her, confess, and seek counsel. But from whom? Once again she longed for Amesbury, the wisdom of her aunt, and the understanding confessor Sister Beatrice had found for her young novices.

"The priest I choose for my own confessor cannot be Brother Thomas," she said, grinding her fist into the curved wooden railing. "Nor Brother Simeon, that boisterous and arrogant man. And certainly not Prior Theobald. I believe a rock would have more understanding of either God or man than he. In all of Tyndal, surely there is just one priest to whom I can speak freely!" Eleanor rubbed her hand as she closed her prayer book, turned away from the small prie-dieu, and glanced up at the wall hanging covering the stone masonry just in front of her narrow bed.

The tapestry of Saint Mary Magdalene sitting at the feet of Christ fascinated her. A beautiful piece of work, she thought, walking over to touch the fine embroidery as she often had since her arrival. When she was first shown her new quarters, Eleanor had commented on its beauty.

"What is the origin of this piece?" she had asked Sister Ruth.

The older nun hesitated. "I do not know such details, my lady," she had mumbled with some irritation. "Prioress Felicia commissioned it not many years after coming to Tyndal. Now let me show you where you will receive guests." With that terse comment, Sister Ruth had quickly led her from the room to the public chambers.

It was a curious luxury, Eleanor thought, looking around at the austere private room with its simply carved prie-dieu and even more spartan bed. The choice of subject for the tapestry was understandable enough. Mary Magdalene was the patron saint of hospitals, and other than maintaining the parish church and providing a hospice for the few travelers to this dank coast, Tyndal's main purpose was the care of the sick. As she felt the skillful, even stitches and admired the finely dyed yarns, Eleanor now looked at the faces of both Jesus and Mary Magdalene more closely.

It was their expressions that surprised her. Indeed, the saint did sit humbly at the feet of Jesus and her hands were raised in the standard attitude of chaste adoration, but Jesus looked down at her and she at him with a gaze of deep understanding and mutual appreciation. Sister Beatrice had pointed out to Eleanor similar looks in the faces of long-married couples who came to Amesbury to provide for their burial together.

"These know the fullness of love and thus are halfway to Heaven already," she had said to Eleanor. "They have suffered much together and have grown close in a way quite unimaginable in youth. Without sharing passion, grief, and loss with another, we can never understand the true meaning of love or attain the peace which is its highest manifestation."

That was one of her aunt's many teachings that Eleanor had locked away in her heart to think on at a later time.

Yet surely it must be blasphemous to suggest such a thing between the two in the tapestry, Eleanor thought with a shake of her head, and once again wondered why Prioress Felicia had had such a design made.

A rustle at her feet brought her back from her distraction and she looked down. The orange cat, now ennobled with the name of Arthur, stretched first with front legs extended and then the back. Having finished this exercise, he sat down in the rushes, looked up at her with round, green eyes, and began to purr.

"And I suppose you want something to break your fast?"

The volume of purring rose significantly.

Eleanor laughed. She had known of prioresses, indeed abbesses, who had lap dogs. Although the practice of keeping pets was much frowned upon, censure rarely followed the discovery. She herself had never before felt any desire for such a thing.

"Yet I seem to have acquired you, haven't I?" she said to the eagerly rumbling, young bundle of fur in front of her. "But I'll have no pampered pet here. You'll work for your meals. Is that understood?"

Eleanor would have sworn the cat nodded.

"Very well, then. Let's see if I still have some fish left over from last night."

That was a rhetorical statement. There was far more than a scrap of fish left. Eleanor had been unable to eat the undercooked fish brought to her, setting it aside with rarely felt disgust. In fact, she now wondered if her vow to fast today wasn't more a wish to avoid unusually unpalatable meals than a true penance for her sins. True penance might be to eat what was placed before her, she thought, but after a questioning glance heavenward, quickly decided otherwise.

Arthur, however, had no such problems with the spurned fish. Eleanor watched with affection as he devoured his morning meal with little growls and joyful feline snorts.

Although the cat might have no problem devouring the results of Sister Edith's kitchen leadership, Eleanor knew she had to find a way to improve the fare. Simple meals in the priory were to be expected, but inedible ones were a waste and an insult to God-given bounty. And then there was the state of what little bounty Sister Matilda had wrested from the priory gardens under her less than tender stewardship. Here lay another problem to address before the growing season was completely gone and Eleanor was forced to purchase food for the coming winter.

Thus her thoughts came round to the accounts she must review with Prior Theobald and Brother Simeon before even more time had passed. Her discussions with the nuns about what they might have seen on the day of Brother Rupert's death had been fruitless, although her attempts to calm each about the threat suggested by such a horror had been more successful. The economic disarray at the priory demanded immediate attention. She would send a message this morning that she wished to meet with both men tomorrow afternoon on the subject. And should her fast today fail her and the naked incubus in the shape of Brother Thomas appear tonight to destroy her rest, she would will herself to bore the vision into an impotent state with a detailed discussion of tithes, hides, and grain production.

She shut her eyes tight and forced herself to think upon Prior Theobald. What had he been like as a young man, she wondered. It was hard to picture him as other than an old man who hadn't had a thought of his own in years behind those bushy eyebrows. Had he always hidden behind others more competent or stronger than he? How sad that a man should grow old with nothing better to recommend him than his skill at speaking the words and thoughts of others.

Theobald might be dismissed. Simeon could not. Now there was a conceited boor for cert. First impressions were hardly fair judgements, as she well knew, and she had been far too distracted by the arrival of Brother Thomas to deal at once with the receiver's rudeness, as she should have. She would not invite Thomas to the review of priory finances tomorrow, she decided. She did not need the distraction, and his presence was not critical. A long meeting where she could study Simeon with care and listen to his reasons for decisions made was too important. She must decide whether Simeon was still a competent receiver or whether he was to blame for the current financial crisis. Perhaps his value to Tyndal lay in some other position. Her mind must remain alert and agile so that her decisions would be, above all else, practical.

Today, however, she would visit the hospital and had sent a message to Sister Christina that she wanted to meet with her. Despite Anne's assurances that Christina was a good choice to head the hospital, Eleanor still had her doubts and had yet to see how the young infirmarian performed her task. Although she agreed that prayer was critical to the wellbeing of souls, she wondered if the young nun spent too much time in chapel to be an effective administrator.

Even Sister Ruth might be a better choice, Eleanor thought. Despite her rigidity, the dour nun had shown flashes of compassion with Sister Christina and at Brother Rupert's burial. She had also gained sufficient respect amongst the nuns to be elected prioress before Eleanor's arrival. That suggested the nun had demonstrated some competence and leadership to her fellows.

She shook her head in frustration. How best to handle that particular and stubborn adversary of hers continued to elude her.

The unfortunate experience Christina had had with Crowner Ralf in the chapel reminded Eleanor that she needed to assure the young woman that she would not have to face the rough invader again. "Peace of mind is tenuous enough at Tyndal these days with all my charges," she said with a sigh. "May there be a quick solution to the crime!"

The death, nay, murder of Brother Rupert had not only grieved the nuns, it had understandably terrified them. Death was never a stranger to any of them, but murder in a house of God was unthinkable, an abomination, a violation that permeated each soul with a feeling of uncleanness as well as personal dread.

If Eleanor had been greeted with skepticism and contempt at her first chapter, the mood of her charges had changed by her second. When she had called them together the afternoon of Brother Rupert's death to announce that their beloved priest had been hideously slaughtered, she could see growing hysteria in the pale faces and unblinking eyes staring back at her. Then they had looked to her for wisdom and calm leadership. Again and more fervently, Eleanor had prayed to be equal to their needs.

"Armageddon is surely coming," she had heard some mutter. "Why else would our sanctified ground be so befouled?"

"Satan is an assassin and has surely killed our priest," others suggested. "Only the Prince of Darkness could have breached our walls."

She had not shied away from telling them the truth of what had happened that day, but just as quickly she had turned their thoughts from that horror to the story of Cain and Abel. It was a comforting tale of the inevitability of justice, of Good prevailing over Evil even in a sinful world. God had not only seen Cain in the unimaginable act of killing his brother but had also justly punished him for it, she emphasized, and, with an unwavering voice, she announced she had certain confidence that God would lead the crowner to the perpetrator quickly. Justice would prevail.

Many had visibly relaxed after her speech, their burning eyes shutting in weary relief. Those still undecided had nervously looked about them; but seeing others take comfort in her words, they took solace in the general shrinking of the atmosphere of terror. A few, like Sister Anne and Sister Ruth, seemed never to have feared that Armageddon was imminent. Eleanor had expected such of Sister Anne, but seeing the same calm strength in the abrasive Sister Ruth pleasantly surprised her.

Once calmed, a simple certainty that the vile murderer had been from the world outside Tyndal's walls and that he would be captured soon infused most of the priory inhabitants:

"Someone forgot to lock a gate," one had said.

"Not likely to happen again if we have guards," a second nodded.

"Carelessness. A lay brother must have…"

Eleanor had encouraged this conclusion, promptly announced her plans for improving the security of all walls and gates, then quite visibly oversaw strict compliance.

"I may not afford myself such blithe assumptions, however," she said to the cat, which was licking his paws. "Murder done by a member of the priory, by a soul committed to God, might be unthinkable to most, but it is an eventuality I have to prepare for. If the culprit is a member of Tyndal, the Church will take him from the secular crowner's hands for ecclesiastical trial. Depending on how that situation is handled, the reputation of Tyndal might be tarnished for years to come."

Eleanor looked back down at her feet. The cat had finished his post-meal scrub and was curling up for a nap. "Nay, sir! Enough woolgathering for me and enough leisure for you. It's back to work for both of us."

She walked to the door of her chamber, carefully letting the cat go first, then firmly shut the door behind them.

⟠

Tyndal's hospital could house thirty patients, somewhat evenly divided between the sexes, and treat many more. Not all Fontevraud houses were linked to hospitals, but Tyndal had once been a Benedictine house dedicated to the care of the sick, a much needed service in this lonely part of England. When that old priory had fallen into disrepair and eventual abandonment due to inadequate revenues, one affluent nobleman, deeply penitent in his old age for some regretted but undefined sins, had begged Fontevraud to resurrect Tyndal for the good of his soul.

The Abbess of Fontevraud had agreed, with the understanding that he grant the priory some very profitable lands to keep the establishment solvent. Shortly thereafter, the noble's wife, with his concurrence, begged admission to the Order and became the first prioress of Tyndal. It was she who had the hospital building repaired, thus allowing Tyndal to continue to care for the sick and dying.

The priory began to acquire some reputation for successful treatments, especially in more recent years. Two special areas of accomplishment were the easing of joint pain and the surprising absence, even cures, of often terminal infections. Although the local villagers, the fishermen, and their families were the primary recipients of monastic care, wealthier patients sometimes came for ease of their mortal aches and donated quite generously when the treatment proved favorable.

Thus the hospital not only provided a service to the sick but also helped Tyndal remain reasonably solvent, a condition the current prioress wished to maintain in view of the diminishment of other revenues. Eleanor wanted it run efficiently.

⊙≈≈≈o

"My lady!" Sister Christina bobbed awkwardly.

What age was this young nun, Eleanor wondered, as she reached out and gently touched Sister Christina's shoulder. Life seemed not to have placed the slightest mark of passage on the infirmarian's face. Even the skin on her plump hands was as smooth as a babe's. How could such an innocent be in charge of the sick and dying?

Eleanor looked around at the clusters of suffering people waiting near the door to the hospital. Some were mobile. Some had been carried. Eleanor passed one family who had brought a young woman on a litter. Glancing down, Eleanor had shuddered. The woman's mouth was frozen open in the silent scream of death. The body was beginning to reek. When she looked at the faces of the two older women, two young men, and three children who had brought the body here, however, she saw blind hope as they patiently waited their turn to be seen.

Eleanor gestured in their direction to Sister Christina. "I think Brother Thomas should attend that family. His services would be of great use."

"We have not seen the good brother this morning."

"How odd. Surely he neither forgot nor got lost."

"Perhaps Prior Theobald had need of him?"

Eleanor bit her tongue and nodded. She would have to change the prior's, nay, Simeon's assumption that his needs took precedence, at least without first requesting her approval or sending an immediate explanation.

"My lady?"

"Sister."

"If I may, I would tend that family myself since the good brother isn't here. Indeed, I have seen such grief before and believe I can give them some ease of spirit."

"You needn't ask my permission. We are here to give succor. By all means, go. I will wait."

As Eleanor watched the round, ageless nun walk hurriedly over to the huddled group, she saw the normally awkward, dithering woman change into a gentle, calm, and confident figure. Sister Christina lightly touched each person's hand before she gathered them around, then gestured for each to kneel with her next to the corpse of...of whom? Their mother? Their sister? Daughter? Someone's wife?

Soon their eyes were closed and they seemed to be praying with her. As they did, tears began to flow from the eyes of the two women closest to the nun. Without stopping her prayers, Christina reached out and pulled each of them closer to her in a motherly embrace.

Eleanor continued to watch as the nun wept with them all until the wails of anguish reached a crescendo, then fell to moans of more bearable grief. Soon Christina rose, spoke quietly with each, and comforted the children with hugs and soothing caresses until two lay sisters came for the body. Although sorrow followed the family like a shadow as they trailed in mourning after the corpse, Christina had been able to give them the courage to face what they had been unable to see.

Eleanor shook her head in amazement. Sister Anne was indeed right. The plump little nun had a gift. She could soothe the souls of the grieving. It was a skill she herself did not have. However deep her faith, it would always be a very pragmatic one. Eleanor had long accepted that she would never be a saint. Sister Christina, on the other hand, just might.

As the nun walked back towards her prioress, her gait once again became awkward and her head bobbed nervously. Eleanor reached out and took the young woman's hands. Christina's bright blue eyes widened in confusion.

"You have the gift of comfort, sister. I can see why Prioress Felicia made you infirmarian. She was wise in her choice, and I am pleased as well."

The nun blushed, but it was the first time Eleanor had seen her smile at another mortal.

❧

The prioress gestured to Christina to precede her and they began their tour of the hospital.

Near the entrance to the building itself stood a hut. Lay brothers and older lay sisters or nuns with some medical knowledge screened the patients for type and seriousness of ailment. Those most likely to die were often admitted for the good of their souls; home treatment was ordered whenever possible for all others.

Eleanor had a basic understanding of herbs and cures herself. Every woman did, whether she was meant for the convent, a lord's castle, a merchant's stall, or a villein's hut. Healing at home was woman's work, but some were better trained than others. Tyndal was lucky to have several sisters, as well as some lay brothers, with both talent and knowledge in the healing arts. Being a small establishment, they could not always eliminate those women from care-giving who were still subject to monthly bleedings, women such as the infirmarian herself, but the patients had suffered little from their ministrations despite the common medical opinion that menstruating women were polluting, thus dangerous to the sick. The de facto leader of all caregivers was Sister Anne, whose background Eleanor continued to find intriguing.

Eleanor had heard of women who were trained in the apothecary trade and even of some who were physicians. Hildegard of Bingen's medical works, as well as those of Trotula of Solerno, were known to her aunt. These days, however, such women were quite rare. According to Sister Beatrice, most of the women physicians in the present day were of the Jewish faith. Although Marie of France had celebrated the medical expertise of a wealthy woman from Solerno in her lai, "Les Deus Amanz," less than a century ago, Eleanor knew that was just a tale.

But to be familiar with texts from the Holy Land itself? How unusual even for Anne's physician father. She had finally pressed Sister Anne ever so slightly on this question, and the nun had explained that her father knew physicians in Paris who had shared the works with him. Eleanor wondered how he had been able to read the language in which they were written. Translations from the infidel tongue were even rarer than these texts themselves. Perhaps Sister Anne meant that her father had received training in these skills from mentors who knew the languages he did not. No matter. She was grateful to have such a knowledgeable practitioner of healing arts as Sister Anne in the priory.

"…and we all wash our hands after attending to every patient." Sister Christina was gesturing down the long room on the women's side. Each patient not only had a private bed but was protected from curious eyes by wooden screens.

"An interesting practice."

"Something Sister Anne insists on. Prioress Felicia did not approve. She said it was ungodly and unhealthy, but then Sister

Anne asked Brother Rupert to bless the water every day so our hands would be cleansed with holy water."

"And?"

"It did seem to help the sick, so our prioress allowed us to continue. It was clear that our hands thus washed were imbued with God's grace. Should you..."

"We shall continue the procedure, of course." Eleanor glanced into one screened-off area and saw the tall figure of Sister Anne lifting a skeletal woman into a sitting position, then slowly giving her sips of some liquid. The hand washing was not only an unusual thing to do, she thought, but the good sister had also chosen an interesting way of justifying it. None had noticed that no one had replaced Brother Rupert in the blessing of the water, and Sister Anne had certainly not stopped the routine. Perhaps this was yet another practice out of her father's texts from the Holy Land.

"My lady!"

Eleanor spun around as a breathless nun skidded to a stop in front of her.

"Calm yourself, sister! What has happened?"

"It's Brother Thomas, my lady. He lies dead in the forest!"

Eleanor could not stop the small cry of anguish that escaped her. "Tell Sister Anne to follow me immediately after this treatment," she quickly said to Christina, then turned her head away before anyone could see the tears starting up in her eyes.

Chapter Fifteen

"Indeed he's lucky he is not dead."

Eleanor realized she had been holding her breath as Sister Anne examined the bloodied but breathing monk.

"Fa!" Thomas spat out the liquid Sister Anne had just given him.

"And he may be yet, if he does that to me again," Anne said, wiping away the fluid he had just spewed all over the front of her habit.

Thomas groaned.

"Can you understand me?" Sister Anne asked.

"My head hurts." His voice was a whisper.

"It should. Someone laid a good blow on the back of it. Cut your scalp, but you'll live. You have a suitably thick Norman skull."

Thomas turned over and vomited, a little liquid but mostly air.

"Didn't eat much last night, did we?"

"I don't suppose you know who did this to you, brother?" Eleanor asked.

Thomas sat up slowly with Sister Anne's help and shut his eyes. "If I ever find out, the whoreson won't live long."

"Not a sentiment I'd expect to hear from a priest. You'll want to remember that for your next confession." Eleanor kept her voice stern as she struggled not to laugh in nervous relief at his spirit.

"At least I should get exemption from the next blood-letting."

"You're feeling better." Sister Anne smiled, then looked up at the tall, green-eyed monk standing beside her. "Would you give me that cup? I think I can try again with the medicine."

"You said you found him?" Eleanor watched the man pass the cup with care to Sister Anne so that their hands did not touch.

The monk nodded and lowered his green eyes with courtesy.

"I do not know your name."

"Brother John, my lady. I am in charge of both the male novices and monk's choir at Tyndal. "

"And what did you see, Brother John?"

"Not much, I fear. I came out this morning after chapter to pick lavender to strew on the floor of the novices' quarters. They are suffering from a surfeit of fleas, you see. We grow only enough of the plant for medicinal use so I look for the wild herb. It serves the purpose just as well."

Eleanor nodded with some impatience.

"And as I came to this spot, I saw the brother lying just there." He pointed. "After what happened to Brother Rupert, I fear I didn't check for signs of life. I thought he was dead with those eyes so staring at me. I ran to the nuns' gate and asked Sister Ruth to summon you, then waited in the outer court until you came so I could lead you here."

"I see," she replied. "But first tell me, brother, how you found your way out of the monks' cloister without a key to the passageway?"

John blinked. "The door was unlocked, my lady." He hesitated. "Perhaps Brother Thomas forgot to lock it behind him when he left the cloister."

Eleanor looked back at Thomas, who was grimacing in the direction of the other monk. He must hurt so, she thought. "Do you find the passage door unlocked so often that you would check first before asking permission to leave?"

"Not at all! After Prime, as I led the novices back for lessons, I saw the door open and sent the boys on their way to consider further some questions I had already set them. I wanted to take the opportunity to get my lavender while I could. You see, when Brother Rupert was alive, he allowed me to accompany him when he left to attend to the nuns if I needed to go into the woods for herbs. Both Brother Simeon and Brother Andrew are quite busy, and I had yet to speak with Brother Thomas about a similar arrangement. I'm afraid I saw my chance this morning and took it without permission."

"And by so doing, found our injured brother. The good of your impulse outweighs your failure to seek proper permission," Eleanor said. "You would say, however, that leaving the door unlocked was a rare occurrence?"

"Indeed, my lady. Brother Rupert was very careful and strict about such matters. He would never lend the key out and only let another go with him if the need was reasonable."

Was the same true of the door to the nuns' quarters, Eleanor wondered. She would have to ask Sister Ruth. In the meantime, she had to question Thomas no matter how much pain he was in. He had no reason to be so far outside priory walls, nor should he have been so foolish as to leave the door unlocked with a murderer about.

"And why were you out of the priory, Brother Thomas?"

"A call of nature, my lady. Sometime after Matins."

"The monks do have a proper latrine for that. You needn't have come all the way out here…"

"Forgive me, my lady, but I am still unaccustomed to my quarters and lost my way. I did not wish to waken anyone to ask directions."

Eleanor felt her face flush with hurt anger. Did he really think she was that stupid? His reason for being outside the priory walls in the middle of the night was so ridiculous it was an insult to her intelligence. First of all, the latrine was just off the monks' dormitory, as it was in almost every monastery in Christendom. Second, if the call was so urgent he didn't have time to find such an easily located privy, did he really think she'd believe he could have waited long enough to find his way outside and wander so far away from the priory? She snorted in contempt. If he did, then he was the fool, not she.

As she looked at his bloody head and pale complexion, however, cold logic fled and she softened. This was not the time to joust with him over inconsistencies. He had not been here long enough to have found a willing woman in the village on his own for less than priestly purposes, and a staff of monks so frail that they could not even say Mass, if Brother Simeon were to be believed, would be unlikely to have a list of local whores any younger than they.

She would wait until he was feeling better to search out the real reason for his nocturnal meanderings, and she would do so privately. Indeed, her aunt had told her about monks who awoke at night, suffering from dreams conjured up by Satan as she had herself endured of late, and slipped away to spill their seed in the manner of Onan. Perhaps it had been thus with Thomas, and, if so, he might well be embarrassed to say so in front of three nuns and a monk.

Sister Anne stood and looked down at the monk who was struggling to stand up. "Can you walk to the hospital, brother? I need to treat that wound further with remedies I have there."

"Of course."

"With help." Sister Anne gestured at the tall monk. "Brother?"

"Aye. I'll steady you," John said, as he reached out his hand to Thomas.

It was with some interest that Eleanor noted Brother John used his left hand, as he had when he passed the cup to Sister Anne.

Chapter Sixteen

"You've got yourself quite the wound, brother." Crowner Ralf stared fixedly at the back of Thomas' head, then reached out his hand as if to touch it.

"Keep your hands to yourself, Ralf! Brother Thomas is no corpse that you can prod and jab with impunity. I'll describe anything you need to know."

It was the morning after the attack against him and Thomas sat on the edge of his bed in the hospital while Sister Anne removed the dressing and examined the injury. He winced slightly and she patted his shoulder once in sympathy before reaching over to a nearby basket for a fresh poultice of yarrow and bandaging. "It's healing well, brother," she said.

The crowner looked at her, his eyes twinkling with mischief. "Very well, Annie, then describe to me in detail the man who did this to the good brother, for I haven't the slightest idea."

"A strong one," the nun said without hesitation, "and left-handed."

"Ah, our sinister friend again? And how, may I ask, did you come to that conclusion?"

"The wound slants thus." Sister Anne drew a line in the air about an inch from Thomas's skull from a high on his left side to a low on the right of the head. "He swung from the side. If he had hit him here..." she pointed to the top of Thomas' head, "he'd have killed our brother."

"Are you saying you don't think he meant to kill him?"

"I don't know, Ralf. You'll have to ask the man who did it."

Ralf snorted. "If I can find him, and so far he has left few traces. We have had no recent problems with highwaymen or any other masterless men, but no one has seen or heard anything unusual around the village. I would guess that the culprit might be the same who killed Brother Rupert only because Tyndal has never suffered such a spate of crime in my long memory. Nonetheless, I have been unable to unearth a reason for either the murder or the attack you suffered, brother. Perhaps you were just in the wrong place at the wrong time. What do you remember?"

"Nothing much." Thomas raised his head gradually to avoid the pain of any sudden movement and turned just as slowly to face Ralf. Behind the crowner stood the prioress. She had said little to anyone this morning, but Thomas noticed that her face was unusually pale. Her right hand was clenched in a fist and she held it tight against her waist.

"Perhaps you can start with the reason you left the priory in the first place, brother," Ralf suggested.

As Thomas started to speak, Eleanor raised her hand in a gesture of precaution. "Please do leave out the call of nature. That story wasn't even clever."

"My lady…" Thomas began and then stopped as he watched the prioress's face flush pink. He wondered if she was feverish.

"Lest you were in doubt on this matter, brother, I am neither ignorant nor stupid. The truth, therefore, would be quite refreshing. It might even make it easier to discover who did this to you, and, perhaps, to find Brother Rupert's killer."

Thomas shut his eyes. The pain had diminished from yesterday, but his head still ached and the prioress's tone was harsh. He was not in the mood to be treated thus even if he had lied to her and she was the prioress to whom he owed obedience. The cowardly attack on him was a matter of honor, an attack on his manhood, and no woman should hold authority over him in such an affair. He would deal with the man who had hit him in his own way. Nor did he want the crowner here either. It was none of his business. He'd find the perpetrator himself, although he was almost certain it was that grim-faced, green-eyed Brother John. "'S blood," he muttered.

"Presumably you can find your confessor better than you could find the privy. Profanity is unacceptable in a man dedicated to God. You must have known that long before you took your vows."

Thomas covered his face with his hands.

Sister Anne turned to Eleanor. "He hurts, my lady."

The prioress drew in a deep breath, let it out very slowly, and started again with a gentler tone.

"I know you are in pain, brother, but we need the truth if we're to prevent more violence. First, we had Brother Rupert's death, and now we've had the attack on you. We don't need a third such incident because you are suffering from the sin of pride."

Thomas nodded. Ralf and the prioress were right. It hadn't been that clear to him that the two incidents were related, but he did not want someone else killed or injured. Still, what truth could he tell? What made sense and what should he or even could he explain?

He remembered following Brother John and the young man as they ran out of the chapel. Following them had been an instinctive act; thus the reason he had done so was quite inexplicable. Nor was he sure he wanted to try. He might be chary of the somber monk with glittering green eyes, but he wasn't sure he wanted to tell what he had witnessed either. The scene between monk and youth had been intimate, poignant. Thomas' interest had been piqued for sure, but he also felt protective of them.

Perhaps there had been no sin between the two, although the observed encounter rather lent itself to the darker interpretation. The youth he had seen with the monk was no high-voiced child. He had had the shoulders and height, if not the girth, of a man. No, he thought, he would never be guilty of doing to another what had been done to him. Thomas shook his head to shatter the image of Giles in his arms and turned his thoughts back to what had happened outside Tyndal Priory.

It had been difficult to see far in the outer court. Clouds or fog had drifted across the sky. The moon gave only meager light and the stars were hidden from view. The area was still strange to him, and he had stumbled on the unfamiliar, rough ground as he tried to keep the shadows of monk and youth in sight.

He remembered crossing a small wooden bridge below which he assumed must be the priory mill from the sound of groaning wood and splashing water. Then he had seen the silhouette of the mill itself. It loomed blacker than the night along what had suddenly become a smoother, well-worn path.

Distracted by his attempt to keep his bearings, he had tripped. As he picked himself up, he saw the two had gained on him, their outlines growing fainter in the distance. Then he spotted them as they opened a creaking gate in the wall. It must have been used by the townspeople who had need of the mill, he guessed. Perhaps a monk or lay brother guarded it during the day, but there was none such to be seen in the gloom of that night.

When he passed through the gate, however, the shadows he was chasing had vanished. There was no sign of them to either left or right. Ahead of him was the forest.

He stopped, held his breath to keep the hoarse sound from masking what he hoped to hear. His ears were straining, listening for any sound of human life.

Nothing.

Then he heard something, deer or man, running through brush. He raced headlong into the trees, but they had slowed and confused him. Soon he knew he was lost. Sweating and tired, Thomas had lurched through snagging vines and rotting tree limbs until he came into a clearing of sorts. He stopped and tried to get his bearings, staring into the dark, moving shadows for two more. The shapes he saw were eerie impish things, not human, which seemed to reach out to him and snatch at his cowl and habit.

He remembered taking a deep breath, then hearing the gurgling of a brook nearby. And just as he thought he detected the sound of hushed voices above the noise of the water, something hit him, forcing a cry of surprised pain from him as he fell into the soft leaf mold and slipped into total oblivion.

So what could he tell the crowner and Prioress Eleanor? If the voices he thought he had heard were those of the lad and the monk, then the man who hit him was a stranger. If he had imagined the voices, then monk was still the most likely suspect. Perhaps the less said, the better, Thomas decided. For the moment.

"You are long silent, brother." Ralf was looking at him with curiosity.

"I was trying to remember what had happened, crowner, but I fear I can summon up little." Thomas nodded to the prioress. "Indeed, it was not a call of nature, my lady, but I was shamed by my foolishness in leaving the passage door open. The truth is simple enough. I was unable to sleep and slipped down to the chapel to pray, but my body was restless and sleep still would not come. So I did what I used to do as a boy and took a short walk, albeit outside the priory walls. I had no evil purpose. I am not yet familiar enough with the priory to know where I could walk and meditate without disturbing others at such a dark hour."

That much, Thomas thought, was reasonably true.

"When I entered the forest, I became confused but when I came to the clearing, I stopped. I thought I heard a brook and remembered that such ran through the priory. Just as I was thinking I could follow it back to the grounds, something hit me and I remember nothing more."

"What was the first thing you do remember?" Ralf asked.

"I was cold. Then I felt a hand on my shoulder and someone turned me over. The morning light hurt but I was able to see Brother John's face clearly." Thomas laughed. "Indeed my head hurt worse than it did the time I fell down some stone steps as a boy when I was wrestling with…" With Giles, he thought, and winced.

"And still does, I see," said Sister Anne with such a steady look that Thomas feared she could see into his very soul, stained as it was with half-truths, lies, and dreams of Giles.

Thomas turned his head away.

"And when did you leave the chapel, brother?" asked Ralf.

"It was long after Matins but before Prime," Thomas replied. "I felt the sharpness of the morning mist and saw it covering the stars."

"Indeed, Brother John found you not long after Prime," Eleanor said. She seemed lost in thought, her chin in her hand as she looked at him. He could read nothing in her gray eyes.

"Not much to go by, son, but at least you are alive and lucky indeed to have the good care of Sister Anne at the hospital here." Ralf glanced over at the tall nun. His smile as he looked at her was surprisingly gentle for such a rough man.

Despite the look from her that made him fear she saw all his secrets, Thomas could understand how a man might become fond of such a remarkable woman as Sister Anne. For all her unfeminine candor and logical mind, the nun had gentle hands and thoughtful ways. Her binding of his wound had been quick, almost painless, and she had not only given him a soothing mixture to aid sleep but also a comfortable bed last night well away from those so sick they moaned despite her herbs and calming draughts. In truth, he had slept well.

Although he had had two strange dreams, which made him wonder what had been in that sleeping potion to cause such fantastic imaginings. The first one was almost spectral. In his dream, Thomas had opened his eyes and seen nothing but darkness. All was quiet in the blackness except for the low, uneasy muttering of the sleeping sick. Then, through the opening of the screen which gave him privacy, he saw two shadowy forms standing close together in whispered discussion and softly silhouetted by the light of the candles each held. When one figure moved his taper, Thomas recognized Brother John. The monk's murmuring was rapid and intense, and although Thomas could not hear what either said, he recognized Sister Anne's voice when she briefly responded.

Thomas looked around but saw no sign of another sister, monk or lay person present and remembered thinking that surely it was not allowed for the two to be together without proper attendance. Then Brother John put his hand on Sister Anne's shoulder and kissed her on the cheek before slipping away into the darkness. Thomas must have fallen back into his deep sleep for he remembered nothing more of them.

The most troubling fantasy came later. Again he had dreamed that he had opened his eyes. And, again, all was dark. He could hear only the steady or irregular breathing of the other sick and wounded. This time there were no candles or ghostly figures, but he did hear a soft rustling. A mouse or rat, he remembered thinking, and closed his eyes. At that moment, he felt a presence next to him, the movement of a garment against his arm, and the sound of breathing above him.

Instinctively, he kept his eyes shut and waited, wary but oddly not unnerved by the quiet figure. It was a man, he was sure. He could smell his sweat, an acrid scent, not the sweetish, sometimes metallic smell of a woman.

The man did nothing. He just stood there. Then, with a stroke as soft as a feather brushing against his face, he touched Thomas. A lay brother perhaps, he thought, tensing ever so slightly. Someone checking for the dead amongst the quick? Then the robe swept across his arm once again as the man turned and moved away. He heard the man's feet crush the floor rushes with that whishing, rodent-like noise he had heard before.

Thomas opened his eyes. He would have sworn that the bulky shadow moving away from him was Brother Simeon, but as he fell back into a profound sleep that lasted until the morning bells for prayer, he decided he must surely be mistaken.

Chapter Seventeen

Ralf the Crowner had been the first to leave, shaking his head with frustration over this additional complication and at the unexpectedly slow pace of his investigation into Brother Rupert's murder. As he marched down the length of the hospital, he had muttered curses at himself, and the young lay sister accompanying him must surely have blushed at some of the things she overheard.

Soon after, Anne returned to her treatment of the earthly pains of mortal bodies while Sister Christina soothed whatever ailed the trembling souls of those seeking to be healed at Tyndal. Thomas was left under strict orders to do nothing more strenuous than wander in the safety of the monks' cloister gardens.

Eleanor went back to her chambers and was grateful to be alone at last. Picking up the orange cat, she sat staring at the tapestry of Mary Magdalene with Jesus.

"I am furious with myself," she muttered. "I was harsh to the wounded brother, not because of his lies, although I might have had the right in that, but out of fear of my own frailty. In that, I was wrong." Tears stung her eyes. To keep herself from one sin, she had committed another. Indeed, she had longed to reach out to soothe his pain with gentle caress, not only to comfort him but also to satisfy her own hunger to touch him.

The previous night she had slept little, and, when she had, the dreams were so violent she had awakened, sweating in terror.

Some of her night horrors were about Thomas. The attack on him had frightened her, and not beyond reason, but it were not the sole cause.

"There is a brutal and twisted wickedness loose, not just in the world outside Tyndal's walls but, I fear, within the priory itself," she said aloud, looking down at the contented bundle of fur on her lap. "Evil in some form has invaded this house dedicated to peace and to God."

And that house was her house. Ultimately, it was her responsibility to protect everyone within these walls, and she was failing.

"Against my better judgement, I have allowed myself the same easy comfort I have encouraged amongst the brothers and sisters here. For cert, I may hope Brother Rupert's murder was a chance thing and the murderer some common outlaw, but for the safety of us all, I may not assume it."

She shifted. Arthur, the cat, looked up at her and expressed a mild complaint. "Hush, sweet one. I have recovered my wits." She smiled as he resettled in her lap. "When I awoke from my nightmares in the harsh green moonlight of the midnight hour, a manly reason did prevail over my weaker self."

Eleanor looked away from the tapestry and toward the window that looked down on the priory grounds. "No purposeless killer would drag a body, not only into the outer court of the priory grounds but further into the walled nuns' quarters. That had to have been a deliberate act, meant to send a specific message, and thus most likely the murderer has a close connection with Tyndal."

Was the slayer a monk? Was he a lay brother? Could it have even been a woman? Perhaps one of the village people who used the mill or had other commerce with the priory and knew their habits well? The idea that any religious would do such a thing to another was not beyond her comprehension, but she prayed it would not be so. Besides, what could an old man like Brother Rupert do to anyone in this priory, or what would he know, for that matter, that would make that person choose murder to quiet him? A murder, moreover, committed in such a horrible way? There were few sins so abhorrent that confession would not remove both the shame and the sin. Monks knew that best of all. Or should. Surely the killer was from outside the priory, perhaps the village. Surely from the village.

"Then there is the attack on Brother Thomas," she said, rubbing the cat's forehead. "The crowner suggested that the killer of one monk might be the attacker of yet another. Thus the reasons for the more heinous crime become twisted and complex. No, this is no easily caught, ordinary malefactor. This is someone with the cleverness of Satan himself." She hesitated. "However, even the Prince of Darkness did not escape punishment for his defiance of God's supremacy. Neither will the killer of Brother Rupert," she said emphatically. Like her nuns and monks, she, too, had to believe that God would render justice, whatever form it might take. To believe otherwise was heresy. And madness.

"The crowner continues to be thwarted by lack of evidence, however, and Brother Thomas is still not telling the truth." She had no good reason for thinking the latter, none that any man would find reasonable, but her instincts knew well what those little twitches in his face meant after his long pause and the quick glance to the side before he began his new tale. Some of his most recent story might be true. He had been found in a clearing near where the large stream ran toward the priory, and most certainly he had been struck from behind.

"Nay, I do not believe his tale of the need for a walk any more than the call of nature story, but for whatever reason he left the priory, he must have seen something he wasn't meant to see. Did he accidentally walk to a place he shouldn't have been, at a time he shouldn't have been there? Could the reason he left the priory grounds be related to why he was attacked? In that case, who or what was he protecting?" She shook her head in puzzlement. Surely a man so new to Tyndal could not have formed such strong bonds of loyalty so soon with anyone.

"Perhaps he strayed into something similar to what Brother Rupert encountered? Not quite the same thing or he would have been killed, of course, but near enough to merit a warning?" Eleanor mused aloud as she looked down at the curled creature now sleeping in her lap. "He was struck in a clearing in the forest at night. Might he have ventured too near the meeting place of evil spirits?" She rubbed her weary eyes. Although she had no doubt that evil spirits existed and often lurked at night, she had never personally known any that did not come in a very earthly form. No, if Thomas had trespassed on land claimed by agents of evil, they were human ones.

She stood up and gently lowered the cat to the ground. Arthur had left a fine layer of orange hair on the skirt of her habit. Briefly, she brushed at it. What little she dislodged floated down and reattached to her hem.

"Well, my good friend, it seems I must carry some of you with me as long as my gown lasts! Perhaps it will keep me warmer come winter and I shall be most grateful."

The cat sat at her feet, rumbling softly, his green eyes round and his gaze intense.

Eleanor reached down and scratched him behind the ears. "It is time for you to go to work in the kitchen, fine sir. And it is time for me to take a walk, in the manner of our good Brother Thomas, to see what lies outside our priory."

It was a warm day, mellow as late summer days could be, a day that lulled mortals into forgetting the sharp sleet and chill sea winds which came with punishing force as the life-giving seasons slipped into the long months of damp gloom. As she walked into the grove to the clearing where Thomas had been found, Eleanor thought about the dark time ahead and could understand why her pagan ancestors had woven such vivid and often cruel tales to explain the changing of the seasons. It was easy enough to see how they could interpret the end of spring and the harvest season as a time of cruel devastation, hopelessness and, aye, even murder. What amazed her was their ability to rebound and find hope in the renewal of life long before they had ever heard of Christianity. Giving His man creature such resilience of spirit, even in the benighted days, spoke volumes about God's love. The thought gave her comfort as she walked through the trees where a man of violence had stalked not so very long ago. Such love would surely bring this person to justice in some way and soon.

Eleanor caught herself wanting to talk to her aunt about all that had happened; then she felt a quick pain. "Now it is up to me to answer my own questions, is it not?" she asked aloud in a quiet voice. "And it is certainly up to me to keep my mind to the mark and my eyes open for whatever there is to find," she added as she walked into the clearing.

The birds twittered as they flew in search of insects. The insects hummed as they went about their business in spite of the birds. And Eleanor stood with her hands tucked into her sleeves, looking about her.

The clearing looked innocent enough in the daylight. There were no signs of midnight fires or foul, rotting holes from which Satan's creatures might have burst forth upon the earth during the night. No, the evil that had skulked here so recently had had a mortal form.

Yet the crowner and his men still found nothing. If Lucifer's most monstrous deeds had been imperfect, and he had been one of God's highest-ranking angels, then surely no mortal man could commit a crime without leaving behind evidence of some kind. There must be something…

Eleanor turned slowly around. What might the crowner and his men have failed to notice? They were, after all, men. She smiled with both love and gentle amusement. The image of her solemn-faced but sweetly earnest brother Hugh came to mind. A warrior in the mold of his hero, King Richard, Hugh could always see where a castle's defense was weakest, but he would then trip over a sharp stone on the way to scale it.

The eyes of most men are more used to looking at the grander plans of intrigue and battle, she thought, and, in so doing, they often miss some small thing, perchance a commonplace thing that an eye impatient with tiny detail would pass over. A woman's eye might be more useful here, an eye trained to the domestic and the mundane, and therefore more likely to note a simple object out of place. Indeed her own training had hardly been domestic, but, in learning to joust with the finer points of philosophers' arguments and in the minute study of her mortal fellows, she had found great pleasure in details of a sort. Hers was still a woman's mind trained to minutiae, she argued to herself, albeit somewhat different concerns than occupied most of her gentle sex.

As she walked passed the place, she looked down and saw the bloodstains in the grass where Thomas had lain. She recoiled slightly. Her feelings for him were still too tender and uncontrolled. Then she pressed her hand flat against her chest as if binding her heart with a bandage and walked away, up the slight hill toward the trees and the rushing sound of the nearby stream.

ome

The brook was pretty in this season, the bubbling water flashing bursts of light where it flowed into the sun. After a storm, the stream might become a dangerous torrent, but now the water was low, although running swiftly. As it entered the priory grounds, it served to give Tyndal fresh fish and clean water for watering gardens, bathing, washing, and making ale, although few drank the water, knowing how dangerous it could be to their health. As it left the priory, it washed away the refuse from the latrines, and the kitchens, and carried all into the sea. Truly one of many gifts from God, Eleanor thought, as she started down the slope toward the banks.

Her foot slipped in the moist brown earth of the embankment, and she caught herself by grabbing an exposed tree root. A reminder that she was doing something she shouldn't, perhaps? Of course, she should not be here alone. Even a prioress was required to have proper and prudent companionship wherever she went.

"Indeed, that is true, but I am still too new at Tyndal to know whom I can fully trust and whom I cannot," she sighed. With a murderer possibly in their midst, she felt safer by herself than with someone who might be of danger to her, especially as she wandered around, looking for something to uncover that very culprit. Even the seemingly open and pragmatic Sister Anne had shadowy corners in her soul, although Eleanor felt increasing comfort in the company of the nun.

"No, I am safer alone," she said aloud to nothing in particular.

As she walked along the edge of the stream, she knew she hadn't the vaguest idea what she was looking for. She stopped and glanced around, in part to mark her path back to the priory and in part to look for something out of the ordinary.

The ground was rocky near the stream. No footprints surely.

As she looked up at the high banks, she imagined this charming little stream as it turned into a raging river and gouged this deep channel into the earth. Indeed, several of the trees, not just the one at her descent, extended tangled and naked roots into the space above her head. She would have to check whether the stream's course through the priory was sufficiently constrained when she got back.

With her mind distracted and her gaze turned upward, Eleanor stumbled and fell on the uneven, rocky ground. She cried out when her ankle turned and her hands scraped against the gravelly surface as she broke her fall. For just a moment, she shut her eyes tight against the sharpness of the pain; then she twisted herself around into a sitting position and concentrated on feeling her throbbing ankle.

"Not broken," she said with relief and considerable gratitude. It would be difficult enough to get back to the priory by herself with a sprain, let alone with a cracked or shattered bone.

She looked around for a broken branch close by that would be sturdy enough to support her. Nearer to the bank, there were a couple of promising limbs. She half-crawled, half-pulled herself toward the branches.

The first one was rotten and broke in half as soon as she put pressure on it; however, the second held, and she began to pull herself up. As she did, an intermittent breeze rose and fell, and she noticed the movement of something against the bank.

She eased herself back into a sitting position. Close against the bank lay a huge boulder, over which a netting of roots lay, attached to a large tree. The tree sat precariously balanced between rock and bank, some of its roots still bound deep into the earth. From one of the largest roots a woven grass mat hung down between rock and cliff. One edge of the mat was weighed down with a heavy stone, but the other, the one that moved in the breeze, had lost its weight.

Eleanor once again pulled herself up with her strong branch, and, grabbing the broken one as she did so, limped closer. The breeze moved the matting again. Behind it, there seemed to be a small gap.

"Is anyone there?" she asked.

Silence.

Cautiously, she extended the point of the broken branch and pushed the mat aside.

No one was there.

She pulled the mat away. It covered a narrow entrance between rock and bank to a cave, presumably gouged out by the stream and deep enough to provide shelter for two or three people. Had the boulder not been there to brace it, she thought, looking up at the huge trunk above her head, the tree would have fallen and the remaining roots would have ripped away the roof of the small cave, destroying the shelter entirely.

As she looked further into the enclosure, she could see marks in the walls where nature's results had been deliberately enlarged. There was no sign of a fire or utensils for cooking, but there was a narrow, raised, and sturdy wooden bed frame with a clean straw mat and some pegs jammed into the earthen wall. Over one peg was hung what appeared to be a small whip.

Eleanor hopped awkwardly up to the peg and looked with care at the object in the dim light. There was no question that it was a crude whip made of twigs bundled together. It was darkly stained. Was this blood?

"Whatever is this all for?" she asked quietly as she fingered the stiff switches and looked around the small space.

She shuddered, then spoke aloud to calm herself with the sound of a human voice. "This is something for the crowner to look at, not me. And, methinks, I would be wise to leave!"

She pushed the mat aside and hobbled into the feathered sunlight, but the shadows playing on the sparkling water were no longer beautiful and the utter silence of the birds was ominous.

Eleanor looked around quickly. There was no one and nothing to be seen. Bracing herself with her makeshift crutch, she bent and replaced the rock that had held the mat down. With the mat securely anchored and pushed into the shadows of the narrow opening, she realized that the cave entrance was barely visible.

As she straightened, adjusting the branch to support her weight, she heard a rustling sound just above her and looked up.

Standing on the bank above her, a bearded and unkempt man stared at her for what seemed a very long time, a knife glinting in his hand. His left hand, Eleanor observed with the icy precision of fear.

Then he turned and ran. Eleanor stood frozen in place until the sound of his escape, crashing through the brush, had faded into the sound of the stream flowing beside her.

And in that instant, she understood what it meant to meet Death face to face.

Chapter Eighteen

Sister Anne stood up, hands on hips, and looked at her prioress with undisguised disapproval. "If I may be so blunt, my lady…"

"And you may, sister."

"You put yourself in unnecessary danger out there beyond the priory today. Although I agree that you may have found something of interest, perhaps even of great value to our crowner in his investigations, the risk you took was, well, rash."

Eleanor was sitting in her chambers with her injured foot bound and propped on a stool, a goblet of watered wine at hand and Arthur in her lap. She sighed.

"Blunt indeed, but tactful considering. Let me speak your true thoughts. I was reckless, thoughtless, and stupid to do what I did."

Anne nodded, then smiled.

"And I have learned my lesson. I was quite happy to send word to our crowner and let him investigate the cave more thoroughly." Eleanor shifted slightly, and the cat meowed with instant feline annoyance.

"Let me take him." Anne reached out. "His added weight is not helpful to you."

"Let him be." Eleanor looked fondly at the furry creature. "He has a soothing softness."

Sister Anne started to laugh, then stopped. There was a sharp rap at the chamber door, and she turned toward it with a frown.

"Enter," Eleanor called out.

Gytha rushed in and curtseyed awkwardly. "My lady, the crowner is here. He begs an audience with you."

"He has done his investigation quickly," Eleanor said, turning to Anne and raising her eyebrows in surprise.

Gytha spun around on one foot and was about to speed out the door.

"Gytha! A moment, if you please. I will need you to provide refreshment for the good man."

"Shall I bring bread as well as wine, my lady?"

"And cheese. He will need something to regain his strength after all his efforts. And perhaps something for..." She pointed to the cat. "I understand he brought three fine dead rats to Sister Edith today."

"Who squealed loud enough the whole priory knew of his success at the hunt!" Gytha giggled, then rushed from the room to fetch the food.

"Such energy!" Eleanor chuckled.

"Such youth," Sister Anne sighed.

⟨※⟩

Ralf stood over the heavy wooden table and, with ravenous eagerness, eyed the already razed stack of bread and hacked mound of cheese set before him. "Blood it was on the whip. I'm sure of it," he said as he reached out with his stained knife to spear another piece of deep orange cheese. He wrapped a hefty chunk of fresh bread around it before taking a huge bite. "I'm grateful for this, my lady. Haven't been able to break my fast yet today." Crumbs flew as he chomped at the food with dogged enthusiasm.

Eleanor glanced up at the angle of light coming through her window. The day was well into the afternoon hours. "Do sit and relax. I can wait for a report," she replied.

Anne rolled her eyes heavenward with gentle amusement as she watched the crowner saw off another slab of cheese.

Ralf shook his head. "If I sit, I'll fall asleep." Then he took another monstrous bite and couldn't quite close his mouth as he chewed. "I must say that the purpose of the cave is still puzzling." He continued munching cheerfully, his cheeks puffed out like a chipmunk with a winter's cache in its mouth.

Eleanor took a sip of wine. "What are your thoughts on it?"

Ralf paused for a brief second in mid-chew. "My first thought was that it was a hideaway for a villein running away from his lord, but the pegs suggested it was being used for more than a temporary hiding spot. They and the raised bed were not things a poor tenant farmer on the run would bother with. At most he might make a mat of leaves or a pallet of dried grass."

"Did you find any evidence of cooking?"

"No evidence of fire at all, or discarded bones from eating, and that was passing strange as well." Ralf shook his head. "The whip did make me wonder about one possibility. Have you heard of any hermit recently come to the area?"

Eleanor looked up at Anne, who shook her head. "No. We have heard of no one. I would not expect a hermit to make himself an elevated bed either. Although, now that you raise the question, I wonder about the man I saw."

"Surely a hermit would have come to us by now, my lady. He would want to have the services of one of our priests," Anne suggested.

"I wish I had gotten a better look at the man before he ran from me. Perhaps the cave was his. I also find it strange that the sight of a mere nun would frighten him so."

"A bearded man with long hair and brindled clothes would match most of the men from the village." Ralf grunted. "Fishermen and men who work the fields care not for fashion. And the knife does not surprise me. Perhaps he didn't mean to threaten you at all. Perhaps he was cleaning a bird or some wild animal he'd just killed, but running from you does surprise me. The sight of a nun should not be surprising or strange to anyone in the area. The townspeople have all benefited from your hospital and they come to your church for services. Unless he ran because he did not expect to see a nun alone and did not know what he should do? Perhaps he feared God's wrath if he spoke to you."

"He did not necessarily know I was alone. Indeed, he would have expected someone to be with me. He might have been surprised to see a nun where he did not think to see one, but he would have had no reason to run unless he was afraid. Or had something to hide."

"Or was possessed," Sister Anne suggested.

Eleanor thought for a moment. "I believed he was going to kill me when I saw him with that knife in his hand. Now that I think about it, however, he did look frightened. Certainly, he ran as if he were. If he is possessed, I fear the spirit that has entered his body is more likely to hurt him than another."

"Then he is to be pitied more than feared," Anne replied as she turned to the crowner. "The townspeople have seen us away from the priory on occasion, albeit rarely, and usually in the woods. I have looked for herbs abroad when our garden has run short, and Sister Matilda used to search for mushrooms in the forest when she was in charge of the kitchen." She shook her head as Ralf opened his mouth to speak. "No, the villagers are not there for criminal reasons and steal nothing of interest to the King. They usually come for the same reasons we have. When we meet, they greet us with courtesy and pass on."

Gytha quietly lifted the ewer of cooled wine and filled the goblets for both Eleanor and Ralf. When the girl offered to pour wine for her, Sister Anne put her hand over her cup.

"You've been that far from the priory?" Ralf asked the nun.

"Not I, Ralf," Anne said. "The wild herbs I use require sun or light shade. My needs were met closer by, but Sister Matilda might have gone deeper into the forest for her mushrooms."

Ralf coughed, then belched with immense satisfaction. "I would be most grateful, my lady, if you would speak to the sister. I don't know why, but I seem to frighten your nuns, or else turn them into angry amazons. If Sister Ruth had had a lance in hand when she saw me approach your cloister gate today, I do believe she would have run me through."

Eleanor laughed. "Indeed! Then be grateful we cannot be warrior nuns in the manner of the Templar monks. Still, I will be happy to talk to Sister Matilda. Perhaps you would be good enough to return tomorrow. I will tell you what I have discovered."

Ralf swept the table with one last look, grabbed the remaining piece of cheese, which he raised to Eleanor in salute, then bowed and left. As soon as the chamber door shut behind him, Eleanor and Anne looked at each other and burst out in loud laughter.

Gytha blinked in amazement as the two women continued to howl in shared mirth.

"Fear not, child," Eleanor said, reaching out to touch Gytha's arm. "We are not mad but simply ungracious enough to enjoy the thought of our elder porteress as a warrior maiden, donning armor and baring her breast to joust with our crowner, who, I should think, would be more interested in a fine cheese than her naked breast."

"Forgive me, my lady, but Sister Ruth would need no weapon save her bared breast to slay Crowner Ralf," Gytha replied, eyes twinkling despite her sober look.

The two nuns flushed red, but this time all three bent over in uncontrolled laughter.

Chapter Nineteen

Thomas lied to Sister Anne.

Despite his aching head, he could not stand yet another full day of enforced rest. She had called it a miraculous recovery and let him go with a look that said she knew full well that he was more impatient than fully fit. Out of guilt he had promised not to overdo and to come back at once if he began to vomit or show other symptoms of ill health within the next few days.

As he left the hospital, every muscle in his body cried to run for all he was worth or find a horse and gallop until he and the beast were too exhausted to go further. Then his head began to pound at the very thought, and he knew that Sister Anne was right. He would be cautious, he decided grudgingly.

Still he wanted to be useful so he walked into the hut just outside the entrance to the hospital. There were few people awaiting treatment. A lay brother gave one such person something to treat what looked like a minor cut. Another man blushed as he pointed to his genitals and made a scratching gesture. Tomorrow, Thomas thought, his wife may be in for the same reason and the husband back as well with a cracked skull for sharing the ailment he most likely got from his whore.

No one needed the services of a priest so he left and walked toward the church. As he reached the split in the path that would take him toward the sacristy, he heard the gravel crunch behind him and he turned.

"How does your head feel, brother?" Brother Simeon's expression was grave and his hand gentle as he reached over and touched Thomas on the shoulder.

Thomas put his hand on the wound as if he had already forgotten about it. It was still sore. "Hardly notice it," he shrugged.

Simeon beamed with returned good humor. "Good! Then you'll be back with the nuns soon. Brother John will be most grateful to return full time to his little novices and his music. He does so miss them." He snorted with ill-disguised contempt.

"He may do so today. I am on my way there now."

"Then I shall walk with you," Simeon said and the two monks started back along the path to the sacristy. "Has your memory returned as well, or have you heard anything more about who might have attacked you?"

"No, my lord. Neither. I am beginning to think it was some malevolent spirit whose nocturnal wanderings I interrupted."

"Or you got too close to the hiding place of some villein escaped from his master." Simeon sighed. "Then you have heard nothing either about any progress in the hunt for Brother Rupert's killer?"

A loud laugh made both men spin around. Standing just a few paces behind them was Ralf. Fatigue edged the crowner's eyes in black, but, as he looked down the path at the two monks, his grin was almost boyish. "Neither of you was ever in the army, for cert. Had you been sentries, you'd be dead by now. Never even heard me come up behind you!"

Thomas watched Simeon's face turn scarlet with rage. "It seems I must remind you that this is a house of God, not a military camp, Crowner. Your worldly skills have no value here." Simeon almost spat the last words.

"And if Brother Rupert, or our brother here, had had my worldly skills as you call them, the former might be alive and the latter might be without that bump on his head. And how is your tender pate, my saintly friend?"

"Were I saintly, Crowner, I would feel it less. And if I had your thick skull, I might never have felt it at all," Thomas replied.

Ralf threw back his head and roared with laughter.

Simeon looked at Thomas in surprise.

"You missed your calling, monk," Ralf said. "You should have been a Templar. From what Annie told me, you got quite the crack on your skull, yet your tongue is quick and ready despite your injured wits, and you're walking around quite freely again. Had you been a warrior monk, methinks you'd be back on your horse and ready for battle. The Templars could use someone like you in the Holy Land."

The crowner brought his hand down on Thomas' shoulder so hard the monk saw flashes of light and swayed ever so slightly. For an instant, Thomas' mood darkened. Perhaps he would have been happier with the fighting monks. He was not suited to inconsequential investigations of account rolls, but then he hadn't been given much of a choice. Still, this assignment had not been without its adventures, he decided. His mood brightened.

"Enough childish waste of time, Crowner. Are you here because you finally have some news about Brother Rupert's murderer?" Simeon drew himself up to his full height and stuffed his fists into his sleeves.

"It's only right I tell your mistress first," Ralf said, and, with an impish grin, watched the colors of frustration and anger rise and fall in the receiver's face. "And I must confess I find your prioress a rare sort of woman. What think you of her?"

"A woman is a woman. Whatever her titular position here, she can never be more than what God has made her, a ward in need of man's firm direction."

The crowner winked at him, but Thomas decided silence was the wiser response.

"She has a man's stomach for all her delicate look and short stature," Ralf said. "I would trust her to lead me into battle, I think."

"Then you are the greater fool." Simeon's laugh lacked even the hint of humor.

"No, but perhaps you are. Have you heard nothing of what she found by herself yesterday?"

Simeon glanced quickly at Thomas, who shrugged.

"Ah, I see that neither of you has heard of your brave lady's efforts to protect you all at Tyndal. It seems she was disturbed by this recent attack on one of her charges." Ralf nodded at Thomas. "And decided to go off on her own to investigate."

"What feminine foolishness!" Simeon barked. "And what woman did she imperil by taking her along on this childish game? Since I have heard nothing of this, I know none of my monks went with her."

"She endangered only herself. Seems she went out to the clearing where our good brother was struck and wandered down by the stream he had heard in the distance."

"The woman needs a keeper!" Simeon's face turned red again.

"And there she found a cave."

"What cave?"

"A place cut out by the stream in flood, methinks. Someone had built a bed there, of all things, yet there was no evidence of any fire. And then a strange man appeared..."

Simeon gasped. "Surely one of Satan's imps." Then he leered. "Or else she has odd fantasies like women are wont to have. Did the man perchance have cloven hooves, hairy legs like a goat, and a proud member as well?" Simeon jerked his hips suggestively and winked.

"Nay, monk. He held no lance ready for a lusty joust, but he did hold a knife in his hand."

Simeon hesitated and stared at the crowner in brief silence. "A knife? My jest was unseemly. Did he injure our lady by either word or deed?"

"She had already turned her ankle, but the man harmed her not. He ran away as soon as he saw her."

"And did she describe him? Perhaps I have seen this man. He may be one of our villagers."

"She did not get a good look at him. I thought perhaps he was a holy man just come to the area and was using the cave for his hermitage. All she noted was that grime darkened the creases in his face, that his beard and hair were unkempt, that his clothes were torn and stained, and that he held the knife in his left hand."

"Not a bad observation for a frightened woman," Thomas muttered.

"Indeed," Simeon said with a frown. "We have heard of no hermits in our area. Nor do I recognize the man's description. It could fit many from the village."

"Aye. Her find did lead me to search the cave and the environs, however, and I have brought something to make our liege lady happy. You too, I think."

"A breakthrough in the foul murder of our brother?" Simeon asked, raising his eyebrows.

"Ah, I might as well tell you, good monk, since I have yet to know a monastery without holey walls when it comes to gossip. Here is the broken hilt of a dagger, stained with blood, I believe." He patted the leather pouch at his side. "One of my men found it buried under the rocks just outside the cave your prioress found. And also buried nearby, we found a bloody robe with a knife tear near where Brother Rupert's heart would have been."

⌀〰〰⌀

As soon as Ralf went off to speak with the prioress, Simeon left Thomas and hurried back to tell Theobald of the latest developments. Thomas continued on to the church.

Thomas had never pretended that his faith was other than a thing of habit, unconsidered and at no point in his life profound. Even now he went through the motions of priesthood as a necessary daily ritual and suspected that the majority of others did the same. However, he was not such a fool as to deny the truth of what he practiced. Wiser men than he had said that Hell fire waited for unbelievers, and who was he to question them? He was no scholar and felt no unique connection with God that he might argue he had been granted special enlightenment. He was happy to leave the clarifications on the details of faith to the likes of Saint Augustine and Thomas Aquinas.

Thomas' faith might be mundane. His love of music was not. He had never shown skill on any instrument and his voice was toneless, but when choirs lifted their voices heavenward in the praise of God, it was the only time Thomas felt his soul had gotten a glimpse of Heaven. Thus, when he entered the sacristy and heard singing, he decided to slip out to see who was practicing the chants with such sweet sound.

It was the novices of Tyndal.

He was surprised to see Brother John leading the boys so skillfully. Thomas stood near a pillar just outside the nave and watched the monk rehearse them in their chants. Their youthful voices filled the air with a song so beautiful it was almost too painful to hear. Indeed, the sound was as powerful as that of a full choir of monks, although the mix of just broken and unbroken voices added a purity, indeed a uniquely innocent quality to it. In spite of himself, he lifted his eyes heavenward. At least the attitude of prayer was sincere enough even if no words came with it.

Brother John waved his hand, and the chanting stopped. The monk then gestured and hummed with enthusiastic grace, demonstrating how he wanted them to sing a particular passage. The boys watched him, their expressions solemn and worried, their eyes unblinking. If Thomas hadn't had less comfortable meetings with this troubling monk earlier, he would have warmed easily to him now. The novices certainly had or they would not have cared so much about following his instruction.

This Brother John was a very different person from the one Thomas had first seen. That monk had frightened him with eyes as cold as frosted stones and mouth as stern as if he were sending a heretic to the stake. Perhaps that was what bothered him most about the monk, his icy aloofness. Then he had seen him with the young man in the church. That monk was not aloof.

He quickly scanned the faces of the choirboys. None were of the right height or shape to match the young man he'd seen in the chapel that night. These were younger boys, just on the edge of manhood. The one Brother John had embraced with such tenderness in the pale moonlight of the chapel had crossed the line between childhood and a man's world. When Brother

John smiled at these boys, however, the love Thomas saw in the monk's look came not from the loins but the heart.

Nor could Thomas ignore the gentleness with which the monk had treated him when he found Thomas lying in the clearing. Nor could he deny the attentiveness with which this man had helped him walk to the hospital. Brother John had found him a comparatively quiet bed there and kept him company until Sister Anne came. He was even companionable, touching Thomas' shoulder with tenderness and sympathy from time to time, asking meaningless and non-intrusive questions to distract him from his pain.

Thomas folded his hands into his sleeves, trying to think back to the events in the clearing before he was hit from behind. Once again he asked himself if it could have been Brother John who struck him. He was the most likely person, but Thomas was almost certain he had heard more than one voice speaking across the clearing before he was struck down. If there were two ahead of him, wouldn't they have been Brother John and the youth? He had seen no third person.

Then who might it have been if it wasn't the monk? Newcomer though he was to the area, he surely would have heard if the priory had been plagued of late with lawless men attacking those who came to the hospital. There were no prior tales of errant monks or wild hermits. Had there been a spate of troublesome strangers about, the crowner would have been a regular visitor to the priory, and the word was that Ralf had not ever come to the priory before the murder of Brother Rupert. Had the old man been the first victim of such a band?

Thomas shook his head. Unlikely. Despite Prioress Eleanor's snide comments, the old priest could not have been the first monk to wander beyond Tyndal's perimeters, but, with the exception of Prior Theobald and his large gold cross, monks rarely had anything worth stealing to tempt the lawless. He smiled. Thomas rather doubted that the trembling prior was one likely to seek unholy solace to ease the holy life.

Nor are men seeking coin or jewels prone to violating their victims, Thomas remembered with a wince.

No, Thomas was convinced that Brother Rupert was not the victim of lawless men; however, he might have been the victim of someone who wanted his death to look like the suicide of a monk overwhelmed with guilt over lust.

He shifted his weight against the pillar and watched the novice master demonstrating to one boy how a short passage should sound. The man had a pleasing voice, he thought.

"So why carry him into the nuns' cloister?" he muttered under his breath. Why not just leave the man where he had been killed? And how could the murderer fail to notice that the genitals were in the wrong hand but still have the composure to change the dead monk's clothes? And what was the intent of the murderer? There were just too many questions.

Thomas scratched the bristling hair in his tonsure. It would need shaving again soon. "The man must have known that his attempts to disguise the murder as a suicide were rudimentary at best. How stupid did he think we all are here?" He looked up nervously, hoping his words had not been overheard, then fell back to silent thought.

He...well, it must have been a man surely. A woman could never castrate a man, even after death. Surely, women were too delicate. The young ones, anyway. Thomas gave a mirthless snort. The lasses he had known in his old life might have been too delicate. He wasn't so sure about these nuns.

Sister Anne, for one, was as tall as many men. She had shown no timidity about examining the dead monk, nor had she shown any hesitancy about looking at his horrible wounds. No man, himself included, could have looked upon that brutal mutilation with the calm detachment she had shown. A strange woman indeed, Thomas thought, as strange in her way as Brother John was in his. Had she been plump with age and gray-haired like several of the female servants he had known in his father's house, he would have had no difficulty imagining her indifference over a man's body, but Sister Anne was neither beyond the child-bearing age nor had she gray hair. Her reaction was not womanly, not natural. Could she have killed the monk?

Nay, he thought with a smile. Despite her odd manner, he liked Sister Anne. He felt no evil or anger in her, only compassion and a sorrow with which he felt a certain kinship.

Then there was Prioress Eleanor. He could probably eliminate her as a suspect because she was as new to Tyndal as he was. Besides, she was far too little to stab a man in the heart, unless she was standing on a stool to do it. The image of the small religious leaping upon a bench and flailing away with a knife too big for her two tiny hands even to grasp made him grin in spite of himself.

No, he couldn't see the prioress killing a man, whatever his frailty or age. She might be capable of poisoning, he thought grimly, but she didn't have the heft to wield a man's weapon. Nor did he think she would castrate a man. Despite her religious profession, there was an earthly side to the prioress. He suspected she might not only enjoy the company of a man but might also prefer his manhood to be quite functional. In fact, he wondered how well she kept her vow of chastity. Thomas laughed quietly. If she was looking to lose her virginity at Tyndal, she was in the wrong place. The monks he had met here were too old, too disinclined, or too frightened by women to satisfy any such lusty inclinations. Brother Simeon might be the exception, but that one was far too ambitious to damage his chances for advancement by having an affair with the prioress of a minor house like this.

As a female suspect, Thomas rather fancied Sister Ruth. He disliked the gruff woman. She was exactly the type he preferred to find locked safely away behind the stone walls of a convent, but he doubted even she would have killed Brother Rupert. Perhaps the aged monk had been a threat to the chastity of young nuns when he too had been a youth, but the good priest was far too old to be of interest or danger to any woman at the time of his murder.

Could Sister Christina have done it? No, that one was bound for sainthood if he was any judge.

꿍

Brother John was finished running each of the novices, separately and in groups, through the segments of the chant that needed polishing. They were ready to start again. Thomas looked at the novices and back at the monk, then shook his head. The poignant vision of Brother John with the young man in the chapel would not leave him. If I were a wagering man, Thomas thought, I'd say this monk was a bit too fond of boys.

When the chant began, the beauty of the voices excelled anything Thomas had ever heard before and drove the more earthy thoughts from his head. With a soft cry of mixed pain and joy, he slipped slowly down on his knees to the chapel floor as tears flowed inexplicably down his cheeks. If he had just heard the voice of God, he could not have felt more awe.

And had tears not blinded Thomas, he might have looked up to see Brother John turn and gaze at him with a slight smile and widening green eyes.

Chapter Twenty

Gytha had just finished tossing out the old rush mats and was sweeping the floor in preparation for laying fresh ones when there was a knock at the door of the private chambers. She stopped in mid-sweep, rested against the broom, and looked over at her mistress.

"Enter!" the prioress called out from her chair, her foot still propped and wrapped.

"My lord Prior begs an audience, my lady." Sister Ruth entered, and, as she glanced down at her prioress, her face curdled into puckers of disapproval.

Eleanor looked up in surprise. The purpose of the prior's visit momentarily escaped her. She knew she had planned to spend this day in comparative quiet. The sprain was a bad one, and Sister Anne had ordered her to avoid the long, narrow steps into the cloister until the ankle was stronger. Gytha had even spent the night in her mistress's chambers, rather than returning to the village as she usually did, in case Eleanor needed assistance.

That quiet day had included some plans the sub-infirmarian would have forbidden, had the prioress mentioned them. Eleanor hoped to talk to Sister Matilda about her mushroom hunting forays during her kitchen days, and she thought she might also walk to the chapel for daily prayers with the assistance of Gytha. Other than that, however, she had decided to listen to Sister Anne. If nothing else, obeying the sub-infirmarian in part would allow her an hour to indulge in reading from the copy of Wace's *Geste de Bretons* which her aunt had loaned her from Amesbury. That book might have been the cause of Sister Ruth's scowl this time. Or not. Eleanor shrugged. The nun never seemed to view anything Eleanor did with any approval.

"Of course," she said, closing the book carefully so it lay flat on the lectern shelf in front of her. "Why is he here?"

"He didn't say and I didn't ask, my lady." Sister Ruth sniffed.

Gytha rested the broom against the wall and sprinted over to the corridor door, opening it just enough to stick her head out. Sister Ruth closed her eyes in utter disgust.

"He has that big monk with him," Gytha said, puffing out her cheeks and patting her stomach. "And Brother Andrew, the tiny one, is behind, lugging a box and rolls of something under his arms. The rolls are dropping and rolling around in the corridor, and he's running back and forth after them. The big monk is just standing there and not doing anything. Does that help?"

"Do not make fun of others, child. It isn't kind."

"Yes, my lady."

"At least I now remember why they are here. Please let them into the parlor before poor Brother Andrew exhausts himself. Some wine for our guests, perhaps slightly more for our Brother Andrew after his heavy work, and then I shall attend them." Eleanor winked at the girl, who smiled broadly.

"Do you need me to stay, my lady?" Sister Ruth asked in a tone that suggested she most heartily wished to be anywhere else.

"I do. The good prior is going to tell me what lands are owned by Tyndal and what our income is from each. Since you have resided in the priory for more years than any other sister, you are the most knowledgeable person here and should be present when we discuss our financial health. Someone of competence must be as fully informed as I am should I suddenly be called away. As you are the one most qualified, I am appointing you sub-prioress and you shall act as such henceforth. Another sister will be selected to be porteress."

Sister Ruth's expression first suggested that she had just taken a bite of rotten meat, then that she was rather surprised she had.

"Please ask the good prior to wait while I ready myself." She nodded dismissal to the new sub-prioress.

As Ruth stomped out of the chambers and Gytha returned, Eleanor gestured for the girl to come to her side. The young girl quickly turned and stuck her tongue out at the older nun's retreating back.

Eleanor decided to pretend she hadn't seen the gesture. "I had forgotten I had requested an examination of Tyndal's account rolls today," she said, "but I want to appear as if I had expected them and should enter with full dignity." Eleanor noted the concerned frown on the girl's face. "Help me up, child. I won't fall. Sometimes we must do things which hurt to achieve a higher purpose."

Indeed it did hurt to walk the short distance from her reading lectern to the public room, but once Eleanor had settled into her raised chair, the wrinkles of pain smoothed away and she gestured for the monks to approach.

"My lady!" The men spoke in unison and bowed. Andrew dropped a few scrolls, his bad leg clearly paining him as he stooped to pick them up. He was ignored by Brother Simeon, who concentrated on easing Prior Theobald into the chair indicated by Eleanor. She knew it was vindictive of her, but she offered the large monk not a chair but a seat on the bench at the table next to Andrew. It was her way of putting Simeon in his place after he had so rudely disregarded her during their first meeting.

He looked surprised and a bit confused.

She felt sinfully pleased.

Gytha served cool wine in glazed pottery cups from a simple pewter pitcher, and Eleanor noted the slightly fuller one given to Brother Andrew, who glanced up at the girl, then at the prioress, with amused pleasure. As the men drank and shifted, she decided she would not bother to pretend, beyond the demands of courtesy, that the prior knew anything about the financial situation of Tyndal.

In fact, she probably knew more than he. Prioress Joan of Amesbury had told her what lands were owned by Tyndal and what other assets the priory had before she left to take this new office. Pretending greater ignorance was a ploy intended to find out what she would be told and how. In truth, all she needed to establish was whether the stewardship had been proper, despite the drop in revenues, and whether all resources had been used as efficiently as possible. Courtesy did demand, however, that she address Theobald first.

"Prior Theobald. I appreciate your attendance, and, as I informed you, I would like a summary of our holdings and the income thereof."

Theobald coughed and grasped his cross, an habitual gesture which Eleanor was beginning to learn meant he felt inadequate to whatever task he was called upon to do.

"I have brought our receiver, Brother Simeon, to provide the information you requested, my lady. His eyes are better than mine, you see, and he is better suited to read the documents to you and interpret their meaning."

Eleanor glanced up at the large monk. His expression was quite smug.

"Indeed, Prior, your thoughtful preparation is most impressive, and I shall accept the work Brother Simeon has done in preparation for my questions. Perhaps you did not know, however, that I am capable of both reading text and comprehending numbers."

"The wording of the charters is in Latin, my lady." Simeon's expression had changed but minimally.

"I also read Latin, brother, but I will be pleased to accept your detailed review since Prior Theobald has assigned that work to you. In the future, Prior, I will be happy to accept whomever you assign to provide the information I request." Eleanor nodded in Theobald's direction. "I sympathize with the burden it must put on your eyes which have been strained in the many years of service you have given to Our Lord."

Theobald sighed and lowered his head in a sign of gratitude at her concern and his escape from responsibility. "Indeed, my lady, my eyes have aged in His service."

"Brother Simeon, please do begin."

Brother Simeon did not make the process either simple or short. In fact, Eleanor got the distinct impression he wished to make his presentation so convoluted that she, lesser vessel that she was presumed to be, would either feel obliged to accept his information as fact or give in out of frustration and irritated fatigue.

Eleanor was no lesser vessel. Tyndal was her responsibility and, although she was willing to accept Simeon's past reputation in running the estates in view of the official reviews done on his account rolls, he had to prove his competence now and explain, to her satisfaction, the recent reduction in income. She was also determined to teach him that what might have worked with the good prior and the former prioress was not going to work with her. Rhetoric was lovely in its place, but its place was not in the reporting of figures and balances. Those required clarity. He would learn that she demanded no less. Annoyed, Eleanor stretched out her hand.

"Let me see the charter, brother. I cannot believe that we own the land on which the forest grows but received nothing from the timber removed from it. To my knowledge, we have not given King Henry a gift of trees for any ship. Have we?"

The charter he handed her had sweat stains on it.

She pointed to one line. "See here. It says we have full own-ership of the…"

"My lady, I did not mean we received no income from the sale of timber. I only meant that we granted the poor of the village the right once a year to gather fallen branches free of any charge."

Eleanor looked steadily at the monk. His face was glistening and red from the effort of answering her pointed questions.

"Then say so, brother. I do not count good stewardship by the number of words you use to describe it. I like precision, accuracy and supporting documents."

She glanced down at one of those documents, which showed the accounting of rental income from one of the priory grants, and sighed. She would have to get used to his crabbed numbers and awkward letters. Wherever the good monk learned to write, he had not been taught either grace or legibility in the skills.

"Very well, brother. I will keep the charters with me to study further."

Brother Andrew sighed softly and smiled, then quickly raised his hand to hide his mouth.

"But I am concerned with the share of produce sales we are receiving. I do not believe they are high enough to guarantee the income we will need to buy provisions for the coming winter. Our own garden has failed to yield what it should for our needs and we will be forced to buy additional food."

"Indeed, my lady, crops have not been what we hoped this year from the priory farms either." Brother Simeon took a large drink from his goblet. His eyes were glazed and he looked fatigued.

"In truth? I had heard otherwise about our farms in the area."

"I cannot speak to what you may have heard, my lady. I can only say that I have not seen any farm producing what we had either hoped or expected."

"Then we must either eat less this winter or conserve in other ways. Perhaps on wine purchases this fall. We do make our own ale, I believe." Eleanor smiled as she watched the fleshy monk pale. Was it the reduction in unpalatable food he abhorred or the prospect of a winter without a fine Gascony wine to warm him? Prior Theobald, she noted, had drifted off to sleep some time ago and, from the look of his thin body, would have been disinterested in the lessening of either. Sister Ruth had thoughtfully, and with gentleness, inserted a pillow between his head and the chair.

"Or raise rents, my lady! Indeed, we could raise rents!"

"Brother Simeon, if the crops have been so poor, then the farmers will also suffer from deprivations. I do not think raising their rents is compassionate."

"Their souls, my lady. They will think of their immortal souls and gladly give more money to our house of God."

"Our souls should face a little less comfort more easily than those used to the world, good brother. In fact, I believe it would be better for us to consume less food and wine than to deprive those we have promised God to care for."

"But our strength. We must keep up our strength to better serve Him…"

"Brother, I will make no decision until I have toured our lands and spoken to those who rent as well as to those who manage and work the grants. Perhaps something has not yet been brought to your attention that will save us all from such severity."

"My lady, Prioress Felicia left all such things to…"

"I am not the good prioress and, as you know, I am not from Tyndal. The people who serve us and those who gain from us are as unknown to me as I am to them. It is unwise for any of us to remain so ill-acquainted."

"You will need a horse, my lady. It will take me a little time to find a suitable one."

"I need a donkey, brother. I am a small woman and a nun. A horse is both too big and too grand. Our Lord rode a donkey into Jerusalem. I will follow His example."

"But to find such a creature…"

Gytha put down the wine ewer. "I know where you can find a good beast, my lady."

Eleanor smiled. "I thought you might, my child."

And as Brother Simeon looked down, Eleanor noted that his face had turned the shade of one of his beloved red wines.

Chapter Twenty-One

"What an odd group we make," Thomas muttered as he glanced at the small cluster of dark-robed religious. They were all assembled outside the thick wooden door of the thatch-roofed house belonging to one Tostig, brother of Gytha.

When Brother Andrew first told Thomas that Prioress Eleanor Wynethorpe of Tyndal Priory had decided to buy herself a braying, gray-bristled donkey for riding forth into the world, he had roared with laughter. Then he remembered the story of one fine bishop, and Thomas changed his mind.

The bishop in question, dressed in richly dyed vestments of soft-woven cloth and seated on a horse of rare breeding, had ridden into a mob of querulous farmers. With the arrogance common to both the aloof and the ignorant, he had assumed that such crude creatures would be suitably awed by his eminence and cease their silly arguments over his increased rents. Instead, they had pelted him with offal, vegetation rotten beyond recognition, and unidentifiable animal parts. Later, his chief clerk, dressed in duller clothes, had walked with impunity into the village and negotiated a compromise that was acceptable to both the lowly farmers and the clerk's high-minded master.

Even now the story made Thomas smile, and he nodded with respect toward his wisely humble prioress just as the door to the cottage swung open on its leather hinges and Gytha gestured for the assembly to enter. As he approached the door, Thomas sniffed nervously. There was a strong scent of farm animals in the air, but the smell was the fresh, earthy one of healthy beasts. He would not have to wade through aged cow manure. No matter how long he lived on this forsaken coast, Thomas knew he would never quite become a man of the soil.

⚬⚬⚬

The space inside Tostig's house was small, but the floor was planked and strewn with sweet-smelling straw and herbs. There was no window to let the daylight in, but a centrally located stone hearth both warmed the damp air and provided enough light to see and move about with ease.

The master of the place stood in front of a dark wooden table near the hearth, his arms folded. Tostig was a straight-backed, muscular man in his early twenties, his hair long, thick, and golden like his sister's, but there was none of her gentleness showing in his blue eyes. After scanning the faces of the priory visitors with contempt just barely concealed, he looked down at Prioress Eleanor and bowed with an easy grace.

"I am honored, my lady. Your visit brings a blessing to my home. I would offer some refreshment, but I am a simple man and do not have things that you and your attendant monks are accustomed to. There is only a rough ale, not wine, and coarse bread to give you and your companions. The cheese, however, is a goodly one."

Eleanor noted that his smile at her might have been somewhat genuine, but his words to the party as a whole were spoken in a tone edged with brittle sarcasm. Then Gytha bent over and whispered in her ear. Eleanor burst out laughing.

"Your sister tells me that I should ignore your ale but take your bread, which she has baked herself, and your cheese, which she says is famous in the town."

"My sister is rightly proud of her baking, but the bread is still unsuited to the tender mouths of noble folk," Tostig said as he shot Gytha a glance gentled with love and humor.

Brother Simeon shifted from foot to foot, his nose wrinkling in exaggerated disapproval at the smells of the cottage. "Perhaps we needn't bother with refreshment, my lady. We came only to look at donkeys."

Brother John's green eyes sparkled with ill-concealed laughter as he looked at the receiver. "Indeed we have, brother, but I have heard of Tostig's cheese from our annual fair, as you must have as well." He turned to Eleanor. "It sells out on market days and is gaining fame abroad, my lady, or so I have heard from travelers who have stayed with us."

Eleanor looked at Thomas, who was watching the interchange between novice master and receiver with interest, and then she turned to Tostig with a mischievous smile. "Brother Thomas and I are new to this part of England," she said. "We would be delighted to accept your offer of ale, bread and cheese. Perhaps our good Brother Simeon has vowed to fast today, but I believe the rest of us would be grateful for your hospitality."

Gytha happily ran off to serve the guests. As Tostig offered Eleanor and the monks seats on the bench behind him, he lowered his head so she could not see his reaction to her acceptance of a hospitality he thought would be rejected. For all his obvious dislike of the priory visitors, however, Eleanor felt a modicum of tolerance, even warmth, exhibited to her.

Indeed, the fare served would be considered too plain for a manor house, Eleanor thought, as she ate what Gytha had put before her. Nonetheless, the flavors of the ale, cheese, and bread when eaten together were wonderful, especially after the flavorless meals she had suffered since her arrival from Amesbury. As to ale, she had rarely drunk it. Her family and those she had been raised with at Amesbury much preferred wine to this very English beverage. After the initial shock of its bitter taste, however, Eleanor found she rather liked it. It was lighter than wine, yet warmed the stomach well, and it suited the nutty bread and the robust, marbled cheese served with it.

She looked up to see Gytha and Brother John studying her with smiles twitching at the corners of their mouths. Turning to Gytha first, she pulled her eyebrows together in a slight frown.

"You were wrong, my child."

"About what, my lady?" The girl looked worried.

"I must either stop teasing you, Gytha, or you must learn when I am." She put her hand on the girl's arm. "Everything is all right. I only meant that you were wrong about the ale. It is delicious. Indeed, whoever brewed this is superior in the craft."

Brother John pounded the table lightly in evident delight. "My lady, not only is Master Tostig's cheese famous, so is his ale. The local ale-wives praise his even above their own."

"It is made in competition with the priory's ale," Brother Simeon said, his deep voice lowered to a growl. He had tasted nothing offered.

"Indeed? Do we lose income as a consequence of this?" Eleanor asked, pointing to the sweating crock in front of her and glancing at Tostig's expressionless face.

"We make far more but sell less as a result of this, this..." Simeon waved his hand dismissively in the direction of the aforementioned jug.

"Then perhaps we should cease trying to compete in such a profitless area," Eleanor said.

Tostig's eyes widened slightly.

"You have just seen our accounts. We cannot lose more revenue just because this..." Simeon waved his hand in the direction of Tostig as if Gytha's brother were no more than a piece of pottery.

Eleanor raised her hand to silence the receiver before he finished his sentence and before Gytha's brother could react to the suggested insult. "Master Tostig, I have an idea which may be of benefit to both you and the priory. Perhaps you could come to Tyndal to discuss the possibilities of a partnership in this ale venture?"

Tostig glanced at his sister, who nodded imperceptibly.

"I would be honored, my lady."

Brother Simeon rose to his feet, his eyes narrowed in rage.

"And what did you have in mind? Surely, as your receiver, I have a right to know what sort of scheme..."

Thomas, who was sitting next to Simeon, reached over and tugged at the monk's sleeve. "Brother," he whispered. "Calm yourself. They are speaking of ale. Mere ale."

Simeon looked down at Thomas. The receiver's eyes looked dead, so glazed were they with the white heat of his anger. Then his body shuddered almost imperceptibly as he regained control. He smiled, but his eyes remained narrowed.

"Of course. My apologies, my lady, and I beg forgiveness. I have fallen prey to the sin of anger today. Perhaps Satan tempted me in my weakness from fasting. I succumbed and shall seek penance."

Thomas thumped the monk on the back.

Eleanor said nothing.

"Donkeys, my lady? You came to see my donkeys." Tostig broke the silence and gestured toward the door to his cottage.

Both a prudent and a proud man, Eleanor thought as she rose and walked to the door. She glanced back at him. His face showed no emotion as he waited for her to pass first through the low door. Then she smiled and winked at him.

Tostig's eyes grew round, his head moving a fraction backward in surprise. Then he too smiled. And winked back.

You are a quick judge of character, my fine Saxon, Eleanor thought. I will remember that.

As she stepped outside to the slightly muddy and gouged earthen path between the two rows of village huts and hovels, Eleanor stopped. She trembled as if a cold wind had struck her, and she looked quickly to one side.

A man was staring at her. His black beard and brackish colored clothing were unkempt, ragged.

Eleanor blinked. He was the man she had seen in the forest.

He turned and sped through the space between two huts.

"That man!" she cried to Tostig, who was just behind her. "Who is he?"

Tostig looked around him very slowly, his expression once again blank. "What man, my lady? I see no one."

"Did anyone see that man?" Eleanor asked the monks as they emerged from the doorway.

"No, my lady," they said in near unison, standing aside to let Gytha come out behind them.

Perhaps they had not, but Eleanor saw a fleeting frown on Tostig's face as he gazed in the direction the strange man had disappeared.

Chapter Twenty-Two

"My foot is fine, sister."

Eleanor's ankle still hurt, but she was quickly becoming intolerant of the inactivity forced on her by the injury. She had accepted the help of Gytha on the walk to the village to buy her donkey, but now that she was back in her chambers, she was both exhausted from the pain and frustrated by restlessness.

Sister Anne was gently rewinding the ankle. "Need I remind you, my lady, that lying is a sin. Your entire foot is now swollen twice its size from the walk."

Eleanor sighed. Most assuredly, Prioress Felicia would have reprimanded Anne for such bluntness. Rank did demand due courtesy. On the other hand, respect must be earned else it would be as hollow and short-lived as prayers said without faith. Something her aunt had taught. Nay, she preferred the honesty, Eleanor decided. Anne did not present a false face to her and that was refreshing. Besides, she was growing quite fond of this nun whose bluntness never held malice in it. "Had you been born a man, I would have wanted you to be my confessor," she said. "Yet I would have little to confess, for you would have already seen all my faults."

Anne patted the finished wrapping and stood. "Had I been a man, I would have ordered you to stay in your chambers and not allowed you to go shopping for a donkey. A donkey, of all things!" The gruffness of her rebuke was spoiled by her laugh.

"I like Adam. He is a sweet donkey. I hope he is happy in his new home."

Anne rose with a slight creak in her knees and walked over to the window. Eleanor noticed that the nun stretched her shoulders as if they were stiff. Over Anne's head she could see mounds of great clouds rushing across the sky pushed by a moist wind. A rain, chill with the hints of coming autumn, would arrive soon, she thought.

"Most likely he is eating," Anne said, turning back to face her prioress. "Brother Thomas took him to the stable as soon as we got back. He seems quite competent with four-legged creatures."

"And how is he with his two-legged charges?"

"He shows great compassion with the suffering in the hospital. Brother Andrew also commented on that the other day."

"Well and good. I was concerned about choosing someone no one knew anything about to replace Brother Rupert. It was Brother Simeon's suggestion, and it seems to have been a good one. By the way, our good receiver was not pleased with my decision to consider a partnership with Tostig on the ale business. Did I err?"

"No, I do not think so. Tostig is a good man. Brother Simeon would not be happy with the concept, however. He has never thought the villagers any better than animals, and finds some animals superior to the villagers. The idea of joining with Tostig on making ale quite interests me, however. May I ask what in specific you had in mind?"

"I wanted him to join with us in the making of it instead of competing against us. If we can produce more but he makes it better, I thought he might first teach us how he makes it and then monitor our process to guarantee the product was consistently good. For this I would suggest giving him a high percentage of the profit. We would gain by increased sales, and he would lose nothing, probably even gain from our mutual success."

"Brother Simeon would never be pleased with a man from the village telling Normans, albeit monks, what to do. Our receiver aside, however, I do not think most of the monks and certainly none of the local lay brothers would have any problem with the arrangement. Tostig is well respected here."

"Then Brother Simeon needs to be reminded that Saxons are not beneath us. Fontevraud has taken in monks and nuns of all ranks and origins, including prostitutes, as Jesus did Mary Magdalene. And after all these years of doing as he pleased, the good brother also seems to have forgotten that it is the prioress who makes the final decisions about the running of the priory. If he does not approve, he should ask to leave the Order and become, perhaps, a Cistercian."

"If I may say so, my lady, the practices of which you speak have been true at the mother house, but, except for the primacy of the prioress, we have seen little of the rest of it in England."

"Are you not a physician's daughter?"

"And I have never been accepted by Brother Simeon, nor, indeed, have I been fully accepted by some of the sisters here."

"Until they are ill, I would think."

Anne smiled.

"We shall see what Tostig thinks of my idea. Perhaps he will object himself to being under the authority of a woman while he works with the monks. Do you know if he has a woman sharing his life?"

"I do not believe he is married, my lady."

"Sister, not all relationships are as the lords of the Church would prefer. Does he have any woman to comfort him and tend to his needs?"

"Not to my knowledge."

"Then he is unaccustomed to being ruled by one of us. He may not know what he is getting himself into with me."

There was a fond warmth in Anne's smile as she replied, "I will not argue with you on that, my lady."

"Now tell me about our crowner. You know him well. He has made no progress in finding either the murderer or the one who attacked Brother Thomas, yet I feel he is a capable man. He quickly found the bloody garment and the knife hilt."

The nun blinked and turned her face away from Eleanor.

"Speak freely, sister. I need honesty. But if the subject brings you grief..."

"Ralf is both kind and competent, my lady, but he grew up wild. He was a frail child at birth, the last of those his parents bore, and his older brothers tormented him. He found his comfort more with the villagers than with his kin. He has great contempt for the courtly life his elder brother, the sheriff, loves; and, unlike his brother, Ralf is respected here as a diligent and just man."

"And he has contempt, I think, for the Church as well."

"There is no question of his faith..."

"Nor was I suggesting otherwise. There may be as many ways of showing faith as there are honest believers. The contempt I heard was reserved for those men and women who have taken vows."

"He respects you, my lady."

Eleanor sat back and, in silence, studied the nun in front of her. Anne's head was still bowed and her face turned away. "Sister, you are protecting the man from something. Should I know the reason?"

When Anne looked up, Eleanor saw tiny rivulets of tears flowing down her cheeks. "I grieve for Ralf, my lady, but my feelings for him are chaste. As a sister, I love him. As a sister, I want to protect him for his spirit is in much pain. There is nothing more."

"You still fear answering my question about his contempt for those dedicated to a religious life?"

"If I may be so bold, my lady, your views and ways are very different from those of Prioress Felicia. The change will take some getting used to. Plain speech, while not punished in the past, was not often welcome."

"As I told Gytha, sister, I respect honesty without malice. If I do not like what I hear, I try to reflect and pray on it, not condemn out of hand. Now, please, answer me."

"Ralf's second eldest brother is high in the Church, my lady. He is known more for his acceptance of bribes in matters of canon law brought before him than justice. This and his brother's childhood cruelty to him have colored his view of men in the Church."

Eleanor sighed. "I hope we may one day teach your Ralf that we are not all corrupt."

"I believe you have begun, my lady," Anne said. She wiped her cheeks dry.

"I would return to Adam, the donkey." For I have asked enough of you for one day, Eleanor thought. "Do you think he's lonely?"

Anne tilted her head in puzzlement.

"Might we consider whether to get a fellow for him?"

"Why?" Anne frowned.

"In case I need someone to ride in attendance when I go abroad." Eleanor smiled with mischievous delight.

"Brother Simeon is much too large to ride on a donkey, my lady. And if he were not the one to attend you, then perhaps Brother John or Brother Andrew, but they are..."

"I was thinking of you."

Anne's eyes widened in shock. "Me? Why, surely if you need a nun to accompany you, Sister Ruth or..."

"Who but you would remind me of my failings when I needed it? Who but you would be comfortable outside the priory and would not mind being in the world when it was necessary?"

"You flatter me, my lady. I am grateful for your confidence and accept..."

"...out of duty, but will you come with some gladness of spirit as well?"

"With pleasure, but only if I can find and train a novice talented enough to learn about herbs and potions to replace me in my treatments at the hospital. Prioress Felicia would not allow me to do so. She was not completely convinced my methods were sanctioned by God, although Brother Rupert had so assured her many times."

"You shall have a novice, more than one if you find others to your liking. Question them and select the most promising. You will have time to do the training. I am not planning any visits except to the local farms and tenants. Brother Simeon could ride his horse for those."

"Then I agree with both gratitude and gladness, my lady."

"Good. That gladness is a first between us then! Now I need Gytha to help me down the stairs. Weak ankle or not, I must see Sister Matilda about her former trips to the forest as I promised our good crowner."

Anne looked at her with a frown, but, knowing she would lose this battle, gave in. "Just one question before I get Gytha, if I may?"

Eleanor nodded.

"Why did you name the donkey *Adam*?"

"After the first man."

Anne bent and looked directly into Eleanor's eyes. "And?"

Eleanor laughed. "My father. As my newly chosen beast was roped, he dug his hooves into the earth and brayed in loud protest. I was reminded that those who are enemies of my lord father claim he can be bloody-minded in both action and speech. Those who love him concede that he is often strong-willed but with the speech and action of an honest man."

"Just like his daughter, I'd say," Anne replied with a grin and a glance at Eleanor's wrapped foot.

Chapter Twenty-Three

Brother Simeon paced in tight circles around the room, hands behind his back, face scarlet from too much anger and too much wine. Thomas watched in silence.

"How could she have embarrassed me like that? After all my years of service to Tyndal. After all I've done to keep the priory solvent. After the praise I have received from our Abbess for my fine annual accounts! And to do such a foul thing in front of a Saxon churl and his crude runt of a sister. For cert, the woman shows no judgement. She allows far too much familiarity from these low orders! A woman should never be put in charge of things she knows nothing about. Surely our founder never intended such a thing to happen."

"Indeed, brother, I understood that he meant only for us to experience humility by putting a woman above us. Surely he never meant for her to actually lead us." In fact, Thomas cared little for why Fontevraud's founder did anything, but agreement with Simeon seemed the wisest course in his ongoing effort to gain the receiver's confidence.

"Well said, brother. Something a man could easily see."

Thomas held up the pitcher of wine and raised his eyebrows in a question.

Simeon glanced at his empty goblet and nodded. "Of course," he said, taking several long swallows from the replenished supply, "Robert d'Arbrissel never was made a saint. Rome must have known he had gone too far against nature with his radical ideas." He staggered slightly and slid with a heavy awkwardness onto the bench across the table from Thomas.

Thomas looked at Simeon, who was staring back at him with an intense but somewhat unfocused gaze, and felt pity. Here was a competent man, a man who was comfortable with responsibility but who was now being shoved aside into a secondary role after running Tyndal for years. Even though Thomas doubted the monk would lose his position as receiver or even sub-prior if the prioress found his account rolls acceptable, the prioress quite clearly intended to take back full charge of the priory. Simeon might have accepted such a change from a new prior, but never from someone he saw as an inferior. It must all seem so unnatural to a man of Simeon's cast of mind.

"Indeed." Thomas hesitated. "Forgive me for my bluntness, brother, but I cannot help but wonder that a man of your ability and stature ever entered the Fontevraud Order. Why not the Benedictines or the Cistercians?" Thomas glanced at his own, nearly full goblet and took a small sip.

The corners of Simeon's eyes grew moist. "I was the youngest of too many boys. My father was of good birth but had little land and could not afford a knight's training for all of us." He gulped some wine. "He held the Benedictines in contempt. Too corrupt, he said, and two of my brothers were already Cistercians. He needed to put me somewhere and Fontevraud is small but powerful." He blinked, then wiped a hand across his mouth. "Told me I could at least be in the company of queens since I wasn't suited for that of kings." Two large tears slid from the inside corners of his eyes and dropped from his jaw onto the table.

Thomas winced at the cruel implication of the remark but nodded sympathetically. He also knew better than to ask Simeon if the monk had felt even the slightest hint of a religious calling.

"But he never would have put me here if he had thought a woman would so humiliate his son." Simeon sat up in brief defiance. The goblet wavered near his mouth, and a tiny rivulet of red wine slipped down his chin, dribbling onto his robe. "He died almost two years ago," he said in a whisper.

"And you must grieve for his loss," Thomas said, lowering his voice into concerned tones. "Surely your father must have loved you to have given you to such a powerful order." He deliberately emphasized *powerful*.

Simeon swayed, took another long gulp of wine, then reached over and put his hand over Thomas', caressing it in silence. "He hated me, you know. I knew it. He called me fat, soft like a woman. Then one day he caught me with another boy." Simeon ran his fingertips down Thomas's arm. "We were doing nothing more than other boys often do when manhood arrives, but he mocked me and took my clothes, saying I could walk home naked so the world would see what a slut I was."

"Surely he must have relented. You were his son."

"You are a sweet boy to say so," he said, his lips and chin trembling. "No, he beat me when I got home. Called my brothers in to watch while he tied me to a bench and whipped my bare buttocks until the blood ran down my legs. Just like a woman's courses, I remember him saying." Then Simeon closed his eyes, his head dropped, and he slid across the table. The receiver and sub-prior of Tyndal had just passed out.

Thomas sat looking at the monk for a long time. He glanced down at his hand, which the receiver held like an overgrown child would his parent's or a lover would his beloved's, then gazed at the gold cup that Simeon still clutched. Perhaps this man was guilty of diverting some priory income to pay for these visible symbols of his competence in managing Tyndal. Surely no man of logic and reason would blame him for that. An ill-judged act it most assuredly was but no greater sin than men of higher authority in the Church had committed. If gold cups were the reason for the vague accusations of impropriety, luxuries that would enhance the standing of the priory amongst honored guests as much as they signified the competence of the receiver, Simeon would have little to fear. A jealous, petty monk was probably the source of the letter. As soon as he identified him, Thomas would be through with this assignment.

He felt a stab of pity as he looked at the receiver. How humiliated this proud man would be if he knew anyone had seen him in this drunken state, a small pool of drool from his open mouth puddling near his cheek. Thomas, however, would not mock him for it. He had grieved for the story he had just heard. As distant as his own father had been, he had been far kinder to his by-blow than Simeon's was to the issue of a lawful wife. No wonder the receiver held on to his well-earned authority over the priory with such ferocity. No wonder he hated the woman who threatened to take it from him, despite her right in the doing. And, Thomas thought, looking down at the drunkenly snoring monk, no wonder he was taking solace in fine wines.

Very gently he removed the monk's large hand from his and slipped out of the room.

Chapter Twenty-Four

"What if you fall, my lady?" Gytha said, "and no one came by. The stones of the cloister are uneven. If you are further injured, I would have failed you."

Anne had just left for the hospital with firm instructions to her prioress to stay off the foot for the remainder of the day, instructions which both she and Eleanor knew would be ignored as soon as the sub-infirmarian was out of sight. As Eleanor stood with her weight on her sound foot and looked down the steep stairs from her chambers to the cloister, however, she had to concede that both Gytha and Anne were right.

"Very well, then. Help me down the stairs, but bring that sturdy branch I brought back from the forest. It will give me support on level ground, and I will let you watch me for a bit so you can see for yourself that I am able to walk safely on my own."

So the young girl, who was slightly taller already than her mistress, agreed and the two walked with cautious, slow steps down the stairs. At the bottom, Eleanor braced herself against the wall and rested. Gytha put her hands on her hips, watching with an worried expression.

"Tostig bred a fine beast, my child. Your brother is a man of many talents," Eleanor said, trying to switch the subject away from herself.

Gytha glowed with pleasure.

"You are proud of him."

"He is a good man, my lady. When our parents…well, he has been father and mother both to me."

"Not married?"

"Not yet. He wants to regain some land and wealth first."

"Regain?"

Gytha blushed. "I'm sorry. I should have…"

"Honesty, child. You promised me honesty." Eleanor smiled.

"Our family were thegns to Harold before…"

"And lost your lands to those who followed William, but it has been a long time since then, Gytha. Your family has surely had opportunity to prove your worth and advance your interests with men who are now your neighbors, not your enemies?"

Gytha was silent, her head bowed and her face turned away from the prioress.

"What is it? What are you trying to say?"

"You will not be angry, my lady?"

"If honesty angers, it is not true anger but rather confusion over what is truth. I would not punish you for my failure to understand something when no spite was intended. I promise to think about whatever you have to say."

"My lady, I am an ignorant person and my words will be ill-chosen, but I would never intend malice or insult against you, nor would Tostig. I will try to explain as best I can what my brother's thoughts are. Please do not condemn him for my inadequate expression of them."

Eleanor nodded.

Gytha gestured toward the land beyond the priory. "You may see neighbors out there, and for sure they are to you, perhaps even kin, but my kin are a conquered folk. We may speak your language, but we speak it with an accent. It is not our tongue. And we have learned your customs, but, no matter how hard we try, we will never quite look, sound, or act like you. Your barons look at me and do not see the daughter of a thegn, worthy of marriage to one of their sons, but a lowly creature, unsuited to anything but service to their ladies or labor for their fields. Yet we once held all this land and had honor in our king's eyes, more perhaps than a Norman baron has in King Henry's. Now we have little land and little honor with this king. We work land for others that once belonged to us. My brother makes ale and cheese, and breeds donkeys. For this our new lords respect him, but no Norman will trust Tostig with land. Should Tostig have land, he might think himself the equal to a Norman. There can never be two lords over one land, my brother says."

"Surely enough time has passed to forget which family has been here longer and to whom our kin owed allegiance so long ago? A good man is a good man whether he be Norman or English."

"Nay, my lady. One man sees goodness in another only if there is trust; and trust can only exist between equals, my brother says. My family is not on equal footing with yours. We hold none of you in fiefdom. Again, I believe these to be my brother's words."

"So you fear us still?"

"And you, us. There is a lack of trust, my lady."

Eleanor nodded. What Gytha told her had saddened her. Perhaps she even disagreed with some of it, but she grieved that people innocent of any wrong should be afraid of someone like her or her kin.

"I can only say that I will think about what you have told me, Gytha, and pray for wisdom beyond myself. Until those prayers are answered, you must believe that I have no desire to hurt you or your family. I would earn your trust."

With that, Eleanor hugged Gytha, who hugged her back with genuine affection; but, with her eyes closed and her arms around the Saxon girl, Eleanor remembered the disheveled forest man who ran from her a second time near Tostig's house. She saw again the frown on Tostig's face, and once again she wondered what lay behind his silence.

Chapter Twenty-Five

Sister Matilda was leaning on her hoe and weeping softly. Eleanor watched her in silence from the cover of the bower, then lowered her head, ground her foot noisily into the pebbles of the path, and slowly walked into the sunlight.

"Ah, Sister Matilda!" she said, raising her head just as she approached the woman. "I am so glad to find you here."

The nun had had time to wipe the tears from her face, but just barely. "I am at your service, my lady." She curtsied.

"I see you have been working hard at the garden. Let us take some ease and talk awhile." Eleanor gestured to a stone bench in the corner.

The nun dropped her hoe, picked it up with an awkward gesture, and rested the implement against a tree. It fell again. With a sigh, she left it lying in the dirt.

Not a tool with which Sister Matilda felt much comfort, Eleanor thought. "Tell me, sister, how you are progressing with the vegetables for this winter's store?"

The poor nun put her hands to her cheeks, threw her head back, and began to wail piteously.

"Come, come! Nothing can be that bad." Although Sister Matilda was clearly older than Eleanor, her cries were as piteous as those of a child suffering a bee sting. Eleanor reached out, took her hand, and stroked it soothingly.

"I have failed everyone!"

"Whatever do you mean?"

"Look!" Sister Matilda gestured at the dusty garden. "The poor plants. I am so sinful I kill them. I mean only the best and I work hard, but I cannot make them grow. Sister Edith has tried to teach me, but I cannot learn. She says Satan has given me brown thumbs." She raised the offending digits and stared hard at them. "I don't see the change in color, but she has to be right. I must be so sinful I cannot see what Satan has done to my thumbs. I…"

"Hush! Let me see your hands." Eleanor reached out for both hands.

The nun thrust them at her and turned her head as if afraid she'd see the Horned One sitting in her very palms, painting her thumbs as dark as the soil.

"Now pray with me, sister," Eleanor said, holding the nun's two hands gently in her own.

The two women lowered their heads.

"Were you able to pray?" Eleanor asked after she heard Sister Matilda's breathing return to normal.

"Yes, my lady. After just a moment."

"Then Satan has little hold on you. I think we can get rid of him quite easily."

The expression on Sister Matilda's face grew almost beatific with relief. "I will do anything, my lady. I will don a hair shirt and never take it off. I will care for lepers and wash each of their wounds. I will fast every other day for the rest of my life. I will…"

"Perhaps none of that will be needed. First I must ask why Prioress Felicia chose you to care for the priory gardens."

"It was to punish my sinful pride."

"What pride?"

"In the kitchen. I love to cook, you see. Even before my sister, Edith, and I came to Tyndal, we would slip away from our lessons when the servant fell asleep in the sun, I to the kitchen, she to the gardens. Neither of us could embroider an even stitch, but Edith could coax a plant to grow from anything and I seemed to have a talent to cook whatever she grew. When we were older, Inga, our cook, finally let me take charge of one dinner as I had been begging her to do. Our parents told her it was the finest she had ever prepared, but she said nothing about my efforts. They would have been angry that their daughter had done such menial work, but when we came here, Edith gave her talents to the priory gardens with joy. I took over the kitchen."

"And did the plants grow for Sister Edith?"

"Oh, yes, my lady! Prioress Felicia said her harvests were more plentiful than they had ever been before."

"And your meals?"

Sister Matilda lowered her eyes. "Prioress Felicia was kind and said her guests were always pleased. Our own fare is simple, but I heard no complaints."

"Still, your prioress said you suffered from excess pride. Why?"

"I tried too hard to please, my lady. I had overheard someone say our woods had fine mushrooms." She gestured toward the woods surrounding the stream. "I asked permission to look for some when our prioress was expecting important guests. It was granted and my pasties pleased right well."

"That is not undue pride, surely?"

"No, but I went often after that. During the Lenten season I found that many of our recipes for meat dishes suited dried or fresh mushrooms quite as well."

"Again, no sin."

"It was, my lady, and I was given an unmistakable sign of it."

Eleanor raised an eyebrow. "Do tell me."

"One day after Chapter, when I was harvesting mushrooms near a ledge overlooking the stream, I suddenly heard piteous cries coming from the direction of the water. I ran to the edge but could see nothing. The cries, now only whimpers, seemed to be coming from within the earth itself. I was frightened and stepped back. As I did so, a wild, screaming demon burst forth from the earth just under the ledge. His eyes were wild, his arms flailed, his beard was black as smoke. I fled, my lady. I ran in terror back to the priory and told Prioress Felicia and Brother Rupert."

"And they…?"

"They told me that I must have found a hidden pathway to the dark regions and had heard the cries of lost souls. Surely Satan knew I was coming to the forest, as I had so often done, and had sent one of his devils to drag me down to the fiery pit for my sin of pride. It was only God's grace that saved me, they said, and forbade me ever to go to the woods again. Henceforth, I should work in the garden as penance."

"And Sister Edith was to work in the kitchen?"

"She would not know a mushroom from a toadstool, my lady. She would never be in danger of stumbling over that hidden hole to Hell."

Eleanor smiled at this little hint of pride still exposed in Sister Matilda. "Nor has she ever done so. But tell me, sister, do you remember anything else about the demon or where you found this secret path?"

"The demon came from the earth near the bend in the stream, just below the tree whose roots were exposed by the flood two winters ago. Of the demon, I remember little other than what I have said. He was dressed much like a man, but very ragged." She hesitated. "Indeed, Satan does not provide for his minions quite as well as I had thought he would."

"For cert," Eleanor said, as she remembered the wild-haired man looking down at her as she stood by the cave entrance hidden with matting near the bend in the stream.

Chapter Twenty-Six

Thomas watched the nuns of Tyndal file out to chapter after Mass. Prioress Eleanor had not requested his attendance this morning, for which he was most grateful. He hated the inactivity of just sitting and trying to look stern over one more confession of petty vanity or inattention at prayer.

After Sister Anne had released him to normal activity, he had volunteered to work in the stables, a task he actually looked forward to. Keeping the stables clean was too much for the elder monks and had lately fallen to two younger lay brothers, but Thomas was fond of anything equine and had extended that feeling to the new donkey. He quickly proved that mucking out this stable was satisfying exercise for just one young man, yet not sufficiently absorbing that it cut into time needed to comfort the sick, hear confessions, and do whatever else was needed at the hospital. Much to their disgust, the two lay brothers had been quickly assigned to other duties where their diligence to the task assigned was more closely supervised.

The priory had always had a couple of horses, Brother Andrew told him. Recently the prioress's donkey had been added, and only a few days after its arrival, a stall for a second donkey was being prepared. This beast had been purchased for whoever would accompany Prioress Eleanor on journeys abroad. Thomas smiled. The prioress was spreading humility over them all, albeit slowly and with gentleness. He liked that.

As long as he could stay active physically, Thomas was finding his work as a priest much more satisfying than he had originally thought, the hospital especially. Taking individual confessions from the nuns might be boring but had proven less onerous than he had feared. Most of the women at Tyndal suffered but minor sins. If only they knew what real sins were, he thought grimly. Theirs were but laughable ones, although serious enough to them, he supposed. For their sakes, he listened courteously and passed out due penance with a properly somber face.

Thomas walked into the sacristy and began to change into the worn and rough robe he used to muck out stables.

On occasion, however, he did hear rumblings of deeper ills in the confession booth. One skeletally thin young novice had wailed for an hour over her unconquerable lust for food and had begged him to let her whip herself in penance since vomiting had failed to purge gluttony from her. Thomas shuddered in horror at such an extreme reaction and had refused to allow her to punish herself so. At such times he wished he were a wiser priest and feared he knew nothing of a young woman's tribulations. Instead, he had ordered her to talk to the nun in charge of novices who, he assumed, would be better able than he to cope with the problem.

And then there was Sister Ruth, who still felt rage toward the woman she believed stole the position of prioress from her. How naïve she was, he thought. Men made such decisions about who ruled whom. Sister Ruth must have spent most of her life with the foolishly simple if she thought any woman could attain priory leadership if the court of kings had other notions. Her reasoning was feeble indeed.

Thomas left the sacristy and looked out toward the sea. It was a clear day, although wispy clouds did drift high above him. The morning sun warmed the naked spot on the top of his head. Life here could be pleasant, he decided.

Although he was still inclined to believe that most women, like the elder sister, were incapable of sustained logic, he excepted both Prioress Eleanor and Sister Anne and did so with delight.

He quite enjoyed discourse with such intelligent, competent creatures, and, he thought with a slight smile, he had always wanted to please women. Now that he no longer pleasured their bodies, he found it just as satisfying, if not more so, to pleasure their minds.

It was something he could not do with Sister Ruth, whose hatred of the new prioress was so unbalancing her humors that she seemed to find no pleasure in anything. Indeed, Prioress Eleanor's recent decision to appoint her sub-prioress angered her even more. Nor did Brother Simeon help matters any with his remarks to the former porteress about the injustice she had suffered and with his praising of her superior abilities over those of the woman who had supplanted her at Tyndal. Satan had a fertile field in the older nun. Thomas had oft been tempted to suggest she scourge herself for her less than charitable thoughts. To order a nightly penitential whipping, however, would satisfy his own dislike of the woman more than it would help banish the Devil, so he had resisted. Not surprisingly, she had expressed no desire herself to perform such a penance.

He crunched along the path that led from the church and listened to the soft wind whispering through the tall grass, dry after the long summer.

None of the other nuns had cared much for the method of choosing Eleanor either, he'd heard, but he was seeing a slow change in their view of her. Her youth still bothered most, although he now heard more about her kindness, modesty, and willingness to listen. The extensive changes they feared would be made had not occurred. The small ones that had been made seemed to please them.

He had even heard some compliment her on being more in their midst, something the old prioress had rarely done. When she was obliged to entertain, they learned that the food served was what they themselves ate. And rumors had come from Amesbury kin of a couple of the Tyndal nuns that the new prioress had spent a year in the world before making her final vows, a fact that argued somewhat against the inexperience which had troubled many.

In addition, Eleanor had been seen in conversation with the crowner. It was noted that this older man, a representative of King Henry, showed her due respect despite her youth. This pleased the nuns. When respect was shown to their leader, honor was bestowed on the priory.

Thomas stopped just at the rise of the hillock near the monks' quarters and breathed in the salty air. Bracing, he thought. Perhaps he was growing accustomed to it. He walked on toward the small bridge leading to the stables.

Nonetheless, Brother Rupert's murder had still not been solved, a reality that cast a long shadow over both nuns and monks at Tyndal. Although lay brothers visibly watched the gates and walls of Tyndal and the prioress was observed overseeing such efforts, Thomas still heard voices turn hoarse in terror as nuns recounted awakening during the night after dreaming that some demonic creature was standing over them, bloody blade in hand. It troubled Thomas as well that nothing had come to light since the discovery of the knife hilt and bloody garment. The murder seemed no closer to being solved.

Thomas looked down from the bridge and watched the sparkling stream flow beneath. It had a soothing babble, and the occasional dark shadow wriggling through the clear water suggested there were fine fish to be caught for dinner. He turned away and crossed to the other side.

Truth be told, however, his concern over the murder had been momentarily diminished by another decision just made by the prioress. All nuns at Tyndal came to him for confession except Prioress Eleanor. Of course he was used to those in power choosing their own priests, but it seemed strange that a prioress, noted for being more with her flock than prioresses were wont to be, should behave in only one respect as he would have expected her to do in all others. What bothered him most, however, was that Brother John was her choice for confessor.

Thomas continued up the path that led to the stables and smiled. At least the smell of horseflesh was the same, he noted, whether in London or in the country.

Nay, he was not jealous of Brother John. After what he had survived in his London prison, ambition and competitiveness dwindled to insignificant passions. No, the problem lay in his opinion of the man. Thomas was of two minds about him. The monk's eyes could be as cold as green ice or as warm as gem fire in the sun. He had treated Thomas both with disdain and with gentleness, neither of which seemed contrived. Indeed he was a curious man, intriguing enough that Thomas had followed him on occasion and had even spent more time in his company.

Just two nights ago, Thomas had seen the monk slipping quietly out of the dormitory and he had followed him, once again into the clearing in the woods. This time no one attacked Thomas, but he watched as Brother John stripped off his habit and spent an hour whipping his naked body in the moonlight while praying in a quiet voice for unspecified forgiveness. As the monk stood with arms raised to the sky after his strange penance, Thomas found himself inexplicably seized with lust for the first time since he had arrived at Tyndal, but in the few moments it took him to quiet his own unruly flesh, Brother John had disappeared. Thomas had spent the rest of that night troubled by sporadic and now forgotten dreams.

The next morning, the monk had greeted Thomas with good cheer and asked if he would like to accompany him when he took the novices fishing after Mass. The man he had seen caressing a lad in the chapel behaved properly during the fishing trip, and Thomas noted no hesitation on the part of any boy to be close to him or to join in the physical roughhousing usual between elder and younger males. Although no man had ever groped him as a youth, he knew other boys who had been, and one who was raped by some knights in his father's company. Those boys had tried to avoid the men thereafter. Brother John, however, seemed genuinely loved. A puzzle, Thomas thought, for he was sure the monk had shown more than brotherly love for the youth in the chapel that night of his attack.

Thomas walked into the stable, stopped, then looked around. His pitchfork was not where he had left it yesterday. Had one of the two lay brothers he had replaced hidden it out of spite? He chuckled. He hoped they liked slopping hogs and cleaning up after the chickens better than stable work.

He kicked around at mounds of hay and checked in the stalls. It had neither fallen nor been put elsewhere. Perhaps someone had taken it up for some task and hadn't thought to return the tool where Thomas had propped it.

He walked outside and around the back into the shadows of the stable building. There, sticking out of a mound of filthy straw, was the pitchfork. As Thomas tugged at it, he realized it was stuck on something. He grabbed the handle with both hands, then pulled with a sharp jerk.

The tines emerged from the straw. For cert, they were quite stuck. Deep into a man. He was dressed in ragged, stained clothing; his beard was black and unkempt. His eyes stared fixedly at Thomas. He did not blink.

Indeed, the man was quite dead.

Chapter Twenty-Seven

The wooden door to the prioress's chambers creaked on its hinges, then slammed shut, the wooden panels shaking quite visibly from the force.

Eleanor raised one eyebrow.

"I swear that woman hates me," Ralf the Crowner said as he stared at the still quivering door.

"Sister Ruth shares the concerns of many over yet another death in our priory." Eleanor gestured toward a stool, and Ralf sat.

"I join with your charges in that concern, but I have found no traces of the person who murdered Brother Rupert. I suspect there is a link to this second death, but I have not found it. I am not used to being so thwarted, my lady, yet thwarted I surely am."

"Have you identified who the poor man was?" Eleanor watched as Gytha carefully poured a goblet of wine for the crowner, then put the ewer down and began to cut some cheese.

"No one has come forward and claimed knowledge of him, nor do I know him."

"Well, he is certainly from here. I saw him by the stream that day I turned my ankle and once again in the village when I was buying a donkey. No one else did, however."

A softened squeal of pain caused Eleanor to look up. Gytha was sucking on her finger.

"Are you all right, my child?"

"The knife slipped, my lady. It has almost stopped bleeding. I will bring the…"

"Come here and let me see."

Gytha hesitated, then came forward and gave her hand to Eleanor.

"The cheese will wait. Run to Sister Anne and let her bind your finger. The cut looks deeper than you thought."

"But…"

"I will brook no argument here, nor do I need your presence for decorum. Sister Ruth stands without the door."

Gytha left the room with a backward glance at her mistress.

"Perhaps it is just as well the child has left. Now I may ask whether you have shown the body to anyone in the village, Ralf."

"Tostig. He claimed no knowledge of him but promised to ask others. No one has come forth."

"And you believe him."

"I trust most Saxons as much as most Saxons trust me."

"That is blunt enough. What have you in mind to get at the truth then?"

"Not what you might think I would do. I have never believed that torture brings forth the sound of truth, although it soon brings loud promises to say anything that will stop the pain."

"You have no paid friends then in the village?"

Ralf laughed. "You surprise me, my lady. How could you think such a thing?"

"My father is at court and my elder brother fights at Prince Edward's side in the Holy Land. I am naïve neither about the mechanics of intrigue nor about how men retain power."

Ralf coughed.

"Lest you fear you have been too unguarded with a nun whom you now find to be less unworldly and perhaps better connected than you thought, let me assure you that I like a plain-spoken man. And men who are blunt to hide a soft heart I like even better." Eleanor smiled, resting her chin in her hand. "So explain to me now why is it that you have no paid *friends?*"

"I bent the truth, my lady. Although many Saxons do not trust me, nor I them, I have true friends in the village that are so because they have learned I will be equitable to all and keep good order. Tostig is one such. What troubles me is that none of the Saxons I have befriended have come to me about this new death."

"Then they are either afraid or have a higher loyalty than their friendship to you."

"Well observed."

"Tell me of Tostig's reaction when he saw the dead man. What did you note?"

"He is a man who does not allow the color of his thoughts to be painted on his face, but I did detect a blink of his eyes and a twitch at his jaw when he first looked on the man."

"Which suggested to you that his denial of any knowledge was false."

Ralf nodded.

"That would confirm my own suspicion. When I saw the man in the village, the day I purchased the donkey, Tostig claimed he had not, although he was standing immediately behind me when I cried out. He could not have missed seeing him. I believe he not only noticed the man, I think he knew him."

"Then he and the villagers do have reason either to protect themselves or him."

Eleanor leaned back in her chair, stared at the ceiling in silence, then sat forward and sipped some wine from the goblet in front of her. As she put it down on the table, she watched the red liquid swirl and thought unpleasantly of blood.

"There may be another way to get at the truth of who this strange man was. Since you were last here, Ralf, I have had some discussion with the nun who used to pick mushrooms in the forest. She told me a strange tale of a demon that burst out of the earth in front of her near the bend in the stream where a tree hangs nearly suspended in air. It is the same place, I believe, where the cave of unknown purpose is."

"A demon?"

"A demon with disheveled clothes and a black, unkempt beard. Unusual for a minion of Satan, I'd say, but not unusual for a man. Since I first saw our dead man there, I wonder if he might have been the very same demon."

"Or it might have been a true son of Satan," the crowner suggested.

"My aunt at Amesbury once told me that the demons we are unable to see or recognize are of far greater danger to our souls than those we can. I will ask my nun to view the corpse, but I will have Brother Thomas accompany her lest she need protection from otherworldly dangers. Indeed I fear she may remember all too vividly the image of her terror in recognizing the cause of it. Would you come as well? You should note her reaction and not hear it second-hand from me."

"I will be there even if the corpse proves to be unholy and Satan himself comes to protect one of his own. Tell me, my lady, do you think there is a connection between this death and Brother Rupert's? I do, yet it is a question, the answer to which eludes me."

"And eludes me too. Something is indeed deeply amiss here. That something caused our dead man to both run in terror from the cave, yet be drawn back again; to run in fear from me at the village, yet come back to Tyndal, only to be found dead on the priory grounds as was our good monk."

"I would not dismiss Satan's hand in the incomprehensible, my lady."

"Nor I, good Crowner, but if Satan has sent his minion to Tyndal, he remains quite invisible to us all."

Chapter Twenty-Eight

Sister Matilda screamed.

Brother Thomas held the cross in a tight grip, both hands stretched rigidly in front of him. Ralf stood behind him, eyes as unblinking and dry as if they had been painted on his face.

Eleanor pulled the wild-eyed nun into her arms, pushing her head into the curve of her neck so she could no longer see the body.

"Hush, sister! There is nothing to fear. Brother Thomas has the Evil One at bay with the cross in his hands. We are safe."

"It is the very Devil who burst from the earth. He has found me!" The nun's cries were muffled, but Eleanor could feel her body shaking with terror.

"He is powerless against you, bound as he is in the chapel near the altar, sister." Eleanor gestured to Thomas to follow her out, then turned and pulled the trembling nun away with great gentleness. "We shall leave, and I promise you will never see him again."

Sister Anne was waiting outside the door as the four emerged into the fading light. She helped Eleanor seat Sister Matilda, then gave the nun, whose eyes were now tightly shut against the sight of any further horrors, a drink from a cup she had close at hand.

"She needs to sleep, my lady," Sister Anne whispered. "I will have someone sit with her tonight in case she wakes from evil dreams, but with this potion I think she will sleep well."

Eleanor, short as she was, took the sitting nun's head and pulled it close to her breast and gently rocked her. "You did a brave thing tonight, Sister Matilda. I believe you will rest now, and, in the morning, we will walk together in the garden after chapter and speak of your return to grace from this penance you have endured."

Sister Matilda turned to look up at the prioress, her eyes already unfocused from the draught the sub-infirmarian had given her. "Penance, my lady? I did penance?"

"You did indeed! Remember? It was for your pride. Now that you have done this thing tonight, I believe you may be relieved of your work in the garden."

The nun sat up and swayed, her face filled with blissful relief and joy.

"Say nothing more, my child. It is your duty now to sleep. We will speak in the morning."

Sister Anne gestured, and a lay sister came out of the shadows. They whispered together for a moment, then the lay sister and Sister Matilda wobbled away in the general direction of the hospital.

"I will stand just there until you need me," Sister Anne said, gesturing to a yew tree a little distance away.

Eleanor turned to Brother Thomas. "You look shaken yourself, brother." She meant it kindly, but she saw him stiffen. "It is one thing to cross swords with a human enemy, but yet another to face Satan himself," she added quickly. "Your courage was impressive."

"I faced a corpse, not Satan, my lady." His expression was unreadable.

"You did not know that when I asked you to protect us against a possible demon." Eleanor wanted to reach out, take his hand, and clutch it to her as she had the terrified nun. The sweet pain she felt at the thought of his hand on her breast was less than chaste. She dropped her gaze, and there was silence between them.

"As you will. I am here to serve and am pleased if I served as you wished."

"You served well, brother." Eleanor took a deep breath and looked up. "I have one thing more to ask of you."

Thomas bowed his head in silence.

"Should you see or hear anything of note in the matter of this death as you perform your tasks, I would hear of it, and hear of it first. Anything unusual. Anything out of place. We are both new here, but I have learned that you are a thoughtful and observant man. Crowner Ralf can only search the outside world for signs of this murder and that of Brother Rupert. I need your skills for noting anything untoward within our priory, especially amongst the monks and lay brothers."

"Aye," Ralf said. "I concur, good brother."

Had the light not so failed that his face was in shadow, Eleanor might have seen Brother Thomas turn pale before he nodded agreement.

Chapter Twenty-Nine

The rock bounced off the stone walls of the priory, and the curse spat after it was quite Anglo-Saxon.

"Who knows me here? Who is her spy?" Thomas snarled, as he threw another rock in impotent rage at the priory. "And what fool gave a woman the right to order men around? Unnatural, it is. This whole place is fucking unnatural!"

This rock shattered. Thomas sat down on the ground and put his head in his hands. He was shaking, but rage no longer masked his fear. Indeed, he had been afraid when the prioress had told him to come to the chapel and hold a cross against any demon still residing in the corpse of the man he had found.

And when Sister Matilda screamed, he thought he had seen a Son of Darkness rise from the body, smelling of smoke, his grinning image flickering in the candlelight. Thomas would have sworn to that. And when he held the cross in front of him, for cert he had heard the thing sigh before it disappeared, then all he heard was the calm prioress crooning to the nun in her arms as if she held a baby there, not an adult woman. Truth to tell, there was a instant when Thomas wished she would soothe him as well, but, along with the innocence of childhood, he knew he had also lost the right to such a comfort for himself.

Thomas began to sob, his body shaking uncontrollably. He had wept little since he was a small boy, yet in this place dedicated to peace and God, tears came to him easily and often.

"Aye!" he cried into his hands. "She is a better man than I. I hate her for it!"

In truth, he did not hate the prioress. Had she been a man of the world, he would have admired her coolness. Had she been a prior, he might have sat at her feet and begged to learn how she blended her piety with pragmatism. Had she even been a saintly woman, he could have worshiped her holiness. She was none of those, but rather a young and earthy woman who was so very different from all the others he had ever known. He did not understand her at all, but he did respect her.

Whatever could he tell her? What was pertinent and what would be the betrayal of secrets with no relevance to these crimes? As Brother Andrew had said, many inhabitants of Tyndal had secrets buried in their hearts. Those were things between them and their God, as far as Thomas was concerned, and of no moment to mortal men, even to prioresses. Someone had a very dark secret, however, and that secret must have led to murder.

Should he speak of Brother John and his solitary penance in the forest clearing? Or of his own suspicions that the monk might have a youthful lover, a lad perhaps from the village? The consequences were dire if two men were found, as Thomas had been with Giles, and brought to trial. Men had been burned at the stake for it. Excommunication was common. Thomas shivered. He might have escaped all this himself either by the grace of God or Satan, but few did and he would never point a finger at another man for a love he could not even now condemn. Were the things he had seen or suspected about Brother John even related to the two murders, or were they unconnected? He did not know.

And what about Brother Simeon, a competent man who had taken control of Tyndal and run it well when the prior could not and the prioress would not. When Prior Theobald faltered, Simeon whispered words and decisions into his ear to use as his own, thus saving the old man's pride. And both Brother Rupert and Prioress Felicia had seen the wisdom in letting him run the tenant farms and see to the other businesses of the priory.

It was not until this year that things had faltered. Thomas was no farmer, but even he knew crops varied. So Simeon liked his wine and comforts. So what? Others in the Church took their ease with women as well as wine, and few were called to account as long as they helped the Church prosper. Surely, the sins of Brother Simeon were but laughable amongst worldly men, and Simeon worldly enough to know that.

This receiver, however, had an enemy at Tyndal. Someone had written the Abbess and suggested serious problems here, but Thomas had heard nothing from any of the monks or lay brothers to suggest who the author might have been. Was there a link between the accusation and these deaths? If so, what? He doubted Simeon knew anything about the letter. The receiver's greatest worry was the arrival of the new prioress and her threat to his leadership of Tyndal.

Had it been Brother Rupert who had written? Thomas had been told he was a man known for direct speech, so surely he would have been more specific about the complaint. Brother John? Thomas smiled. No, he was too busy with his beautiful music and beautiful boys to write vague, yet suggestive letters. Brother Andrew? He seemed a man who observed much, then let it lie. Who, then, had a quarrel with the receiver? Thomas struck his head. Who!

He stood up and walked back toward the sacristy. It was time for Mass again, and time to start on the assignment entrusted to him by Prioress Eleanor. "Fuck!" he muttered in frustration. Thomas was so glad he had met Tostig. The Saxons had such expressive words in their language.

Chapter Thirty

Bedlam would have been a model of calm compared to Tyndal's kitchen the next morning. Sister Edith stood in the middle of the room, staring at the ceiling and screaming orders, many in contradiction to others already given. Steam from overflowing pots boiled into billowing hot fog, the bitter smell of burning meat permeated the air, and a large pestle lay shattered on the floor. Two sisters were in tears over half-chopped vegetables. And the midday meal chicken escaped out the door, squawking in outrage at its proposed fate, just as Eleanor walked in.

"You are a scrawny one," she remarked as the bird raced past her. Then, looking at the scene before her, she wondered how anything, even the inedible, could emerge from all this disarray.

Sister Edith's face was red and her eyes squeezed shut as if she were in a bad dream from which she might awaken, if only she waited long enough.

Eleanor reached up and put a hand gently on the woman's shoulder.

"Cook it any way you want, for the love of God!" Sister Edith screeched, once again raising her closed eyes heavenward. "Just don't ask me another question."

Then she opened her eyes.

"Oh, no!" she whispered as she looked down into the expressionless face of her prioress.

Eleanor struggled not to laugh.

"Come, sister," she said with immense control. "Let us walk in the cool of the garden and talk."

The two women walked silently out of the hot kitchen, across the cloister and through the trellised arbor into the garden filled with tiny flowers and toward the carved stone seat near the fountain. Despite the warming sun, there was a chill to the air that foretold the coming autumn storms. Sensing the change, bees buzzed with special urgency, but a butterfly or two floated almost carelessly in the air as if they cared not a whit for their fate in the darker season.

Sister Edith's head was bowed, perhaps less from humility than from embarrassment, for Eleanor noted that her eyes quickly looked sideways when they entered the garden, as if she could not keep herself from studying the state of the lush vegetation.

"Please sit." Eleanor gestured to the bench. The sound of the water in the fountain was as peaceful as a primeval brook running over ancient, smoothed pebbles.

"My lady, I have sinned…"

"Brother Thomas is your confessor. He will give due penance for sins of anger."

"I have failed both you and Tyndal."

Eleanor folded her hands into her sleeves, tilted her head, and waited.

"It was my rotation in the kitchen and I have failed in my duties."

"Rotation? Not as a penance for anything then?"

"When Mati…Sister Matilda was taken from the kitchen, I was rotated in. Our prioress that was, Prioress Felicia, said we must all learn to do everything in the priory. In that I have been unable to perform adequately."

"Everything? Indeed, that is not a bad idea, for the good of your soul as well as your experience. Surely you began with the basics of cooking?"

"No, my lady. I began in charge. I had been in charge of the gardens. Prioress Felicia felt it would be unseemly for me to do the base work of chopping vegetables."

"I saw two sisters doing just that."

"They are the daughters of knights…"

"And you and Sister Matilda are the daughters of a baron."

"Yes, my lady."

"Would you have minded serving under women of lesser rank?"

"I want to serve God well. If I serve best chopping parsnips, so be it, my lady, but I have not done well directing in the kitchens. Even with Sister Mat…" She stopped and looked sheepishly at the prioress.

"Even with your sister's help?" Eleanor smiled and put a hand on the nun's arm. "Fear not. I have seen each of you struggling to help the other, but I have also seen the anger between you."

"She will never learn not to water in the high heat of…" Sister Edith stopped as her own voice raised in indignation. "That is no more her fault than it is mine that I cannot remember how long to boil a pot of stew or the right flame for meat."

"No, it is not, and you both must make peace. Anger is sinful whether it be between kin or with any child of God."

Sister Edith squirmed uncomfortably on the bench. "Aye, but I still don't know how to cook."

"And I have a solution for that. Would you be willing to do anything, no matter how humble or unsuited to your station, to correct your faults?"

"I wish only to serve, my lady. True station exists only in the grace of God."

"Well said! We must all remember that the twelve apostles were men of very simple birth but were chosen to sit at the right hand of God. So take the lowly task I have for you and perform it well in the spirit of those men. Will you promise me that?"

"Aye, my lady."

"I am assigning you to the priory gardens that you may humble yourself in the earth and bring forth flowers for the glory of God and plants to feed us so that we will have the strength to serve Him better."

"What about Matilda?"

"I am bringing your sister back to the kitchen. She has served her time in the field. And I order the two of you to make peace so that she may prepare the fruits of your work to grace our tables within the blessing of unity."

Sister Edith cried aloud and tears flowed down her cheeks again, but both voice and tears were finally filled with happiness.

Chapter Thirty-One

Sister Ruth was droning. It was difficult to read the Venerable Bede's *Life of Saint Cuthbert* and make it sound dull, but the good nun was succeeding with impressive skill.

Eleanor looked down from the prioress's high table to the long line of nuns eating silently on benches in the refectory below her. This night she had invited no one to join her. She was too weary even for familiar company.

Two deaths on priory grounds had been horrible, but daily responsibilities could not be set aside. After days of talking to the nuns, monks, and lay people at Tyndal, studying the account rolls taken from Brother Simeon, and making small changes she hoped would be beneficial to both body and soul, she was exhausted, her humors out of balance. She needed to spend an evening in restorative prayer and contemplation, something she had had little time for of late. At least her ankle had healed, she thought, quickly adding something positive to offset her list of complaints.

She looked down at the trencher in front of her and smiled. The return of Sister Matilda to the kitchens had been a popular decision. Her talented cooking had also helped ease the transition to a more spartan diet than the religious inhabitants of Tyndal had been accustomed to, a necessity in view of the poor monastery harvest and reduced income from priory lands. Fish from the ponds was still plentiful, and Sister Edith had offered hope for an increase in the cooler season's vegetables, but austerity was still required if all were to have sufficient food through winter.

At yesterday's chapter, Eleanor had announced her personal vow to cut her own portions in half, eat no meat, and drink only ale from Tyndal's brewery. What wine the priory had should be saved for Mass and the sick, she declared, for none could be bought until revenues increased. Eleanor had left the choice of what to surrender from meals, other than wine, to the nuns themselves, although she had warned against an excess of fasting. Thanks to Brother Thomas' wise direction, she knew of one young novice who had difficulties with such excesses. At his order, the girl had told the head of novices about her self-induced vomiting and Eleanor had been told that the nun would be especially vigilant, not only with her but others who might exhibit similar debilitating behavior.

Ah, the good brother! He was the other reason Eleanor had given up any meat, and she meant to do so until her body ceased to respond in lustful ways to his presence. It was well known that meat heated the blood, and her blood needed no warming when Brother Thomas was with her. Brother John, her confessor, had agreed, although he had been kinder than others might have been when she told him about her adulterous feelings toward the monk. He might have suggested scourging. Instead, he had ordered her to pray alone in the chapel for one hour each night as she stretched out, face down on the stone floor. The penance had cooled her passions sufficiently in the warmer months of summer. She imagined it would utterly destroy them by mid-winter when the stones turned icy.

Eleanor took a sip of ale. The taste was bitter, watery. She grimaced as she looked at the pale color. Had the drink been urine, surely the physician would have expressed concern over the health of his patient. Even urine might have better flavor than this, she thought wryly.

Tostig had not yet responded to her offer to talk about a partnership. Although Gytha said he had thought well of the idea when she first mentioned it, all of that had been discussed before the death of the man with the black beard. With his death, a kind of silence had descended on the village in their commerce with the priory. Business, per se, continued, but only just. The comfortable social commerce which village and priory had enjoyed in the past had waned. The tension was as ill defined as a hidden cancer but, Eleanor thought, just as palpable by all affected by it.

The crowner continued to remark on the lack of cooperation from his regular sources, men who had once cared more for justice and peace than any two-hundred-year-old quarrel between Saxon and Norman. Oh, villagers still came to him when a sheep was stolen or a border marker moved, but there was a grimness in their faces that Crowner Ralf had not seen since the early days of his tenure. Tostig in particular seemed to avoid him, and that hurt Ralf most. According to Sister Anne, the two men had been friends since childhood. And the crowner was still no closer to solving the murders of the monk and the man, a frustration that did not improve his somewhat impatient temperament.

Her trencher empty and her goblet dry, Eleanor looked down on the nuns and saw that they too had finished their evening meal. With this second death in the sanctity of their grounds, the calm she had just managed to achieve had vanished. In the fear-widened eyes of these women, she saw a pleading for strength from her. She had come through for them after the first murder. Would she be adequate to their greater need now?

She rose. It was time to lead her charges to prayer and whatever peace it might bring them all.

༺⚬༻

On the monks' side of the priory church, Eleanor's orders for more modest fare were not greeted with unanimous joy, at least amongst some in the higher ranks. Or so Brother Thomas thought as he looked around him at the evening meal.

Prior Theobald was the exception to that. He seemed content enough, picking up odd bits from the half portion he had put on his trencher, but then Thomas doubted food had ever been of major interest to him. He'd probably not notice if horse piss were poured into his cup instead of wine. Indeed, considering the taste of Tyndal's finest ale, it might have been. Thomas shoved his goblet aside and briefly wondered if even well water might be preferable.

Brother Simeon, on the other hand, looked positively gray. As receiver and sub-prior, he did no work in the fields, and the prioress had directed that heartier food and drink should be given to those who did hard labor, since they needed it most. That included the lay brothers. Thomas saw him wince at the arrival of the vegetable stew and noted that he had gone so far as to rip small pieces from his own trencher, which normally would have been passed on to the poor. However improved and quite savory the simpler meals had become of late, Brother Simeon liked his meat and wine. This would be a hard season for a man of appetite.

Even Brother John looked more somber than he usually did at mealtime. Thomas had noticed that the monk cared little more about his food than did the prior, although he did not fast in excess. His lean body and lonely midnight scourgings might point to a dedicated religious sternness, but there were clear limits to his asceticism. He usually ate what he was given with grateful appreciation, and drank wine in moderation but also with some pleasure. Tonight, however, he seemed troubled and poked absently at the food. If his grim mood was not over the meal, then it surely stemmed from something else.

Thomas was curious.

Chapter Thirty-Two

Eleanor walked slowly up her private stairs from chapel to chambers. The evening communal prayers were complete. Her own hard penance on the stone floor had been performed. The evening air was cool and no man in the moon's chilly face peeked through the drifting clouds of the evening sky. It would be a black night tonight, she thought, as she stood in her chambers and looked out the window near her narrow cot.

As she prepared for sleep, folding her head veil and wimple neatly before placing them into the chest at the bottom of her bed, something soft brushed up against her leg, causing her to smile.

"Well now," she said with a gentle tone, looking down at the orange cat. "I suppose you are looking for a warm bed after your hard work in the kitchens today?"

The cat looked up at her with hopeful green eyes.

"I did hear from Sister Matilda that you hunted well. She seems more pleased with your efforts than Sister Edith was. Perhaps you have improved on your presentation."

The cat reached out with a paw and tapped her leg.

"One of these days I suppose I should ask Brother John whether there is any sin in a cat sleeping with a nun. And a male cat at that."

The cat jumped up on the cot.

"Perhaps I will just leave the question be. You've earned a soft, warm bed after your good work keeping the vermin at bay who set siege to Tyndal."

And as Eleanor lay down on her back on the cot and crossed her hands over her chest, the orange cat stretched himself out along her side. In a minute, both weary ones were sound asleep.

ᏝᏝᎧᎧᎧ

Eleanor sat straight up.

The orange cat had used her body to hurl himself, hissing and snarling, out of the bed.

She cried out, as though from a bad dream, not yet awake, eyes still shut. The brush of something down her back, the yell of pain not her own, and the sound of running feet against the rushes on her chamber floor did not arise from any dream.

She opened her eyes. In the dim light, she could see the cat standing by her open door, back arched, growling angrily. With heart pounding, Eleanor flew out of bed to the chamber door and heard the footsteps running down the stone steps to the cloister below.

"Help!" she shouted. "Someone has been in my chamber. Stop them!"

Sister Anne ran through the prioress's private entrance to the chapel. "My lady! What has happened?"

Eleanor grasped the nun hard as if her very sanity depended on the human contact. "I don't know. Someone was in my room. The door is wide open. I heard footsteps running down the stairs."

"I will alert the monks, then return to you immediately." With that, Anne dashed from the room.

Suddenly Eleanor felt chilled. She turned back toward the bed to pull a warming blanket from the chest, then stopped. Her hand covered her mouth in horror.

On her bed lay a knife.

ᏝᏝᎧᎧᎧ

Thomas couldn't sleep. He had tossed and turned since Compline and it was still many hours until Prime. Giving up, he put on his shoes and slipped down the stairs from the dormitory to the cloister. Perhaps some exercise, followed by kneeling on the stone slabs of the chapel, would be sufficient penance and God would grant him a few hours of rest.

As he walked along the outside wall of the refectory, he heard a commotion behind him, coming from the area of the passageway to the outer court. It was a moonless night, and he could see nothing, but curiosity piqued his interest. He turned toward the sound. From the passageway under the dormitory, he saw two dark figures racing toward him.

"Stop him. Stop him! He is a murderer!" The voice sounded like Brother Simeon's.

Thomas did not hesitate. He ran toward the figure coming at him. The man's face was turned to look behind him as Thomas dived at his feet and brought him down. The man struggled but Thomas held him pinned to the ground.

As Simeon came up, panting, Thomas forced the captive onto his back. Staring back at him was the face of Brother John.

"He tried to kill Prioress Eleanor," Simeon puffed.

Chapter Thirty-Three

"Wine for all, please, Gytha. It is no luxury today," Eleanor said, her voice echoing in her ears with more steadiness than she felt. "Even I will have some, albeit well-watered." The pallor of her face matched that of the morning light coming through her chamber window, but Eleanor sat with back straight as she looked at Simeon and Thomas, sitting on stools in front of her. Their faces were gray from lack of sleep and from the shadow of beards yet unshaven.

Sister Anne sat in silence next to the prioress, her eyes staring at the floor, her back hunched as if in pain.

Crowner Ralf paced.

"He refuses to confess to anything, my lady." Ralf took the goblet from Gytha and drank deeply. "He refuses to speak at all."

Simeon waved away any water for his wine. "This is no longer your concern, Crowner. Brother John falls under the jurisdiction of Church law. This is not a civil matter."

"It will be my concern until I know whether he was responsible for the deaths of our unknown man and Brother Rupert as well as the attack on Brother Thomas. If he had some special reason for attacking Prioress Eleanor alone, then he is all yours and I still must catch the culprit, or culprits, who did the other deeds."

"It would be strange indeed if he didn't commit all the crimes. Why only attack our prioress? Surely this house of God would not have two murderers, even three, in our midst at the same time?" Thomas asked.

"Indeed, good brother. My very point!" Simeon waved his empty goblet at Gytha, who scowled and refilled it without water. "Our prioress would not be his only victim."

"Good sirs. If you don't mind, I am still with you. Perhaps you would stop discussing the events of last night as if I were just a corpse placed in your midst to fill a chair." Eleanor managed a half smile.

The men muttered apologies.

Eleanor nodded at the crowner. "I agree with Ralf that we cannot assume Brother John was responsible for both deaths and the attacks on Brother Thomas and me until we either get a confession or find more evidence."

"Nonetheless, I saw him running from the direction of the nuns' quarters, my lady, and I gave chase. He refused to stop when I called out to him to halt. In fact, he ran faster. I say that points to his guilt." Simeon downed his wine, then scowled at the cup as if it had offended him by being empty. Gytha refilled it without a word.

"You first said that you saw him running from the church, Brother Simeon," Eleanor said. "Which now is correct? And if the latter, has he said why he might have been in the church? Perhaps our real culprit has disappeared, and Brother John was in the same vicinity for good and legitimate reasons."

"The man is as guilty as Satan himself or else he would say what he was doing," Simeon replied.

Ralf shrugged in half-hearted agreement. "'Tis usually the case, my lady."

Eleanor nodded and turned to the two monks. "Then you and Brother Thomas would not hesitate to tell me why each of you was abroad last night, also contrary to the rules?"

Simeon flushed. "Forgive me, my lady, but I do not appreciate such insinuations. I was the man who chased him and risked my life to do so. Why should I fall under suspicion of breaking priory rules?"

"I did not say you were, good brother. I was merely suggesting that reasons for not being where one is supposed to be might be difficult to give, however satisfactory."

"Then I shall speak for myself first," Thomas said. "I was unable to sleep and thought a walk in the cloister and an hour of prayer in the chapel might help. I had just entered the cloister near the refectory when I saw two dark shadows running toward me. One shouted to me to stop the other. And I did."

"And I do believe you, brother. This time." Eleanor smiled. "Sadly, your good works did not bring you the desired sleep. For that I am sorry."

"The reward is but delayed. I am sure that God will be gracious in granting me rest some night in the future." Thomas smiled back.

Simeon glared at her through puffy eyes. "Very well, my lady. I, too, was troubled with worries over our failure to bring in enough income to feed us with proper fare for the winter months, and sleep evaded me. I rose and walked toward the church." He raised his chin. "I feel closer to God in my prayers at the high altar than in our small chapel so I go there." He hesitated but continued when no one spoke. "Before I got to the sacristy door, I thought I'd check to see if the brewery was locked for the night." He shrugged. "I do not trust the villagers not to damage…"

Eleanor cleared her throat and gestured for him to get on with his story.

"As I began to walk in that direction, I heard a noise behind me. I turned and saw a figure running from the direction of the nuns' quarters near the sacristy. I immediately called to him, but he ran from me into the monks' quarters through the passageway door I had foolishly left unlocked…"

"And thus you have both reasonably explained your actions. Do you think any man should have a good excuse as readily at hand if he is innocent of any evil?" Eleanor pointedly looked at Thomas and raised her eyebrows.

"He should!" Simeon's voice was slurred.

"Perhaps not, my lady," Thomas admitted quietly.

"There is also the matter of a wound the guilty man may bear somewhere on his face or hands," Eleanor said. "The cat must have scratched him. I heard a cry of pain before he ran."

Thomas raised his hands, twisting them to show the scrapes on both sides. "I fear scratches may not be good evidence, my lady. As you see, my hands are cut from sliding along the ground as I caught Brother John. Both his hands and face are equally scratched, but the abrasions might have been caused by his fall. Brother Simeon as well has…"

"A wound in the service of God's justice is nothing," Simeon muttered.

"Well said, brother." Thomas patted the receiver's back. "I believe I've made my point. There is no simple evidence here."

"Nothing about this case has ever been simple," Ralf growled.

"Perhaps it is time to make it so." Eleanor looked at each man in front of her as she continued. "Perhaps I should speak to Brother John alone."

"Never!" both Ralf and Simeon said in unison. Thomas, however, nodded approval.

"He is quite probably a murderer, my lady," Ralf said, glancing at Sister Anne, who continued to stare in silence at her tightly folded hands.

"We will all take due precautions, but he may say things to his prioress he would not to any of you. Although temporal justice must be served, the peace of the soul is both spiritual and eternal. As a woman, I cannot be his earthly judge in either secular or religious court. As his prioress, however, I am his spiritual guide. He may listen and talk to me."

Ralf raised his eyebrows and nodded.

"It is not well advised, but perhaps we could arrange some protection for you if you insist." Simeon downed his third goblet of unwatered wine. Gytha ignored his perfunctory nod at her for a refill and turned to the crowner with the ewer.

Ralf waved away her offer of wine. "We could come up with a plan to protect you while you speak with him alone as you wish. Allow me to further suggest that you should not do so until at least a day has passed. If he be truly innocent, then some time alone with minimal bread and water in his window-less room by the monks' latrine will surely bring the man to his senses. Whatever embarrassment he might now feel over some relatively minor sin should fade into reason after many hours of thinking about what could happen to him if he continues to act like a guilty man."

Eleanor nodded. "Very well, good sirs. Let us meet tomorrow after Chapter and I will go speak with Brother John alone at that time with your discreet protection."

Dismissed, the men rose, bowed, and left.

Sister Anne also rose to leave.

"Stay, sister. I would have a brief word," Eleanor said.

The tall nun turned toward her prioress, shoulders stooped and expression even sadder than usual. "Of course, my lady."

"You were unusually quiet. May I ask why?"

Tears slowly brimmed and began falling in great drops down the nun's cheeks. "I have something to tell you in private."

Eleanor nodded to Gytha to leave them, then took Anne by the hand, pulling her back down into the seat beside her. "What is troubling you?"

"You never asked me why I was so close to hand when you cried out."

"Indeed, it did not occur to me to ask."

"You should."

Eleanor looked at Anne, but the nun turned her face from the prioress. "Tell me, then, why you came from the church when you should have been at the hospital or even in your own bed." Her voice was gentle.

"I was to meet Brother John in the church last night, my lady."

"A meeting not proper within the letter of our vows, for cert, but you know that as well as I. Tell me why you were meeting him at such an hour and alone, Anne?"

"He asked to do so. It was not for lustful purposes, my lady. He wanted to talk to me about something where no one would hear us."

"Why did he say he wanted to meet you?" Eleanor asked, squeezing the distraught nun's hand.

"He did not say."

"And was he with you when you heard me cry out? If so, he is not guilty of the attack."

Sister Anne began to weep in earnest. "My lady, he was not!"

"Poor child!" Eleanor said and pulled the sobbing nun into her arms. "If he is indeed the murderer of two innocent men and the man who tried to stab me, then Brother Simeon may have frightened him away from the church and saved your life...."

"Brother John is a kind and gentle man! He is no murderer."

Eleanor gently shook her. "You cannot say that for sure, Anne. Despite all our work with them, we may not always know what is in the hearts and souls of our brethren...."

"My lady, I know Brother John very well. He was my husband."

Chapter Thirty-Four

"Sin! The man is full of the blackest sin!" Simeon was weaving off the pathway.

Thomas reached out and tried to pull Simeon gently back to the safety of the level walk. "Surely God protected our prioress from Brother John's black heart."

"God's hand is stronger when supported by a weapon in a good man's hand!" Simeon waved one of his own hands drunkenly.

"Aye, and you have been wounded yourself in the good fight against the instrument of Satan," Thomas said as he caught the waving hand.

Simeon looked down at his bandaged left hand held by the young monk. "A minor scratch. I fell as I chased Brother John from the church and scraped my hand on the rocks of the path. A minor wound in the battle against God's enemies!" He belched with evident satisfaction.

"Has Sister Anne looked…"

"Eve took the apple from the serpent, brother. I will have no woman touch me with that poisonous hand. In battles between kings, each man aids his fellow. In the wars against sin, wounds must be treated in the same fashion. We monks have no need for the daughters of Eve. I know enough to wrap a scrape."

"I meant well, brother. Forgive me if I angered."

Simeon slapped Thomas on the back with his free hand. "You did not anger, my son. I know you meant no ill, but once again

I would advise you to beware of Sister Anne. She is an arrogant woman and not as holy as she should be."

"How so? You have suggested such in the past but never told me your meaning."

"She and Brother John were married in the world, brother. I have seen them behave in ways here that make me question their devotion to their vows of chastity."

"Surely our prioress has seen this as well, yet Sister Anne has gained her confidence…"

Simeon snatched his hand from Thomas' grip. "I do not share your trust in our prioress, Brother Thomas. She is a young woman and inexperienced in the ways of the world. She needs firm guidance in her friendships. I fear that Sister Anne may have blinded her by showing a fine face. Being a woman, Prioress Eleanor is weak and lacking in good judgement. She has been easily beguiled and cannot see the corruption in the nun's heart."

"I am grateful for your wise instruction, brother. Perhaps our prioress would benefit from your words of warning too."

"Our descendant of Eve suffers much from the sin of arrogance, I fear, and shows no signs of realizing she needs guidance and the greater wisdom of Adam. After all, whom did she pick as her personal confessor? A murderer! She certainly did not consult with me on that or I would have warned her away from him. And you heard her join with our boorish and irreverent crowner in expressing some doubt that Brother John was guilty of both murders and the attack on her person. Does any of that suggest to you that the woman is rational or a good judge of character?"

"Perhaps she will see the error of her ways, when she has gained some distance from these horrible events, and be guided by you in the future."

Simeon snorted and marched ahead. His anger, it seemed, had burned away the effects of too much unwatered wine. His step was now firm.

As Thomas stood and watched the man, he sighed. He doubted the good prioress would ever listen to Brother Simeon in the manner he wished, and Thomas thought it equally unlikely that Simeon would ever become reconciled to his new subservient role. In the meantime, Thomas wondered about Brother John's guilt. He had been surprised to learn that he and Sister Anne had once been married. From what he had observed, he doubted that the monk was a threat to any woman's chastity, even his own wife's. He must learn more of what Simeon knew.

Thomas gathered up his robes and ran after the receiver.

⚭

"It is all my fault," Gytha wailed.

As soon as Sister Anne had left the prioress's chambers, Gytha had knocked at the door and begged for a private audience. Eleanor was beginning to wonder if God had suddenly changed the rule prohibiting women from being priests, with so many confessions crowding in on her.

Gytha now stood in front of Eleanor with her head bowed.

"Child, you should have told this to Crowner Ralf, but you are not to blame for what has happened. Indeed, you warned me of the distrust between village and priory. Although I listened, I failed to hear with my whole heart what you were telling me."

"Neither my brother nor I meant to do wrong, my lady."

Eleanor cut some bread and cheese, then pushed the serving across the table toward the young girl. "Sit. Eat. And tell me all, child."

"There is little but that Tostig knew who the dead man was. He was not a village man but he had worked on Tyndal's farms and came to our market days. My brother knew him from that."

"And when he died on our grounds, all believed one of the monks had killed him?"

Gytha nodded. "Some did for cert."

"Why?"

"Brother Rupert visited him not long after Prioress Felicia died. After that, Eadnoth refused to go near either priory or farm. He wouldn't say why but he acted like a badly frightened man. Some said he was losing his wits, a few that he was possessed, but many more thought that someone in the priory had threatened him."

Eleanor stood up, got another cup from the cabinet, poured some wine into it and watered it well. "You are not eating, child. I do not want you ill over this. And drink the wine. It will strengthen you." She watched while Gytha took a small bite and then another. "Did I not promise you that no harm would ever come from telling me the truth, however hard it might be for me to hear it. It grieves me that so many fear the inhabitants of the priory because most of us are Normans. Perhaps they do not know that not all of us are, although your brother should. Whatever the case, we are all children of God and equal in His sight, whether we be Saxon, Norman, or even a Scot or a wild Welshman," Eleanor said, trying to make Gytha smile.

"Sometimes that has been forgotten, my lady." The girl's expression remained solemn.

"During the time of Prioress Felicia?"

"She was a kindly woman and meant well. Brother Rupert was gentle and ministered to the spiritual needs of everyone without hesitation. Neither seemed comfortable in dealings with the secular world, despite all that, and they did little to protect us from those who were harsher in their commerce with us."

"And who might that be?"

"Brother Simeon was one. He did not treat us as if we were all equal in the sight of God. When crops failed or sickness came or times were hard for other reasons, he called us sinful creatures that deserved whatever evil had befallen us. He gave no mercy in the matter of tithes. When we took our complaints to Prioress Felicia, she told us to see Prior Theobald. And when we spoke with him, he would just shake his head in sadness and say that the world was full of evil and grief or that mortal men were weak creatures in need of greater prayer. Homilies but no action."

Eleanor shook her head. "And Brother John?" she asked with sadness in her voice.

Gytha put her head in her hands. "Brother John is a good man like Brother Rupert was. I cannot believe he is guilty of murder! Must he die like Brother Rupert and Eadnoth? Is the end of the world coming that good men now die like dogs, even in a community dedicated to God?"

Eleanor's eyes widened in shock. She reached over to take the young girl's hand. "Don't be afraid! If Brother John is innocent, he will not die. Evil may have attacked this house of God, but this house is not evil. I swear it on my own honor!"

Gytha squeezed her hand and wiped her cheeks dry. "My brother did say your coming to Tyndal might bode well for change. He..."

There was a sharp rap at the chamber door. The prioress straightened up and answered with anger in her voice.

Sister Ruth entered, pushing a dirty young fellow about Gytha's age at arm's length in front of her. The lines of her scowl were so deeply etched into her forehead they were black.

"This foul-smelling creature demanded entry. I tried to keep him out, but he would not take my nay for an answer. Fa, but he stinks!" The nun stepped backwards in disgust.

The lad did smell like something rotting. His clothes were rags and his shoulders and chest were bursting what few seams held. Tears had cleaned two paths down his blackened cheeks. Gytha started at the sight of him

"Your name, my son?" Eleanor asked, reaching out her hand.

"Eadmund, the son of Eadnoth." He hawked and spat at the sight of the prioress's proffered hand. Although his body was not fully fleshed and muscled, his voice was that of a man.

Sister Ruth started to cuff the young man for his rudeness, then withdrew her hand when she realized she would have to touch his filthy cheek.

Gytha had no such qualms. She reached over and shoved him so hard he rocked back on his heels. "Show some manners, Eadmund!"

Eleanor looked back at Gytha with a silent question in her eyes.

"He is a good lad, my lady, for all his ill manners."

"Then leave us with our thanks, Sister Ruth, and we will hear what he has to say."

"My lady, it is not safe to leave you alone with such a ruffian."

"Then get Brother Jo…Thomas, who may be in the sacristy still. He can wait outside my door in case of need."

Sister Ruth rushed from the room so quickly she left the chamber door open. Eleanor rose and slowly shut it.

"Will you have something to eat, my son?" she said and pointed at the food still on the table.

He looked ravenously at the hunk of cheese and bread but angrily shook his head from side to side.

"If I were to guess, lad, I'd say you hadn't eaten in awhile. Please take something."

"I take nothing from the priory."

"Eadmund!" Gytha said, putting her hands on her hips. "You cannot eat pride, and Prioress Eleanor will not hurt you."

The lad looked wildly back and forth between Eleanor and Gytha, then charged at the table, grabbed both bread and cheese and began stuffing huge chunks into his mouth. Bits dropped from his lips. He ate like an animal that knows it might never find another meal.

Gytha looked at him, sorrow casting a shadow in her eyes, then she glanced at Eleanor to see her reaction. The tiny nun sat calmly, her expression sad as she watched the boy, nay, both man and boy, bolt the food. Finally, the feeding frenzy over, Eadmund belched loudly. Then he looked wide-eyed at the prioress and began to cry.

"You've poisoned me, y' have," he moaned.

Eleanor started in shock. "Poison? Why would I do a thing like that?"

"'Cause you killed my pa, you did. You're bloody devils!"

The door opened. Eadmund jumped up and ran to the wall just under the window. Sister Ruth stuck her head in, glaring in fury at the youth. "Brother Thomas is no longer here, my lady. While we wait for him, I shall…"

"Sister, please leave us. Should the young man wish to depart, he is free to go. In the meantime, stay without and shut the door behind you."

"But…"

"As I said, sister."

The chamber door slammed shut.

Eleanor turned to Eadmund, who was looking up at the window like a cornered cat calculating a jump. She wanted to reach out to him but knew such a gesture would only make matters worse.

"Eadmund?" she asked in a soft voice. "Stay there and I will stand over here." She gestured to the wall on her right. "If you want to run, you can reach the door and leave any time you want." Then she calmly walked to the far corner, gesturing Gytha to follow her. "You can see that you are free to leave if you choose, and neither Gytha nor I could stop you. You heard me give orders to let you go when you open that door."

The look in the young man's eyes grew less feral. He slid with his back still against the wall into a sitting position and stared at Eleanor.

"You must have wanted to talk to me if you braved Sister Ruth to get in," Eleanor said with gentle voice and a slight smile.

He looked at her, his expression still wary. He jerked his head in Gytha's direction. "Her brother said you were trustworthy. And he's a trusty one himself, aye, although his sister works for you black devils."

"Has anything happened to Gytha despite her being here?"

Eadmund belched again. "Nay. Other than she is now fat and fine."

Gytha snorted.

"Then we are not all devils, surely?"

The young man's look darkened. "Maybe not but I cannot say who is and who isn't."

"You know Tostig's judgement is good and that he would not have sent you into danger alone. He'd have come himself if he thought you had anything to fear. He seems to be both a brave and a decent man."

Eadmund nodded. "He said he'd come with me if it would make me feel safer, but I said I would come alone. He gave me his word you'd not hurt me." In puffing out his chest, he now looked more a boy than the man he was becoming.

"And have I?"

Eadmund belched for the third time. "I'm not dead yet...and the cheese was good." He looked around as if hoping, despite his misgivings, that there would be more.

"Then you have shown courage. Perhaps now you will say what you came to tell me?"

Once again, the boy looked like a small and helpless child. "I don't know what to say." He smeared what Eleanor suspected were tears away from his eyes, then looked at Gytha with ferocity. "Get her out!" he shouted. "I'll not tell anything if she's to hear me."

Mentally shoving rules aside, Eleanor gestured to Gytha to leave. The girl hesitated, then realized the boy was more afraid than angry, and she quickly left, shutting the door softly behind her.

"Now then, lad. What did you come to say?"

The boy put his head into his hands and began to weep in gulping sobs. "He threatened me, forced me to fuck him, he did, then drove my father out of his wits, swearing he'd make sure we died if either of us said one word. He took me down to that cave and made me swyve him. He gave us money, but my father grew mad with grief. I couldn't leave my father. He needed me to care for him. I had no choice. I had to....I'll burn in Hell for this!" The lad howled like a wounded wolf in a trap.

Eleanor felt a pain as sharp as a dagger thrust in her heart. "Hell shall not have you, Eadmund. That I promise," she whispered. "Now tell me who did this monstrous thing to you...."

"The tall black monk."

"Brother John?"

"Nay! When I told him my sins in confession after Brother Rupert died, he wept, he did, but said he could say nothing unless I spoke out. He begged me to tell Sister Ruth. I would have none of that!" He coughed from swallowed tears, then wiped a hand across his nose. "She's no different than the others. After you came, he beseeched me to talk to Gytha's brother and ask his advice about coming to you. Tostig said you could be trusted...."

"And thus you bravely came. If not Brother John, lad, then who was the man...?"

"The fat one. Simeon, he's called."

With that, the boy began to wail again, and this time, when Eleanor reached out to him, he fell into her arms.

Chapter Thirty-Five

"The creature lies!" Sister Ruth was shaking with anger as she marched out of the prioress's chambers.

Thomas followed, his face without expression.

"Why do you say that, sister?" Eleanor came last, then closed her chamber door quietly behind. Like a mother would her own child, she had tucked the distraught lad up in blankets from her own bed and sent Gytha running to the hospital for help and medicine to ease him into a dreamless sleep. Although he had calmed, she knew he still suffered from the occasional hiccup of sobs behind the closed door.

"This loutish animal is not worthy to speak his name. Brother Simeon is above reproach. He would never commit such an unspeakable vileness."

"Indeed we would hear what Brother Simeon has to say for himself...."

"How could you even think that such a base thing would be more truthful than a man of our receiver's high station and reputation?" Sister Ruth's face flushed with rage. "Treating low creatures as equals is an error you have been making since your arrival. Forgive me for being so blunt, my lady, but you do show ignorance about much."

Eleanor curled her hands into fists and ground them against her body. This was not the time to lose her temper with the woman. "Then teach me," she said.

Sister Ruth hesitated only a moment before continuing, her now mottled face stiff with hatred for Eleanor. "First, you are ignorant of what occurred before your arrival. Even now, you know little of us all. Prioress Felicia had been long with us and knew she could trust our good receiver to provide her with suitable guidance. It may not be proper for me to speak ill of Prior Theobald, but he is not a man to take charge, as he should. If it had not been for Brother Simeon, we might well have suffered many deprivations over the years. He is an excellent steward. We thought for sure he would become a prior elsewhere, if not here." She waved her hand at Eleanor. "This is the man you now treat with such little respect."

"So I have heard, but Brother Rupert...?"

"Brother Rupert was a kind man, loved by us all, but he was weak in his dealings with Prioress Felicia. Where he should have given her firm direction, she sometimes guided him, but Brother Simeon wisely left the two of them to do what they would within the confines here. As he often told me, work within the priory was woman's work and good enough in its place, but stewardship of the lands properly belonged in the hands of a man."

Eleanor suddenly raised her head. "*Often*, you say, sister?"

Sister Ruth paled. "As porteress, I had occasion, proper occasion, to talk with Brother Simeon."

"And you agreed with his methods of running the priory lands without consulting the prioress?"

"Indeed. As Brother Simeon said, that is as it should be. It is unnatural for Adam to be ruled by Eve. I would not be so unwomanly as to disagree, my lady."

As I have disagreed and will always disagree, Eleanor thought, biting her lip. "And such would have been your approach to running Tyndal when you became prioress after the death of your former superior, had I not usurped the position."

"My lady, I would not..." Ruth stuttered, then dropped her eyes.

"You expected to become prioress, did you not, sister? When the priory voted, you were chosen and would have ascended to the position if the King and Abbess had not wished otherwise. There is no shame or wrong in acknowledging a fact."

"Yes, my lady, but I hold no malice...."

"Nor did I think you did," Eleanor said, knowing otherwise but smiling disarmingly. "So tell me one thing, good sister?"

"Yes, my lady?"

"The day Brother Rupert's body was found in the cloister, you left your post at the door to the passageway into the nuns' quarters, as indeed you should have, for Mass and Chapter."

The nun nodded confirmation with a wary hesitation.

"When you left the door, did you leave it unlocked?"

Sister Ruth turned pale. "I did not!"

Eleanor raised her eyebrows in doubt.

"She tells the truth, my lady."

Eleanor, Ruth, and Thomas all turned to look at the person standing with Gytha at the top of the stone stairs.

"It was I."

"At whose instruction, Sister Christina?" Eleanor asked softly.

"Brother Simeon's."

Sister Ruth fainted.

༄

Anne, whose arrival had been delayed by a crisis at the hospital, had just joined Thomas and Eleanor at the crumb-strewn table in the prioress's chambers. With a serene manner, Christina had calmed youth and nun, then led Eadmund and Ruth off to the hospital with Gytha's help, leaving the other three alone.

"How did Brother Simeon know that Sister Christina would be the one to check and then lock the passageway door?" Anne asked the prioress.

"Sister Ruth told him. As we have all noticed, Sister Christina becomes so lost in prayer that she often fails to notice when the other nuns rise and leave for Chapter. She is always the last to leave. When Sister Ruth was elected prioress, she asked our infirmarian to check the passageway door after Mass, in case someone waited without, and then lock the door again so that Brother Rupert and Sister Ruth could come immediately to Chapter after services. Brother Simeon knew that Sister Christina would ask no questions if he told her to leave the door open and that she might well forget he had even done so. Her concerns are not of this world." Eleanor looked down at the rushes under her feet. She did not know if she were more saddened that Christina's trusting nature had been abused or more grieved that Sister Ruth's bitter resentment had caused her to, well, perhaps not lie as much as fail to tell the truth when needed.

"Then you think Brother Simeon killed Brother Rupert and brought the body into the cloister while we were all at Chapter?" Anne asked.

Eleanor nodded.

"I did find Brother Rupert's cross outside the nave near the passageway door to the nuns' quarters," Thomas said.

"Why was the poor man killed in the first place? Surely our receiver could have confessed his sins? The Church allows penance even for sodomy. Murder was not necessary here." Tears slowly filled Anne's eyes.

"Worldly ambition can be a powerful thing, sister. Confession and contrition might save the soul, but men of power in the Church do not view indiscreet sodomy in the lower orders with indifference. Those found guilty of it are removed from any position of authority, if not expelled from the Order and left to beg on the byways with lepers," Eleanor said. "Hard penance for a man used to the sweet honey taste of power."

Thomas chewed on a finger. "Simeon also had reason to fear for his very life, unless his family was influential enough and cared to intervene. If Brother Rupert revealed what he was doing with Eadmund, our receiver might have been burned at the stake as an example to all that sinned in like fashion. Imagining such foretaste of hellfire is enough to unman most of us."

Anne studied the monk in silence for a very long moment. "You speak with authority, brother. I accept what you both say, although I do not understand the need for worldly ambition in a community dedicated to a higher glory." Then her voice turned angry. "But Brother Simeon had bought silence from the boy and his father. How could our good priest have known, and how would our receiver have found out that he did?"

"I can only guess." Thomas shook his head. "Perhaps Brother Rupert began to suspect about Simeon from something he had heard or seen. Perhaps he had even seen the two together in questionable circumstances. Since we now know from Gytha that Brother Rupert had gone to Eadmund's father, he may have wanted to confirm his suspicions with Eadnoth, and Eadnoth might have later told our receiver of Brother Rupert's visit. For cert, Brother Simeon would have feared that Brother Rupert would pass the news on to the mother house in France." Thomas' voice caught as he rubbed his tired eyes. "Paid or not, from the distraught behavior of Eadmund's father before he, too, was killed, I'd say he could no longer endure what was being done to his son. Eadmund did say he had lost his wits. Perhaps the father even meant to kill Simeon himself. That would explain the knife when you saw him at the cave, my lady."

"Still, Eadmund swears neither he nor his father said a word," Eleanor said. "Although the lad may not have known all his father did or said."

Sister Anne looked pensive for a moment. "There was one thing. At the time I thought it was of no moment, but now I wonder...."

"What?" asked Eleanor.

"As Prioress Felicia was dying, she fell into a deep sleep. I thought she would never awaken from it, but she suddenly became quite agitated. She thrashed around in her bed, moaning and reaching out as if she were trying to grab something. To calm her, I took her hand and spoke gently, thinking to soothe her into a quiet passing. Then her eyes opened wide and she grabbed my hand with an uncommonly strong grip and begged me to tell Brother Rupert something. As I remember, she said she had accused wrongly and then she used the phrase: 'it was not the one we feared, but rather the other.' Before I could ask our priest to come to her, she died."

"And did you tell him?"

"Yes, and I saw some light of understanding in his eyes, but he said nothing further to me."

Eleanor bent her head. *I am deeply puzzled by this. What is the connection between her words and Brother Rupert's subsequent visit to Eadnoth? If no one told them about this heinous crime, how could they have suspected it? And her words suggest they thought someone else was involved in what troubled her so much she had to speak before she died. Nay, it is more likely that they would have realized there was something amiss with the account rolls.* She shook her head. *Can that be? To my knowledge, only the receiver worked on them. Who else could be involved or even suspected?* Eleanor looked up at Sister Anne. "What do you think, sister?"

"I have nothing to say, my lady. I do not know what troubled Prioress Felicia so." Anne's expression was both distressed and questioning.

"When I looked over the account rolls myself," Eleanor continued, "I found that harvests had been almost as plentiful as usual, but the incomes from them were not quite as high as they should have been. The discrepancy seemed minor and I told Brother Simeon that I planned to visit some of the nearby lands to ask some questions. It did not occur to me that the harvests had been greater and the rents properly paid but *both* improperly recorded. As far as I can tell, only he was guilty of this act. He was clever enough to modify the entries just enough so they'd appear reasonable to anyone looking for the obvious theft. I find no evidence of a second person being involved."

"In that I concur, my lady," Thomas added. "He did not take me into his confidence on this matter and I know of no one else whom he so trusted."

"Perhaps we will never know what specifically led Prioress Felicia and Brother Rupert to their revelation," Eleanor said.

Sister Anne frowned in thought.

Brother Thomas seemed lost in it. "I find it hard to believe that Eadnoth did not complain to anyone in authority at Tyndal," he said. "How long could a parent turn his head in such a situation? To someone for whom hunger is so sharp that they will sell their child's soul for a mouthful of food, money might buy silence for awhile, but such food would soon fill that mouth with worms."

"As Gytha explained to me, we are still the conquerors in the eyes of many. We may think we treat all with courtesy and fairness, but, when it is Saxon versus Norman, the village believes we protect our own first. There may be some validity in their view."

"And so they distrust the rulers of the priory."

"Yes."

"Although I do not dispute the boy's story, my lady," Thomas continued, "I find one thing strange. Eadnoth would have become a rich man if Simeon had given him all the money stolen from the priory. Yet he was dressed in rags, as is his son, while we must scrimp to have enough to buy food through the winter months."

"Eadmund said his father could not use what he was given. The lad says Eadnoth went to the cliffs above the sea, and he watched while his father tossed the coin into the waves, screaming that Satan could take it all back and return his son's soul and manhood."

"Indeed, Eadnoth loved his son and would have lost his wits over these events," Anne said. "Nonetheless, the sum does seem too vast for one bribe."

"Or perhaps there were others Simeon paid to be silent," Thomas muttered absently. "Others who have not and may never come forward out of fear and shame. The penalties for sodomy are dire ones. Had Eadmund been younger, he would have been found innocent, but he is just man enough to have lost that protection, and all Simeon's victims might be of like age." Thomas winced with unwelcome memories. "Our receiver might have saved his own life by showing sufficient contrition to the right bishop, but those of no influence suffer greatly: public excommunication, an edict announced in every church in the kingdom; to be forever shunned by family and friends. Willing or not, those he committed sodomy with would face hell both in this life and in the hereafter."

Eleanor glanced at Thomas as he rested his chin on his fist, eyes closed. There was something odd in his tone, she thought. "Some probably went to worldly extravagance. Simeon is fond of fine plate and good wine. I have seen the gold goblets in the prior's lodgings and the fine wines served, yet I use good pewter for my guests."

Thomas opened his eyes and smiled at her, a look that gave more joy to her heart than it should.

"It seems the most influential visitors were entertained in the prior's quarters by Brother Simeon," Eleanor continued. "Prioress Felicia supped only with the wives and daughters, for whom fine red gold was not needed. But something else disturbs me. Brother Simeon is right-handed, yet you believe the murderer was left-handed, sister."

"I could be wrong, my lady."

"Or perhaps Eadmund's father killed Brother Rupert?" Eleanor suggested. "He was left-handed and wild with grief at what he had allowed his son to suffer. Maybe he saw the good monk as the servant of Satan."

"Then who killed Eadnoth?" Anne asked. "And do not suggest Brother John! He is as sinful a mortal as any man, but one whom God has forgiven. No, it must have been the same man." She glanced down at her hands clasped tightly in her lap.

"Or not," Eleanor replied, watching the nun's hands nervously clutch at each other. Then she looked at Thomas. "You are deep in contemplation, brother."

Thomas blinked as if suddenly awakened and looked up. "My lady, forgive me, but while I have been listening to all you both have said, I was thinking further on Brother Simeon and Brother Rupert."

"And?"

He turned to Anne. "Besides telling Brother Rupert about Prioress Felicia's dying words, did you tell anyone else?"

"Brother John."

"Did anyone know that you had told him?"

"Sister Ruth was with me…"

Thomas looked over at Eleanor, his face gray with fear. "My lady, if you would take my advice, I would urge that you call the crowner and his men quickly. If you do not, I fear Brother John will not be alive when you go for your announced visit with him tomorrow."

Chapter Thirty-Six

"I like it not, monk."

Crowner Ralf scowled at Thomas and shifted uneasily with impatience. He and one of his men were armed with knife and sword. The other carried a small crossbow. All were dressed in leather armor.

"We have logic on our side, man. Brother Simeon knows that only one other man may know his secret about the theft of funds as well as the reason for it, and that is Brother John. If he kills him, there is only the word of Eadmund. And who credits the tales of villeins against the word of a Norman, a man of good family and well respected for his stewardship of the priory at that? Our only hope is to catch him trying to kill Brother John. Your brother is sheriff, Crowner. Your witness and testimony would be respected."

"So you want Brother John to be bait. I think we should be more concerned with saving his life."

"The souls of one, quite possibly two slain men cry out for justice. If we do nothing, Brother John may be murdered tonight and his body arranged to look like a suicide. Of course I could be wrong and Brother John might live to tell his tale, but I doubt Simeon would take the chance that the monk's tale will be believed over his own. Even if it is not, Simeon may fear that his hope for future advancement will be diminished with the taint of the accusation. Certainly Simeon will never confess to the murders or the attempted murder of our good prioress. If Brother John seems to have taken his own life, surely most will conclude he did so out of guilt for the murders, and Simeon will be exonerated. Eadmund's story will have no credence. Even if you set men to guard him and Brother John survives the night, there is a chance Simeon's word will still be taken over his, a former apothecary, but not if the receiver tries to kill the monk and we witness it."

"You ask me who is most likely to be believed in this ugly matter: Eadmund, the villein, and John, a man of uncertain birth; or Simeon, the son of a man of rank? Satan's tits, monk! The noble brothers in the Church will protect their own. The cleric who literally got away with murder during the reign of our second King Henry was not unusual. Justice has little room to swing her balances in courts ruled by highborn priests." Ralf snorted, then smiled. "You continue to amaze me with your understanding of the real world, monk. If I didn't know better, I'd swear you were only acting a monk's part. "

"The tonsure is real, Crowner," Thomas said, lowering his head to hide his flushing face. "You do agree we have little choice but to follow my plan?"

Ralf grunted. "I never acquired a taste for gambling. Your plan could lose us both Annie's former husband as well as you and still leave Simeon free."

"And you as a witness to it all, remember. Trying to get Simeon to confess otherwise is impossible and would leave us with an innocent man who might be found guilty of crimes he did not commit. And I think John would rather die in a fight to save him than die alone like a trussed chicken at Simeon's hand."

"Aye, but if he died, would he care about the difference?"

Thomas laughed. "Now there, Crowner, is where it pays to be a man of faith. Indeed, in the afterlife, he'd care that we believed him to be innocent."

"Your humor is not like that of any other monk I have ever met either, brother, but I will grant you the logic of your plan."

"And you and your men will not enter unless I give the sign?"

Ralf looked at his two lieutenants and smiled. They nodded. Their eyes never blinked.

As the quartet reached the top of the stairs to the passage, which led on one side to the monks' dormitory and on the other to the latrines, two of them slipped into the shadows. Ralf and Thomas stood looking at the door of one of the small storage rooms that lay along the narrow way to the latrines. All was silent from the room where Brother John lay a prisoner.

"Good luck," Ralf mouthed before he too stole deep into the darkness of the corridor.

Thomas walked quietly into another empty room and crouched along a wall. He could not see the moon from this windowless stone storage chamber and thus could not mark time. It might have been an hour he waited. Or only a minute. It felt like the rest of his earthly life.

In the darkness, he began to distrust what seemed so clear in the earlier daylight. Surely, Sister Ruth had told Simeon about Prioress Felicia's last words. She told him everything, it seemed, everything in return for praise, the warmth of which must have filled her lonely heart like wine. Had the receiver's contempt for women saved her life? And Sister Anne's?

Perhaps the monk thought he could control one woman with flattery and the other with threats to expose some violation of her chastity vow, but Brother John was a man. His word might be given credence. He was a threat.

Thomas felt an uneasy pang of guilt. On the surface, Simeon was a man of the world, rough and jovial, a man he could understand in a world of monks. He had also befriended Thomas, aye, accepted him when he first arrived and understood him well. Simeon, it seemed, had cared for another before he had come to Tyndal and suffered for it too. If the prioress and Sister Anne were horrified at Simeon's acts of sodomy, how would they feel if they knew of his own? Giles was no youth, but to those in the Church, or in the courts of kings, there was no difference. Indeed he and the receiver had a kinship here. Did he not owe Simeon something for that?

Thomas had hesitated about speaking up when he suspected John and Eadmund of being lovers. Why did he now turn on Simeon? Unlike the receiver, John was a strange man, hard on the outside but soft like a woman on the inside, especially in his dealings with the novices. Had Brother Rupert and Prioress Felicia suspected him, as Thomas had as well, of questionable relations with the boys? Was that what the old prioress had realized as she was dying? That they were wrong about Brother John? He hadn't wanted to suggest such in front of Sister Anne or Prioress Eleanor. The shock of what Simeon had done was bad enough, but he did not want either of them to start asking if even more monks at Tyndal were guilty of sexual sins as well. With their quick perceptions, they might, in time, begin to look at Thomas himself.

He shuddered.

Nay, there was a great difference between what Simeon had done and what he thought John had, but was he right now about both men? Thomas had trusted what he'd known, distrusted the strange, and did not question his judgement. He did not, that is, until he realized he was beginning to enjoy the world this gray monastic place offered. Indeed, he was starting to understand how a warrior like Andrew might find peace here, a peace that Thomas longed for as well. And then there were the women like Sister Anne and the prioress, creatures he liked but did not desire. Tyndal was a world turned quite upside down from the one he had known. Neither world was perfect, for cert, yet nothing created by men ever was.

Thomas shifted with discomfort.

Simeon. Simeon had told him how gentleness had been battered from him with whips and mockery as a youth, and Thomas had seen the receiver burning to ash whatever had remained with his own anger and hot ambition.

Brother John. The novices respected and loved John, who loved them back with kindness and understanding. He was a tormented man, for cert, who beat all earthly passions into submission whenever the Prince of Darkness tempted him with whatever sins he longed to commit. Did the man love boys? Aye, love was there but Thomas no longer believed it was a dark lust.

There was much about both Thomas still did not comprehend. How could a man who had taken his hand in understanding, albeit in a drunken moment, so brutally kill two others? Might not John be more tortured and thus more likely to commit such a crime? Thomas cursed this doubting. He must be right about what had happened. He must.

Nonetheless, the question of whether or not the murderer was left-handed gnawed at him. If the guilty man was left-handed, John, or someone else, was guilty, Simeon innocent. Perhaps Sister Ruth had been right to cast doubt on Eadmund's confession. The lad might have yet undiscovered reasons for casting such an accusation at the receiver. Had they all jumped to the wrong conclusions too quickly? Thomas groaned silently. The darkness pressed down on him with...

A faint light fluttered along the sides of the stone walls outside his hiding chamber.

Thomas tensed.

There was no sound at first, and then he heard the soft scraping of shoes on the steps. The light grew brighter.

Thomas held his breath.

For a moment there was absolute silence as the wavering torch flame threw twitching patches of light and black against the walls. Then Thomas heard the clink of a key, and listened as the door to Brother John's cell swung open.

Chapter Thirty-Seven

"Wait!"

Thomas stood in the doorway, his hands resting on either side of the door as he pretended to catch his breath.

"What in God's name are you doing here?" Simeon growled. Brother John was still struggling, but Simeon's sheer weight and height had overpowered the novice master. The receiver stood, twisting the wiry monk's hands with one large fist until John cried in agony. With his other, Simeon held a knife to the monk's throat.

Thomas blinked. The knife was in Simeon's left hand. "I never noticed you were left-handed, brother," he said.

Simeon's laugh was hoarse. "Using my left hand was another reason for my father to beat me. He tied it behind me until I learned to use my right as godly men do. I never quite did so but my writing was serviceable enough."

Sweat began to drip down Thomas' chest. "My lord, I came to help you."

"If this is a trick…"

"Why would I trick you? Didn't you befriend me when I first came to Tyndal? Didn't you see that we two, of all men here, would have a special understanding? I knew that you should be the one to run the priory, not the new prioress, that unnatural woman, and I resented her arrogance but could find no way to show you my full loyalty until now."

Thomas hoped the fluttering light from the torch behind the monk did not deceive him. Simeon seemed to relax his tense grasp of John ever so slightly. Thomas glanced at John's face but shadows hid any expression, and he did not dare to give him a sign. He continued in hurried but hushed tones. "Brother Rupert did not understand your relationship with Eadmund as I do, did he? He must have…"

"He understood nothing!" Simeon whined like a kicked pup. "I loved the young man like a son, but the Prince of Darkness entered my body and transformed me into a lustful woman whenever I saw Eadmund working in the priory fields. I became blind with desire for him. I was under a spell!"

"And you…"

"…fell to my knees before the lad and asked him, begged him, to come to bed with me. Then I took him to the cave and threatened him, forced him to make me his whore. When he left, I beat myself with my whip and Satan fled. For a while."

"Did Brother Rupert discover you?"

"Nay, Eadmund's father did. He came upon us together in the cave, and he ran. Screaming. When I found him later, he swore he'd tell Prioress Felicia or Brother Rupert, but I bought his silence with threats and money. No one would listen to a villein's word over the Receiver of Tyndal Priory, I said."

"Why, then, kill Eadnoth?"

"He came to me and said that money was not enough. He had heard in the village that our new prioress would give as much credence to the word of a simple man as to one of better birth." Simeon's eyes glittered. "That wayward woman who now leads us would never understand that I was not willfully sinning, brother. *She* would not care that I might be burned at the stake for what the *Devil* made my body do!" His last words were spoken in a wail of agony.

Thomas winced. "Indeed, my lord, you are quite right."

"I had to kill Eadnoth. You see, I had no choice."

"Aye, I see that, but why kill Brother Rupert?"

"After the old prioress's death, I saw him leave the priory one day, something he rarely did anymore with his old bones. I followed him. He went to see Eadnoth. I couldn't hear their words, but Brother Rupert came to me soon after and told me there were rumors about a monk having sinful relations with a young man. He did not accuse me but said that the guilty man should be found out and brought to Church justice. At that time, Sister Ruth was elected prioress. She is a proper woman of good birth, one who knew her place in the world of men and would never believe a villein over me. I felt safe. Then a stranger replaced her, this Eleanor, a woman I did not know. I feared Brother Rupert would tell her tales before I could gain her ear, so I told him I had found the man he sought, that he should meet me by the cave so he could see for himself as the man committed the very sin. When he arrived, I stabbed him and hid his body in the cave until I could safely carry it to the nuns' cloister. So I would get no blood on me in the transfer, I changed his robes and buried the bloody ones." Simeon ground his teeth.

"Why castrate him?"

Simeon laughed, his voice thin and high. "Wasn't he a traitor to me, Thomas? Wasn't the King's enemy, Simon de Montfort, castrated after he was killed in battle? Should a traitor to me be treated any differently?"

"Indeed...." Sharp bile rose into Thomas' throat. Simeon was quite mad, he thought, swallowing quickly.

"And wasn't it a clever thing to do! I thought of it after I had killed him. We all knew how close the priest and the old prioress were. A pious man so filled with guilt over his lust might well follow the example of some of our early saints and castrate himself in the cloister, the very center of his sin. Or, perhaps, a lustful nun might have killed him and done the deed out of revenge or guilt. Finding his body in the nuns' cloister might suggest that too. So many reasons could be seen for such an act in such a place. It pointed everywhere. And nowhere."

"You are a clever man, for cert!" Then Thomas turned his head. "But hush, my lord!" he whispered. "I came to warn you.

The prioress is planning to trap you. She has sent for the crowner, and his men may be surrounding us as I speak."

Simeon clutched Brother John to him more tightly. "This is loyalty?" he snarled. "To keep me here while they arrive? And how then did you find your way to me without them knowing it? And how did you propose we escape? I am no fool, Thomas."

"Nor did I think you one, my lord. There is an entrance unnoted..."

"A man new to the priory knows an entrance I do not after all my years at Tyndal? Come, Thomas, I took you for an intelligent man. Surely you can lie better than that."

"Begging your pardon, my lord, but I would guess it has been some time since you have had to escape a lady's chamber when her lord did unexpectedly return."

Simeon's lips twisted into a smile.

"The latrine is not a pleasant ladder to safety, but few men would suspect a monk of knowing that weak point in, shall we say, this castle's defense."

Simeon's throaty laugh cracked like fragile clay. "Thomas, you are a good man. Indeed, I must make up for striking you on the head that night. It was out of my own fear of what you might find out if you caught... But first we must be gone. After I dispatch this troublesome monk...."

"My lord!" Thomas' eyes widened in horror as he pointed behind Simeon. "The torch!"

For just an instant as he turned to look, Simeon loosened his hold on Brother John, the edge of the knife dropped slightly. John threw himself backward, knocking Simeon off balance. As the two men fell on their backs, Simeon's knife flew out of his hand.

"Yes!" Thomas shouted as he dove for the knife.

John rolled just out of Simeon's grasp.

As he seized the knife, Thomas heard a strange whine above him, then a thud, and a grunt. When he looked up, he saw Simeon lying lifeless in the straw, his eyes staring blankly at the ceiling. A crossbow bolt stuck out of his chest.

"How sad," Ralf said with a half frown as he looked at the crossbowman. "I do believe the man is dead. You must learn better control of your weapon."

Chapter Thirty-Eight

"The Church had the right to try Brother Simeon for his crimes, Ralf." Sister Anne's face was flushed with outrage.

"Indeed, Annie, but my man fired the crossbow by accident. A steady fellow overall, but I did reprove him severely. He's been ordered off for more practice. We cannot have deputies carrying weapons they don't know how to handle properly. An innocent person might have been shot." He bowed his head. "When I explained the accident to Prioress Eleanor, she did not condemn me as you have."

"I know you better, and you haven't changed a bit. When you do not trust the authorities to conduct what you consider a proper hearing, you take justice into your own hands. Such an act was capricious and unworthy of a civilized man."

"That was unkind. Come, Annie, surely you know me to be fair and honest." Pain was evident in Ralf's eyes as he looked at the nun.

Sister Anne looked down at her hands. "Aye, Ralf, you are that, but one of these days you will condemn a man for sins he did not commit. You are not God. Do not forget it."

Ralf turned his face from her and said nothing.

Sister Anne reached over and briefly squeezed his arm. "You are still a good man. Brother Simeon was not. Indeed, your sentence on him was kinder and quicker than he would have gotten from any other earthly court." She smiled at him. "Now he is in the hands of God, who will be harsher on him than any mortal man, I think."

"Annie, you know how much I care about what you..." Ralf reached for her hand, but she withdrew it quickly.

"Hush, Ralf, and go. You saved John, for which I am deeply in your debt. I shall keep your secret, but do not think you have fooled our prioress with your story. She is wiser than her youth would suggest, and I suspect she knows as well as I do that you ordered your man to kill Simeon. Still, she will keep her own counsel about it. I think she knows you for the decent man you are."

Ralf opened his mouth, then shut it as he watched Sister Anne walk away from him. After she was gone, he bowed his head and wept, his hand pressed against a heart that ached with a very old sorrow.

⌒☙⌒

Thomas stood at the entrance gate, straight-backed and hands folded into his sleeves, as he watched the man in black ride slowly away. When the rider had disappeared into the dusty distance, Thomas slumped against the rough walls of the priory and did nothing to stop the flood of his tears.

"I have made a bargain with the Devil," he muttered. Indeed, he was beginning to wonder if the man who had saved him from the stake was no man at all, but one of Satan's minions or even the Prince of Darkness himself. "Nay, with that tonsure, he is surely a man of the Church," Thomas muttered, but in his anger he refused to concede that such a man could be godly.

He shook his head to clear his thoughts. The man in black had been contented with Thomas' handling of Simeon. Quite clever, he had said, when he heard about the scene in the storage room, and the man's thin lips had even twitched into a shadow of a smile. Dead men could not testify to dark sins; the creditable living could be trusted not to speak of scandal; any rumors would be quelled. Yes, the demon messenger had said, it was all quite satisfactory. He looked pleased, even happy, if one could interpret anything at all from the man's colorless face and faded gray eyes.

And that was the end of the visit. Or nearly so. After the man had taken a final sip of reddish wine and stood to leave, Thomas had jumped up and demanded to know what else he had in mind for him and when his next assignment would be. He would not be played with like a mouse by a cat, he snapped.

The man had smiled at Thomas' anger and asked in return if he was comfortable at Tyndal.

"This forsaken pile of moldering rocks? This place where the air stinks of rotting fish and slime? What do you think? Of course I am pleased with this place. Who would not be content to stay in such bitter exile?" Thomas had virtually spat at the man, but he had spoken the truth, hidden in the abusive words. He wanted to stay. And he did not want this cursed shadow of Satan to know it.

"Then you shall, good monk. For a while. And when you are needed for some other task, I will come again. Needless to say, I cannot promise when or the circumstances. Nor, I might add, do you have any right to demand anything. You have life, after all, and now..." he waved his hand around the room gracefully, "a comfortable enough haven, despite the smell of the sea."

With that, the man had gestured at the door, and Thomas had led him to the gate where a handsome gray horse waited.

"Brother?"

Thomas started and looked around. Brother John was standing behind him at the entrance gate, his green eyes soft as young meadow grass on a spring afternoon.

"I was looking for you." John lowered his head. "I'm not sure there are words enough to thank you for saving my life."

Thomas looked at the man he had not trusted, a man he still did not fully understand, and was humbled by John's gratitude. "There is no need to thank me, brother," he mumbled and bowed his head.

John reached out and put his hand gently on Thomas' sleeve. "You did not like me, yet you risked your own life to save me.

You distrusted me, but you treated me with fairness. There is much to thank you for."

With John's touch, Thomas began to feel an unfamiliar peace flow through him, and the tension he had felt with the visit of his tormentor started to dissipate. He looked up at his brother monk and said, "Can you forgive me for my thoughts? That would be thanks enough."

John smiled. "There is no need to forgive what never hurt me."

"Then there is peace between us," Thomas heard himself say and realized he truly meant it.

"Peace, aye, and even understanding in time, for I do believe we have some things in common. The love of fine music, for one." John put his arm around Thomas' shoulder. "The novices are ready to practice, and the sound of their sweet voices might give both our souls a needed balm."

Then the two men went back into Tyndal Priory, the late summer sun warming their backs as they walked.

☙

Eleanor stood in her chambers, staring at the Mary Magdalene tapestry. Anne stood next to her, her head bowed.

"I grieve for Prior Theobald," she said to the prioress. "He loved Simeon."

"Simeon took good care of him, and the prior was incapable of seeing what sins were hidden in the man. I understand why he might mourn his loss," Eleanor said, looking away from the tapestry. "Sister Ruth has gone to weep in the chapel as well, but her sorrow is mixed with guilt. She will do hard penance for her willful blindness."

"Although the brother and I did not get along, I knew he had been a good steward at the priory for many years. His sins were grave, shocking, yet..."

Eleanor nodded at the hesitation. "Speak your thoughts."

"Am I sinful to say he had some good despite his evil?"

"Being mortal, we are all flawed and can only pray to keep our wickedness balanced with our virtues. Simeon lost that balance at some point. Do you know why?"

"He was a man I thought I understood, yet I did not. For cert, his gift of stewardship should have been offered up to the glory of God, not to his own credit. In that he had a fatal flaw." Anne looked at the prioress in silence, then said, "Others would say graver sins than ambition were his downfall, yet I cannot find it in my heart to so roundly condemn him."

Eleanor raised her eyebrows. "What mean you?"

"Many would say he was evil, a heretic, because he was a sodomite."

"You do not?"

"Have you not said yourself that love is not a sin?"

"I have. And someone much wiser than I has also said that love is sinful only when it leads a frail human to do evil in its name."

"I recognize that thought, my lady," Anne said, grasping her hands tightly.

"You should. It comes from Brother John. Continue."

"Might not any love be acceptable in God's sight if that love transformed a mortal into a better creature and thus closer to God?"

"I am no theologian, Anne, but, just between the two of us and for the sake of argument, let us say that I agree."

"Fire is said to purify as well as destroy. Had Simeon denied himself consummation of his lust, might not the heat of his passion have transformed him into a more compassionate and understanding being? If he had chosen that way, I would never have condemned him. His sin, I believe, was in rejecting the redemptive aspect of a denied earthly love and thus he became a dark force of Satan."

"You speak only of the denial of love's carnal expression as redemptive, a concept with which we both might well agree in view of our vocation. The Church, however, does condone copulation between men and women vowed to one another;

thus we cannot deny that there are good people who commit carnal acts. Therefore, within the privacy of this room, I do wonder this: what of a couple who falls into lustful acts, man and woman or man and man, whose union has not been blessed? Are they incapable of using that love they share to become better creatures?"

Anne paled. "Could such happen unless the union were blessed? For cert, I am not a theologian either, my lady, and I dare not speak to that. I await your instruction."

"And kindly you do not suggest that I have spoken heresy, Anne. Nor do I mean such, but my heart tells me that there is so much enlightenment yet to be granted from a Wisdom far superior to our own. Perhaps it will be given to us at a time and place when we are most open to understanding. So I, too, shall leave my query to another day and await instruction." Then Eleanor hesitated. "I have another question to ask. You have never told me why Brother John called you to the chapel the night Simeon attacked me. Nor how he came to have his own key so he could so freely come and go."

Anne flushed scarlet.

"You gave him your key, did you not, long ago? And perhaps told Prioress Felicia that you had lost your own?" The prioress's voice was gentle.

Anne nodded and covered her eyes. "You have guessed correctly, my lady, but he did not use the key for sinful purposes. Nor did I. We sometimes met. That is true, but never for carnal reasons. We love each other only as brother and sister and find a comfort in talking together as such."

"I believe you, sister, but in giving him your key, you granted him rights that were not yours to give. Such a decision was rightly left to Prioress Felicia." Eleanor raised her hand as Sister Anne began to speak. "Indeed, there may be good reason for the novice master and my confessor to have his own key, but Brother John must return it to me until I make that decision."

"He will, my lady. You have been most generous to both of us."

"Now tell me why he wanted to meet with you that night."

"When Eadmund refused to tell anyone but John about Simeon, my hus…John wrote an anonymous letter to the mother house. In it, he suggested that our receiver had been committing vague but serious improprieties. Since he could reveal nothing about what the lad had said in confession, he hoped someone would be sent who could discover the truth."

"Then your husband had told you nothing about all this?"

"Nothing, but, when Eadmund told him he was coming to you with Tostig's blessing, John decided you should be prepared to hear horrible things. He did not want the lad condemned.…"

"Nor shall he be," Eleanor interjected. "Brother John will heal his soul, although I have doubts about whether his spirit…Forgive me. Do continue."

"John wanted prompt and harsher action taken against Simeon, not the one who had been forced against his will. Since John did not want anyone else to hear what he had to say to me, he suggested we meet in the church."

"But he never came."

"He was late and I never met with him. One of his novices… well, no mind that. Just as he approached the sacristy door, he heard screams and saw a man rush from the nuns' quarters. He gave chase but the figure disappeared into the monks' cloister. When John entered himself, he saw a shadowy figure at the other end, thought it was the fugitive, and ran toward him. Then he heard Simeon shouting from behind that John was a murderer. That figure at the other end of the cloister was Brother Thomas, who pulled John to the ground. Simeon must have hidden in the shadows when he saw Brother Thomas at the other end of the cloister and hoped it would look as if he had chased John, not the reverse."

"But Brother John told Ralf nothing of this."

"John is an honorable man, my lady. To do so would have meant saying why he was where he had been and thus betraying Eadmund's confession. He could not do so, even if it meant his own life. The boy had to be the one to tell you about Simeon first."

And he was almost a very dead, honorable man, Eleanor thought. "Your husband is a brave man," she said aloud. "You must have loved him well before you both gave up the world."

Anne flushed.

"And you still do, do you not?" Eleanor said quietly. "Perhaps not always as a sister does her brother?"

Anne stood up and walked over to the tapestry. "I pray that you are right in saying there is no sin in love, my lady, and I swear to you that I sin only in my thoughts while John sins not at all in his feelings for me. We once had a son together, you see, a much-adored boy who sickened and died before his tenth summer. Each of us grieved but John's pain was darkest. He believed God had taken our son to punish John for his lust in the marriage bed. Since then, his love for me has been chaste. I long to follow his example, but I sometimes fail."

Thus your grief is doubled, Eleanor thought, the loss of an adored child begetting the loss of a beloved husband.

Anne reached out and gently touched the embroidery in the face of Mary Magdalene. Her fingers slipped down the cheek of the saint. "It has been said by some that Prioress Felicia and Brother Rupert were closer than nun and priest should be. Knowing both, I never believed there was any impropriety. Yet when I first saw this tapestry, I wondered if our former prioress had once been tempted by lust, perhaps for her good priest, and had this made to remind herself that we can choose to let love either transform or destroy us. I found strength in that thought."

Eleanor looked up sharply and studied the sad, but almost peaceful expression on Anne's face. "Thus you teach me once again, Anne," she said and reached out to touch the nun's hand. "Are we not two sisters together, equal in so many ways before God? Anne and Eleanor, not sub-infirmarian and prioress? Indeed, I need a sister to be my conscience and I have none, either here or in the world. Will you act as that for me?"

"A woman of lowly birth such as I, and a sinful one, conscience to the prioress of Tyndal, the daughter of one of King Henry's most favored barons?"

"Remember that entrance to Heaven is harder for me than it is for a camel to slip through the eye of a needle. Thus it is arrogant of me, a most lowly creature in the eyes of God, to ask you to act as my companion and conscience. If for no other reason, would you take on the task as a kindness to one of such mean rank in God's eyes? You have perceptions and nobility of heart that I lack, and I ask with genuine humility for your friendship, unworthy as I may be."

Anne smiled and gently took Eleanor's hand in hers. "I am grateful you came to us, Eleanor. I was so very lonely."

౦៙

Many years later, some of the nuns and monks of Tyndal would swear that they saw a skeletally thin horseman on a very pale horse ride away from the monastery grounds into the forest beyond as the church bells rang for prayer that first evening after Simeon's death. There were many more that claimed the bells had never sounded quite as sweet as they did the following morning when the first day of true peace dawned over Tyndal Priory.

Bibliography

For those who want to read more about the period, the following are a few of the books I consulted. None of these excellent sources should be blamed for any of my errors. I take sole responsibility for any misreading or misinterpretation of their material. For those inaccuracies, not excusable because this is a fictional work, I apologize profoundly—and I am sure I will hear about them, for which I give genuine thanks in advance.

The Lais of Marie de France trans. by Glyn S. Burgess and Keith Busby (Penguin, 1999).

Gender and Material Culture: The Archaeology of Religious Women by Roberta Gilchrist (Routledge, 1994).

Eleanor of Provence: Queenship in Thirteenth-Century England by Margaret Howell (Blackwell, 1998).

Equal in Monastic Profession: Religious Women in Medieval France by Penelope D. Johnson (University of Chicago Press, 1991).

Religious Life for Women c.1100–c.1350: Fontevraud in England by Berenice Kerr (Clarendon Press, 1999).

The Sanctuary Seeker, A Crowner John Mystery by Bernard Knight (Pocket Books, 1998). (Gives the history of crowners and what they did as well as being a mystery.)

Sex, Dissidence and Damnation: Minority Groups in the Middle Ages by Jeffrey Richards (Routledge, 1994).

Women Religious: The Founding of English Nunneries after the Norman Conquest by Sally Thompson (Clarendon Press, 1991).

To receive a free catalog of other Poisoned Pen Press titles, please contact us in one of the following ways:

Phone: 1-800-421-3976
Facsimile: 1-480-949-1707
Email: info@poisonedpenpress.com
Website: www.poisonedpenpress.com

Poisoned Pen Press
6962 E. First Ave. Ste 103
Scottsdale, AZ 85251